To

Melissa

UNDAUNTED

Struggling in a hostile world,
Pursuing your destiny.
You will stand resolute against adversity,
Undaunted.

Best Wishes

Will M/ch
7/22/00

UNDAUNTED

To my wife, Janet

UNDAUNTED

A Stan Turner Mystery

WILLIAM MANCHEE

Book I

Top Publications, Ltd. Co.
Dallas, Texas

Top Publications Paperback
UNDAUNTED

This edition published by Top Publications
1631 Dorchester Dr, Suite 139
Plano, Texas 75075
ALL RIGHTS RESERVED
Copyright 1995, 1998
William L. Manchee

ISBN#: 0-9666366-0-0 formerly ISBN: 1-55197-386-3

Table of Contents

Prologue

At four hundred hours I woke up and couldn't go back to sleep. I dreaded the moment the lights would be turned on and another perilous day would begin. Could I catch up academically with the rest of the candidates or would I fall farther behind and inevitably flunk out? I was scared, really scared. Paris Island and Charlie Russell kept coming to mind. I began to feel the pressure that he must have felt and I began to understand why he committed suicide.

When the lights finally jolted me from my troubled slumber, I jumped out of my bunk and hurriedly got dressed. After making my bed, Randy and I headed to the mess hall. While I was standing in the long line, I noticed two MP's walking toward me.

"Candidate Turner?" one of them said.

"Yes."

"You're under arrest! Raise your hands and place them flat against the wall."

"What's going on?" Randy asked.

"Step aside! Don't interfere," the MP warned Randy as he began to frisk me.

"What's this all about?" I said.

Just then a car drove up and Lt. Burden got out and hurried over to where I was standing.

"Is that really necessary?" he said.

"Why are they arresting me?" I asked.

"They've found some incriminating evidence. They can prove you were at the scene of the crime."

"What?! That's impossible."

"Well, that's what I thought, but they found your fingerprints on the murder weapon."

"Huh? What murder weapon?"

"The knife that was used to kill Sergeant Foster."

"You've got to be kidding. I don't know anything about any knife."

"Well, we'll talk about it later. Right now you'll have to surrender to these two MP's."

"Jesus! I can't believe this. I didn't do anything."

"Candidate Turner, you are under arrest for the murder of Sgt. Louis Foster," the first MP said as the other one tried to cuff me. "Please come with us."

Adrenalin began to explode into my blood stream. I ripped my hands away from the MP.

"I didn't do anything! You can't do this!"

My eyes began to swell up and I struggled to keep from crying in front of 100 stunned Marines. I looked at Lt. Burden hoping he would some how intervene.

"Come on Stan! There's nothing you can do. Just let them cuff you and take you to the brig. I'll come to see you soon and then we'll figure out a way to get you out."

The MP's escorted me to a waiting jeep and sat me down in the back seat for the ride to the Quantico brig. I sat quietly, my head was throbbing, I wondered how in the hell my fingerprints could have got on the murder weapon? What was going on? I was innocent, this couldn't be happening. It just couldn't be happening.

When we arrived at our destination, they escorted me in the back door and led me down a long corridor to an intake room. At the far end of the room was a thick glass window with a retractable drawer beneath it. Immediately to the right of the window was situated a small intercom. Just to the right of the intercom was a large steel door which apparently led into the main cell block.

I waited nervously until the drawer opened. The jailer instructed me over the intercom to deposit all of my personal belongings into the drawer. After emptying my pockets I continued to wait. Several minutes later the intercom made a popping sound and then the jailer told me to enter after the buzzer went off. I waited and then when the buzzer sounded I heard the locking mechanism in door disengage. As instructed I then pulled open the large steel door and entered the main cell block.

As I walked inside, the heavy steel door closed automatically and I heard the chilling sound of the locking mechanism engaging. Looking back, I starred briefly at the door already longing for freedom. Once inside a jailer escorted me to a locker room where I was stripped, examined rudely by a medic and then dressed in a bright orange jump suit. When they were done with me I was taken to a small cell furnished with a single steel framed bed and a forty watt light bulb protruding from the ceiling.

After the jailer left I collapsed on my bed. My mind raced trying to make sense of what had happened to me. How could my fingerprints be on the murder weapon? I hadn't even seen a knife since I had been at Quantico let alone put my fingerprints on one. Depression overcame me, the tears that I had so valiantly suppressed earlier began to stream down my cheeks.

The days passed by. My sojourn in the Quantico brig was into its fourth week and I was still unable to post bond. A hundred thousand dollars was ten times my father's annual income. My in-laws wanted to help but they could only raise $20,000. That would have been enough if I had been in the Portland County Jail, but I was clear across the country in the brig at Quantico

Marine Base, Quantico, Virginia. I was laying on my bunk contemplating by predicament when I heard the jailer calling someone.

"Stanley Turner!"

Startled to hear my name, I jumped up and walked quickly to the bars that incarcerated me.

"Yes, here I am. What do you want?"

The jailer appeared in front of my cell.

"You have a visitor," he said as he unlocked my cell. "Follow me."

The jailer walked down the row of cells to a visitors room, opened it and pointed for me to enter. As I walked in the room I saw an attractive, well dressed middle-aged woman with long brown hair sitting at a table. I sat across from her very curious as to who she was and what she wanted.

"Hi, I am Virginia Stone," she said.

"Hello, Stanley Turner," I replied.

"I am a free lance journalist from Charlotte, North Carolina."

"Really?"

"I know you're wondering why I came to visit you so I'll get right to the point."

"Okay."

"I recently did a story on a platoon of U.S. Marines at Paris Island, S.C. that was the victim of an over zealous drill sergeant. You may have read the story."

"Yes, I did, I read it while I was in the hospital."

"Well, I heard about what happened to you here at Quantico and I was frankly, intrigued. You haven't talked to any other journalist have you?"

"No."

"Good. I want to write your story. I want the whole world to know what you've gone through and what pushed you to kill your drill sergeant."

"But I didn't kill him. I'm innocent."

"Right, I understand. You don't have to confess to me."

"But you don't understand. I'm innocent!"

She smiled and replied, "Of course."

I looked her straight in the eye trying to convince her of my sincerity and continued, "I couldn't kill another human being. I couldn't do something like that."

"What do you mean? You're a Marine."

"Well, if I were in combat I guess I would . . . for my country. But I wouldn't kill someone in cold blood just because I was angry with them."

"It doesn't matter. If you're innocent the story will be great anyway."

"What I'm trying to tell you is there isn't any story. It's all a big mistake. In a week or two my lawyer will have me out of here, I'm sure."

"You're pretty naive Mr. Turner. They found your fingerprints on the murder weapon for godsakes! You're not getting out of here unless you can post bail, and if you haven't been able to do that in over three weeks I seriously doubt that it will ever happen."

Her chilling argument decimated my usually optimistic demeanor. I sunk back in my chair in acknowledgment of the veracity of her words. She smiled at me sympathetically revealing a trace of remorse for the jolt of reality she had inflicted upon me.

"Why should I give you the story?" I said trying to withhold my anger at her words.

"Because I'm the only journalist in the country that wants to write this story right now?"

"Oh really. So why do you give a rat's ass about me?"

"Two years ago my nephew was killed in a bizarre accident at Paris Island. He was two weeks into boot camp when allegedly he fell to his death from a tower on the obstacle course. We probably would have accepted the story except that several days later we received an anonymous letter advising us that Stewart's death was no accident. Of course we contacted the proper authorities but they just dismissed the letter as a prank."

"Were there any witnesses?"

"No, except his Drill Sergeant. No one else claims to have seen it happen."

"Gee, I'm sorry."

"Thank you, but I've gotten over it pretty much."

"Do you think he was murdered?"

"It was a possibility I couldn't ignore so I took a few weeks off and went to Paris Island to investigate in person. I didn't learn much about what happened to Stewart but I learned a lot about the Marine Corps. Then when I heard about the forty-four Marine recruits being hospitalized, I talked one of my editors into commissioning a story on what happened to those recruits."

"So what does that have to do with me?"

"I haven't been able to create a lot of excitement over the Paris Island incident as most of the Marines involved have recovered. The brass at Paris Island have done a good job at putting a lid on the incident. I was at a dead end until I heard about you and your situation."

"I see."

"Your story could be on the front pages of every newspaper in the country, if you'll only let me jump on it."

"I don't know. If my story gets a lot of publicity it could be pretty embarrassing for my family."

"Wouldn't you like to get your side of the story out? If you don't get someone on your side now the Marine Corps, sooner or later, is going to tell this story to the press as they see it and it won't be pretty."

"Ever since I was twelve years old I've wanted to be an attorney. I've geared my whole life to going to law school and fulfilling that dream. If this story gets out, I may be finished before I even get started."

"Don't you see, if you are innocent and you're acquitted you'll be a hero. You'll get a million dollars of publicity and it won't cost you a dime."

"I don't know. Right now all I want to do is make bail and see my wife, Rebekah."

"If I can make bail for you, will you do it?"

"You would do that?"

"Absolutely."

The thought of being free excited me. A sudden rush of hope overwhelmed me.

"Huh. . . . Then how could I refuse?"

"You're right, you can't. . . . That's good. . . . Okay, I'll post your bond as an advance on the contract. Of course you'll get the standard royalty from any news stories, books, endorsements or movie contracts."

"Damn, you're pretty ambitious, aren't you?"

"I've been waiting a long time for this story. . . . I can't wait to write it."

"Well I hope you're not disappointed."

"Don't worry about that just start collecting your thoughts because I want to know everything about you. I want the whole story of your life from the very beginning."

"So how will all this work?"

"I took the liberty of writing up a little contract. Look it over and if it's okay then sign it. Then I'll get you out of here and we can get to work."

"That sounds good to me. Too good as a matter of fact. Is there a catch?"

"No, no surprises. All I want is your story. Nothing more."

I read the contract, we signed it and then Mrs.

Stone got up to leave.

"Thank you so much Mrs. Stone for coming, I feel so much better now. For the first time in weeks I might be able to sleep tonight."

"Don't thank me, it's just business. You got lucky; we both got lucky. Good bye Mr. Turner."

"Hey, Mrs. Stone. Your Nephew-"

"Yes."

"It wasn't murder."

"It wasn't?"

"No, . . . it was suicide."

"Suicide? How do you know?"

"I've seen it happen. Your nephew was driven to suicide. I'd bet this book contract on it. The Marine Corps kept it quiet because it's not good for recruiting. You know-DRILL SERGEANT DRIVES NEW RECRUIT TO SUICIDE-not the kind of headlines the Marine Corps likes."

Mrs. Stone stared at me emotionless and then turned and left. Within two hours she had posted my bond and I was a free man. Just as unexpectedly as I had been imprisoned, I had been liberated. What a bizarre turn of events. I wondered what new surprises might lie ahead. The next day we met in a room at the Holiday Inn in Woodbridge, Virginia to start work.

"Now, just start from the beginning. Tell me about your childhood for starters."

"Well I grew up in a lower middle class neighborhood in Ventura, California. My father was a clerk for an insurance company and my mother was a school teacher. I had a younger sister and a dog. What else do you want to know?"

Virginia smiled and said, "Well I'm going to need a little more detail than that, Stan."

"Well, I hated school, I loved to play baseball and I was a Boy Scout."

"Okay. . . . How about if I just ask you some questions?"

"Sure."

"Now I want you to just relax and tell me everything you remember."

"Alright."

"Okay, when did you first decide you wanted to be a lawyer?"

"Ah. . . . Let me see. . . . I guess it all started when I had my first brush with the law. I was twelve years old and it happened during the Ventura County Fair."

"Okay, good. . . . That's a good place to start. Tell me all about that incident."

Chapter One
Ventura County Fair

The Ventura County Fair was by far the extravaganza of the year for all of us kids. As summer came to a close and the school year was upon us, we couldn't help but anticipate our most cherished holiday, Fair Day. Historically on the first Monday of October every year a huge parade marched down Main Street marking the commencement of the fair which lingered for 14 glorious days. The Fair Grounds were located on the Pacific Ocean directly south of the mouth of the Ventura River. The main Southern Pacific Railway line stretching from San Diego to Seattle abutted to the east. Two long train bridges spanned the Ventura River. Between the two bridges there was a grove of majestic Eucalyptus trees that provided temporary housing for the bums and hobos that rode the Southern Pacific freight trains up and down the California coast. We called it *Hobo Jungle*. The only way to get to Hobo Jungle from Ventura was over the railroad bridges.

The hobos were always a great curiosity to my friend Steve and me. On this particular weekend before the fair we were in the jungle exploring when we came across two hobos cooking their lunch over an open fire. We approached them curiously.

"Hello, what is that you're cooking?" I asked.

"Lima beans," the tall, muscular hobo replied.

"Oh, I hate lima beans."

"Lima beans don't taste so bad."

"Is that all you're going to eat?"

"We got a ham bone in there somewhere."

"That's it?"

"It will keep us alive another day," he said.

"Would you like a ham sandwich?" I said. "My mother made it for me but I am not really hungry."

The hobo's eyes lit up and his mouth started to drool.

"That would be mighty nice of you now, lad."

I grabbed by back pack and pulled out a brown paper bag and handed it to the taller of the two hobos.

"Here, take it. There's some potato chips too." I looked over at Steve and said,"Steve, give your lunch to his friend."

Steve tucked his lunch under his arm and scowled at me. He "But I am hungry."

"It won't hurt you to skip lunch. All these poor guys have are lima beans."

Steve began to loosen his grip on his lunch and finally handed it over to the short, stout, red headed hobo.

"Here. . . . It's peanut butter and jelly."

Steve and I watched them eat their unexpected bounty with great interest. The red headed hobo starred at Steve's bike while he savored the crunchy Skippy Peanut Butter and raspberry jelly.

"You like my new ten speed?" Steve asked.

The hobo nodded and kept on chewing. After about five minutes the hobos got on their feet, extinguished their fire and began packing up their things.

"Thank you boys, that was great," the tall hobo said. "Who are you kids anyway?"

"I am Stanley Turner and this is my friend Steve Reynolds," I replied.

"Pleasure to meet you, boys. I am Sam and this is Red. Sorry we can't stay to shoot the breeze but the 12:02 is due any minute."

Up on the tracks a workman was busy throwing a switch. Sam and Red waited until he had left and then quickly climbed up to the top of the embankment. We could hear the shrill sound of a whistle blowing. The hobos waited next to the railroad tracks and positioned themselves to jump on board. After the orange and silver engine had rolled by, they looked for an open box car. Spotting one they ran along side the train, hurled in their bed rolls, grabbed onto the car door and pulled themselves inside. As the train disappeared over the bridge, I wondered why men became hobos. What were they doing wondering from city to city anyway?

"Why did you have to give him my lunch?" Steve said.

"All Red had to eat was lima beans for godsakes!"

Steve shrugged his shoulders making it clear he didn't care much about Red. "I'm hungry," he said. "Let's go home."

"You want to jump on the next train and go to Santa Barbara?" I asked.

"Are you crazy? We might get caught and thrown in jail."

"Nobody ever seems to catch hobos? Why would they catch us?"

"They know where to hide and when to get off the train so they won't get caught," Steve noted.

"Wouldn't it be cool to be a bum and travel all over the world, never having to do what your mom tells you?"

"Yeah. . . . That would be cool," Steve replied nonchalantly. "But I wouldn't want to eat lima beans every day."

"Oh yeah, lima beams. . . . Yuk! We better get going, the Fair opens at two and we don't want to be late."

We picked up our bikes and headed toward the

railroad tracks. We climbed up the embankment and were out of breath by the time we reached the top. We looked both ways.

"Do you see anything coming?" I said.

"No."

"Why don't you put your ear on the track to be sure?"

"Okay," Steve said as he bent down and laid his ear on the cold steel. "I don't hear anything."

"Okay, you go first," I said. "I'll be right behind you."

Steve pulled his bike up onto the tracks and started crossing the railroad bridge. I followed close behind and peered up and down the tracks warily but saw nothing. The wheels of my bike bounced up and down over each railroad tie making travel across the bridge very slow. I looked up at the steel girders above my head and wondered how anyone could have built such an enormous structure. Steve stopped briefly to tie his shoe. While I waited for him I leaned over the side of the bridge and watched the river slowly winding 20 feet below. As we reached the midpoint of the quarter mile bridge I looked up at the signal light facing northbound trains. A chill darted down my spine as I noticed it was red. I looked down the track anxiously but saw nothing. Then I heard it. It was a soft and distant shriek at first but soon grew in intensity. Steve jerked his head up and gazed nervously down the tracks.

"Oh no! The train is coming," I said. "Run for it!"

We both took off running across the bridge but it was difficult to get up much speed carrying our bikes.

"Ditch the bikes, we'll never make if we don't!" I yelled.

"But it's my new ten speed," Steve replied.

"It will be all right, just drop it by the rail."

We both dropped our bikes and looked back

toward Hobo Jungle. The train was on the bridge, just fifty yards behind us. We ran as fast as our bodies and the rugged tracks would allow but the train was gaining quickly.

"Go out on the ledge! We're not going to make it," I said.

"What?!" Steve said.

"The ledge. Come on. Go out on the ledge. Just hold on tight."

I climbed over the railing putting my foot on a three-inch steel ledge that protruded outward. Steve followed my example but missed the slim ledge and nearly fell into the river. I grabbed him by his shirt and somehow managed to hold him until he could get a foot hold. Almost immediately the bridge began to shake violently as the train rolled past.

Our bikes were sucked up by the turbulence created by the engine and then slammed into the railing. Steve again lost his footing and dangled from the rail by just one hand. I stuck out my left foot so he could grab it and keep from falling. He took a swipe but missed. In order to stretch it out another inch or two, I had to loosen my grip slightly. He took another swipe and connected with my sneaker. His weight was more than I expected. I tried to reestablish my grip, but it was to no avail. Suddenly the bridge shook with greater intensity as the heavy tank cars crossed overhead. The jolt caused Steve to lose his grip on the rail and he fell grabbing my leg now with both hands. My right foot was ripped off the steel ledge by the sudden increase in weight. My fingers began to ache as I tried desperately to retain my grip. Suddenly the vibration stopped as the caboose rolled past, but it was too late, my fingers finally surrendered to the intense pain and we began to fall.

The moment between our separation from the bridge and the plunge into the Ventura River seemed like an eternity. The events of my short life flashed before me. I feared I was about to die. As we saw the water rapidly approaching Steve and I screamed. Steve hit the water first and sunk deep into the river. Then I felt the cold river fluid engulf my body. I sank quickly, plunging all the way to the bottom. Fortunately the river's soft sandy floor cushioned my fall and prevented any serious injury. For a moment I hovered near the bottom, disoriented. Then instinctively I thrust my body upward searching for air. As I swam furiously toward the bright surface, I felt like I was being crushed by the vicious teeth of a steel vice. Just before I succumbed to unconsciousness, I reached the service and sucked in a breath of precious air. After a moment of recovery, I looked around for Steve but saw nothing.

Panic overcame me as the seconds began to tick and Steve was nowhere to be seen. Knowing he must be somewhere close by, I decided I should dive down and search for him. Suddenly from behind I heard the sound of splashing water and frantic coughing. It was Steve. I quickly swam over to assist him as he struggled to remain afloat.

"Calm down Steve!" I said as I put my arm around his waist to steady him. "You're going to be okay."

"Get me out of here," he said as he put a choke hold around my neck. We both began to sink as I struggled to get free. His arm was like a noose around my neck cutting off my oxygen. No matter how hard I fought, it couldn't be budged. My left foot felt the sandy river bottom. Instinctively I thrust us back up towards the surface. We emerged from the water long enough to get one quick breath of air before we descended one more time toward the river bottom.

Finally I broke his tenacious grip, flipped around behind him and pulled him to the surface. As he exuberantly inhaled the cool air he began to relax and I slowly eased him to shore.

"It's not that far to shore. You're a good swimmer, Steve. . . . Come on, help me out."

After awhile Steve began to swim on his own and before long we made it to the riverbank. We pulled ourselves onto the shore and collapsed into the sand's soft embrace. For several minutes we didn't move but just inhaled the cool ocean breeze waiting for our heads to clear. Steve suddenly jumped to his feet.

"My bike!" he yelled. "I've got to find my bike."

I reluctantly got up. "Okay, let's go see if we can find it."

We climbed out of the river bed and up onto the railroad bridge. We looked both ways again for oncoming trains and then walked over to where we had left our bikes.

"Oh no! My bike is wrecked," Steve said.

"You're kidding?" I replied.

Steve pointed to the twisted pieces of metal that just moments earlier had been a beautiful new Schwinn Ten Speed.

"Look at this. Now what are we going to do? My mom's going to kill me."

I walked across the train tracks to where I had left my bike. Unfortunately it was in no better condition than Steve's.

"We're going to have to ditch them," I said.

"What?" Steve replied.

"We'll have to throw them off the bridge and then tell our parents they were stolen."

Steve glared at me in dismay but said nothing.

"Well, do you want to tell your parents what really happened?"

"I guess not."

"Okay then we've got no choice."

I grabbed my bike and threw it into the river.

Reluctantly Steve picked up his bike and dropped it gingerly off the side of the bridge and then peered over the railing and watched it sink into oblivion.

"We can't tell our parents our bikes were stolen until tonight," I said.

"Why?"

"Because they'll come get us immediately and we won't be able to go to the Fair."

"You think so?"

"Oh yeah. My mom will freak out when she finds out someone stole my bike. She'll want to call the cops and contact our insurance agent for sure. We definitely have to break the news to them later."

Steve thought a moment and then said,"Okay."

"Come on then, let's go into the restroom and get some towels to dry off."

"But I'm soaked, paper towels won't help."

"Well, they'll have to do. We can't go home and change clothes now it's nearly two o'clock and the fair is about to start."

After we dried ourselves as best we could we headed for the entrance to the Fair Grounds. There was a large crowd gathered around waiting for the gates to open. When two o'clock arrived the Mayor cut a large ceremonial ribbon and the Ventura County Fair was officially opened.

As we always did, we headed first to the midway to ride the giant roller coaster, the hammer and Ferris wheel. Then it was to the arcade to test our skill with a baseball, darts or at the Kentucky Derby. Finally we strolled through the great exhibition hall to see the marvels of modern technology that were always on display. This year what everyone was talking about was the Univac Computer. It was an incredible machine that could manipulate numbers and information so fast it staggered the imagination. The one at the Fair this year was programmed to analyze handwriting and predict the future.

"Let's get our handwriting analyzed," Steve said.

"Okay, how much does it cost?"

"Twenty-five cents."

"All right, lead the way."

Steve muscled his way through the crowd until he stood before the large Univac Computer. A man dressed in a dark suit with glasses was just finishing his explanation to the crowd of the marvels of the machine.

"And this machine will truly revolutionize your life in the very near future!" he concluded.

The man looked down at us, smiled and said, "Hi, boys."

"Hi, we'd like to find out our futures," I said.

"Okay, step right up. Here are two computer cards. Each of you just sign your name on the dotted line and I'll run them through the computer."

He handed us two long cards each about the size of an envelope. There were many holes punched throughout the cards. We both wrote our names carefully and handed the cards back to the man. He put the cards into a machine and began typing on a keyboard. The machine punched additional holes in the cards.

"Okay, here we go," the man said as he placed the two cards on top of a stack of similar cards and deposited them into the computer. The computer began to whine and lights began flashing wildly. After a few moments the large printer attached to the computer came to life and printed out it's analysis. The operator tore off the two printouts and handed them to each of us. Steve began to read his.

'You are patient, kind and loyal,
A better friend no one could be,
Standing always as a beacon,

Providing light so all may see.'
"It writes poetry, can you believe it?" I said
"What does yours say?"
"Let me see."

> *'Struggling in a hostile world,*
> *Pursuing your destiny,*
> *You will stand resolute against adversity,*
> *Undaunted.'*

"What in the hell is that supposed to mean?" Steve asked.

"I don't know. It sounds like a bunch of garbage to me."

"What I wanted to know was whether or not I was going to be a millionaire," Steve said shaking his head.

I nodded in full agreement. "Yeah, I was hoping to find out if I'd ever own a Corvette."

"What a rip off, huh?"

"Yeah, really," I said as I looked at my watch which fortunately was still ticking. "It's getting late, I guess we better call somebody to get a ride home."

"You can go ahead and call your mom," Steve said.

"No, that's all right. Why don't you call your Dad?"

"Let's flip for it."

"Okay."

I pulled a quarter from by pocket, tossed it in the air and said, "Call it."

"Heads," Steve replied.

The coin fell into my palm and I flipped it over onto my forearm. It was heads.

"Damn," I said. "Okay, let's find a phone booth."

We searched around the exhibition hall until finally we found a bank of phone booths. I took a dime out of my pocket, deposited it into the coin slot and dialed my number.

"We need a ride home, mom."

"What happened to your bikes?"

"They were stolen."

"Stolen! Oh my God. Who would do such a thing."

"I don't know."

"We need to call the police," she said.

I took a deep breath. "Mom, just come and get us, okay?"

"Okay, I'll be right there. Wait for me in front of the main gate."

Mom drove up in our Nash Rambler station wagon. We jumped in the car and were immediately barraged with questions.

"Tell me what happened to your bikes?"

"They were stolen," I replied.

"Well, where did you leave them?"

"In the bike rack in front of the Fair Grounds."

"We'll have to report it to the police tomorrow."

"That won't do any good Mom. They'll never find them."

"You never know. They just might," she said sternly.

"Don't call the police," I pleaded. "It's a waste of time."

"We have to Stan, that's why we have police."

"Mom, come on. . . . Please."

"Stan, that's enough. I don't want to argue about it. . . . Now, how was the fair?"

I fell back into my seat defeated. I said, "It was pretty good until we wasted fifty cents getting our handwriting analyzed by a computer."

"Oh, you mean the Univac Computer. I read about it in the newspaper. What did it have to say?"

I pulled the fortune out of my pocket and began to read it.

'Struggling in a hostile world,
pursuing your destiny,

you will stand resolute against adversity, undaunted.'

"Hmm. I guess that means getting what you want in life won't be easy. But no matter how difficult it might be, you're going to keep fighting until you get it."

"How can the computer tell all that just from your handwriting?" I asked.

"I don't know honey, but computers are supposed to be the wave of the future."

The next day mom called the police and reported our bikes stolen. Officer Barnes paid a visit to our house and took our statement. Steve and I stuck by our story that our bikes had been stolen although we were feeling pretty guilty about it.

The next day Steve and I were sitting on our front porch when a black and white police car drove up. It was officer Barnes.

"Hi boys. I've got good news for you."

"What is it?" I replied.

"We caught the guys who stole your bikes."

"What?" I said.

"We've arrested the guys who stole your bikes," Officer Barnes repeated.

Steve and I looked at each other in sheer horror.

"How do you know they are the right ones?"

"A railroad switch operator out at Hobo Jungle saw them talking to you boys and eying your bikes. He told one of our officers who was out there investigating the theft."

"But you didn't catch them with the bikes did you?"

"No, but that doesn't make any difference. They're just a couple of bums who would steal anything to make a buck. They've probably already sold them."

"What's going to happen to them?" I asked.

"They'll probably get thirty days to six months in

jail."

"They'll have to go to jail?"

"Yeah, is your mom home?"

"She's inside."

About that time Mom walked out onto the porch wondering who we were talking to.

"Hello, Mrs. Turner. I just came by to tell you we have apprehended the men who stole your son's bike."

"Oh, that's wonderful," She said.

"We'll need Stan and Steve to come to court tomorrow and identify them."

"What?" I said.

"It will just take a few minutes. Nothing to worry about."

"Okay, where should I bring them?" Mom asked.

"Just bring them to the municipal court at eleven-thirty."

"Okay," she said. Thank you, Officer Barnes."

Steve and I were sick after officer Barnes left. We couldn't believe what was happening to us. What were we going to do tomorrow when we faced Sam and Red? That night I couldn't sleep. If I told Mom what had really happened she'd never let me go to Hobo Jungle again. Or, worse yet, the judge might put us in jail for lying to the police. Oh my God. What was going to happen to us?

The next day I got up at dawn and ran over to Steve's house. I knocked on his window and woke him up. He opened the window and stuck his head out. I told him to come out so I could talk to him.

"What are we going to do Steve?"

"I don't know. You're the one who said we should ditch the bikes."

"Listen, we've got to keep our stories straight. They'll never convict Sam and Red since no one saw them take the bikes."

"You sure?"

"Yeah. Don't worry about it."

At eleven o'clock, Mom picked us up from school and took us to the municipal court. We were scared to death as we walked in a courtroom for the first time in our lives. Sam and Red were sitting at a table directly in front of the judge. The trial was already in progress. The prosecutor was in the process of questioning a tough looking man with black hair and a mustache. When the judge saw us enter he interrupted the prosecutor and said, "All right boys, come on in and sit down."

We sat in the front row as directed and watched the prosecutor continue questioning the witness. When he was done he said,"Mr. Turner, will you please take the stand?"

Reluctantly I got up, walked to the witness stand and sat down. My hands were trembling so I tucked them underneath my legs so no one would see how nervous I was.

"Do you swear to tell the truth, the whole truth and nothing but the truth so help you God?" the Judge said.

I stood there starring at Sam and Red in a daze as the Judge spoke.

"Mr. Turner. Will you tell the truth?"

I looked over at the judge. "What? . . . Oh, yes, Sir."

The judge looked at the prosecutor and said, "Okay, you may proceed."

The prosecutor, a tall bald headed man, began asking me questions.

"Mr. Turner, have you ever seen these two men?"

"Yes, Sir. We saw them down at Hobo Jungle on Saturday."

"Did you have your bikes with you?" he asked.

"Yes, sir."

"Did you talk to them?"

"Yes, sir. They were hungry so we gave them our lunch."

"They ate your lunch?"

"Yes, sir."

"What happened next?"

"The train came and they jumped into a boxcar."

"Which direction was the train headed?"

"Toward Santa Barbara."

"Did you see them at any time after you saw them in Hobo Jungle?"

"No."

"Now did you have your bikes with you when you went to Hobo Jungle?"

"Yes, I had my three speed and Steve had a brand new ten speed."

"A Schwinn right?"

"Uh huh."

"Where did you leave your bikes?"

"Ah, . . . well, . . . Ah. Out in front . . . you know, in the bike racks."

"Did you chain them to one of the racks?"

"No, I didn't have a lock with me."

"They were gone when you got back?"

"Yes."

"What time was that?"

"About six."

"That's all for this witness your honor," the prosecutor said.

"You may stand down," the judge said. "Call your next witness."

"The prosecution calls Rodney Pelt."

A bald headed man in his forties took the stand.

"Mr. Pelt, how are you employed?"

"I am on the maintenance crew for the Southern Pacific Railroad."

"Were you working last Saturday?"

"Yes."

"Did you see either of the defendants that day?"

"Yes, I saw them in Hobo Jungle cooking their lunch. Those two youngsters were talking to them. Then, later on in the day I saw them near the fair grounds."

"What were they doing?"

"They were acting rather suspicious."

"How do you mean?"

"They were wandering around like they were searching for something."

"Were they near the bike racks?"

"Yes."

"Did you see them take the bikes?"

"No, but I saw them eying them earlier over at Hobo Jungle and they were hanging around the bike racks all afternoon."

"Thank you. No further questions."

"Okay, you may cross examine if you wish," the judge said to Sam.

Sam and Red gave the judge a blank stare. After a minute of silence the judge said, "Okay, the witness may stand down."

The judge looked at Sam and Red and said, "What do you two have to say for yourselves?"

Sam stood up and said, "We didn't take nothing judge. We were just looking for food. We always go to the fair cause there is always a lot of good stuff thrown away."

"Do you have any witnesses?" the judge asked.

"No, I reckon not,' Sam said. "We always travel alone."

"Does the prosecution have any questions of the defendants?" the judge asked.

"Yes, Your Honor, I would like to ask Red a few questions."

"Proceed."

"Now Red, you heard Mr. Turner testify earlier, is that right?"

"Yes, Sir."

"Do you dispute anything he said?"

"No, Sir."

"He and his friend had their bikes with them didn't they?"

"Yes, I think so."

"Now, it's true you took a liking to the new ten speed, didn't you?"

"It was a fine looking bicycle, but I didn't take it."

"Didn't you? You were hanging around the bike racks weren't you?"

"Yes, but we weren't looking to take any bikes. We were just hungry and were hoping to get a handout."

"Isn't it true you had just eaten a nice lunch provided by Mr. Turner and Mr. Reynolds. You couldn't have been that hungry."

"Well. . . . Ah. . . . We were looking for something for supper."

"You took the bikes and sold them, didn't you?"

"No, Sir."

"Come on, do you expect this court to believe you?"

"All right. I've heard enough," the judge said. "Although no one actually saw you two take the bikes I think there is sufficient circumstantial evidence which forces me to find you guilty of this offense. Accordingly, I do find you guilty and sentence you both to ninety days in the county jail."

Sam and Red looked at Steve and me with a cold stare. Suddenly my knees grew weak and I nearly collapsed. The bailiff walked toward Sam and Red and began to escort them out of the courtroom. I couldn't stand it any longer.

"Wait, Your Honor. You can't do this," I said.

"What's that son?" the judge said.

"Sam and Red didn't do anything."

"What do you mean?"

I glanced over at Mom and then back at Sam and Red.

"Our bikes weren't stolen. The train ran over them and we didn't want to get in trouble so we, ... I made up the story about the bikes being stolen."

"Oh my God!" Mom exclaimed.

The judge peered down at me from the bench and said. "Son it's a very serious offense to make a false report to the police and lie under oath. You're in big trouble, young man."

"I'm sorry, Sir."

The Judge starred silently at me for a moment and then said, "Release the prisoners. Does the prosecution wish to bring charges against Mr. Turner and Mr. Reynolds?"

"Well, Your Honor, perjury is a class A misdemeanor punishable by a $2,000 fine and one year in jail . . . but, in view of their age and the circumstances, no, Your Honor."

All right Mr. Turner, I am very disappointed in you and your friend's behavior but I am greatly relieved that you couldn't let innocent men go to jail. Therefore, I am going to overlook this incident this time but I don't ever want to hear about you and your friend ever lying again."

"Yes Sir," I said

"We won't" Steve said.

Steve and I were greatly relieved after the judge let us go. Mom wouldn't let us near Hobo Jungle any more but it didn't make any difference since Steve refused to cross the railroad bridge anyway. Our parents wouldn't replace our bikes so Steve and I had to sell walnuts and mistletoe at Christmas to earn enough money for new ones. We didn't mind, however, we were just glad this whole mess was over.

Over the next few weeks I thought a lot about my encounter with the criminal justice system and started thinking about becoming a lawyer. It seemed like judges and lawyers had lots of power and that appealed to me. I asked by Mom and Dad about it and they told me all they knew, but suggested I talk to Pamela Brown, one of my school mate's mom. I had never realized that Mrs. Brown was a lawyer, she was just Tommy's Mom to me. Anyway the next time I saw her I barraged her with questions.

"Mrs. Brown, what do lawyers do exactly?"

"Well they try to help people in trouble."

"You mean like get people out of jail?"

"Well there are a lot of other ways people get in trouble."

"Like what?"

"Family disputes, financial problems, business problems and lots of others."

"What do you do?"

"I do family law."

"Do you like being a lawyer?"

"Yes. I like to help people solve their problems?"

"Do lawyers make a lot of money?"

"Most of them do pretty well."

"Is it hard to become a lawyer?"

"Yes, you've got to graduate from college and then go three more years to law school if you can get accepted."

"Huh. I always thought I wanted to be a forest ranger until I found out they didn't make much money. Now I'm not so sure. I don't want to be poor like my parents."

"Money isn't everything."

"Well whether you're a forest ranger or a lawyer you've got to work hard, right?"

"Yes, that's true."

"Well then if you've got to work your butt off anyway why not get paid well for it. Yeah, I think I want to be a lawyer."

"Well you're definitely starting to think like one."

Chapter Two
Career Day
January 1963

It was my Junior year at Buena High School and when I wasn't studying or working I was with Michelle. Michelle had just got her driving permit and was anxious to get behind the wheel. I didn't have a car yet and I was relegated to my father's El Camino. The day she got her permit I went to see her. She was in an excited state, jumping up and down and giggling over just about anything. I had never seen her like this and didn't know how to react. When I arrived, she ran out to my car and yanked open the door.

"Look! I've got my permit."

"Wow, that's great, Sweetheart."

Then with no hesitation she looked straight into my eyes, gave me a sexy little smile and said, "Stan, . . . take me for a ride so we can celebrate."

I knew something was up by the look in her eyes and the tone of her voice, but there was no resisting her in the mood she was in. We jumped into the El Camino and headed south toward Santa Paula. Michelle gave me a complete account of her adventure at the Department of Motor Vehicles. I had been driving for two years so I was having trouble getting as excited as she was. Then she dropped the bombshell.

"Stan, now that I have a driving permit, would you let me drive a little?

"What!" I said.

"Please let me drive."

"But this is my Dad's car. He'll kill me if anything happens to it."

"I won't hurt it. Don't worry. . . . Please."

"But Sweetheart, you've never driven before."

"I know, but it can't be that difficult."

"You're not supposed to drive except with someone over twenty-one."

"That's silly. You're a better driver than my mother and she's thirty-eight."

"Okay. Okay. But we need to go out in the country where there's no traffic."

Michelle sank back in her seat in utter delight. She had been victorious and she was proud of herself. After about ten minutes we were out in country amongst the vast stretches of lemon orchards that dominated Southwest Ventura County. I pulled over at a wide spot in the road, stopped the car and reluctantly said, "Okay, let's get this over with."

She jumped out of the car and pulled my door open. I got out and went to the passenger side. I began to give a quick tutorial on how to drive an automobile. "Now look both ways before you go out on the roadway. Put the gear in drive and accelerate slowly."

"This is easy," she said as she pulled onto the highway. She gradually accelerated to 35 miles per hour. "How am I doing, pretty good, huh?"

"Yeah, not bad."

After a few minutes we came to a sharp turn in the road. "Slow down going around this turn. It's pretty sharp."

Michelle looked down to locate the brake taking her eye off the road momentarily. The El Camino strayed into the left hand lane. Suddenly there approached an oncoming truck transporting a cargo of lemons. Michelle looked up just in time to see the truck barreling straight at her. Instinctively, she swerved the El Camino violently to the right to avoid the truck. The tires shrieked as the El Camino swerved. Michelle then turned the wheel sharply to the left in a last ditch attempt to stay on the road. But it was too late and the El Camino ran off the shoulder and settled in the drainage ditch adjacent to the roadway. Luckily neither of us was hurt, but I was very upset thinking of what my father was going to do to me if his car was wrecked.

"Oh shit! Look what you did."

"I am so sorry. . . . I tried to stay on the road."

"I know, but you didn't. Now what are we going to do?"

I wasn't really angry with Michelle. She had actually reacted rather remarkably under the circumstances. Had she panicked we'd both probably be dead. Mainly I was just dejected and scared. We got out of the car and checked for damage. Surprisingly, none was visible, but the car was mired in mud and we obviously needed a tow truck. How was I going to explain to my Dad what happened? I felt sick inside.

"What are we going to do now, Stan? Michelle asked. "Its ten miles to the nearest gas station."

For the first time she seemed scared and upset. I guess the trauma of the incident was just now sinking in.

"Don't worry," I said. "We'll figure something out."

I took Michelle in my arms and held her tightly. Then I closed my eyes and prayed for some divine insight into how to deal with the situation. After a moment our silent embrace was disrupted by the sounds of voices. We looked up and suddenly from out of the lemon orchards came ten or fifteen braceros. Braceros were the Mexican farm workers who came in each year to pick lemons.

"Hey man what happened?" one of them said.

"A truck ran us off the road and now we're stuck

in the mud," I said.

The man shook his head and began talking to his fellow workers in Spanish. Both Michelle and I had taken French so we had no clue what was being said.

"Hey would you like us to try to push you out of the mud?" he asked.

"Yes, would you? That would be great."

"Okay. . . . Let's go men," He said. He barked a few orders to his men and they all gathered around the truck. We jumped in the El Camino and before we knew it we were back on the road. We thanked all of them over and over and then they disappeared back into the lemon orchard.

By the time we got home the sun had set. It was a clear starry night, which is unusual for Ventura in the summer time. Usually the fog rolls in the afternoon and doesn't withdraw until midmorning. I walked Michelle to the door and was about to give her a good night kiss when the door flew open and there stood Michelle's mother. She was a truly beautiful women. I often wondered if her daughter would grow up to be as gorgeous. What was incomprehensible to me was that she was divorced. How could any man divorce such a woman? Embarrassment swept over me as I realized I had been caught kissing her daughter.

Mrs. Schneider, "Hi, how are you?"

"Hi Stan, it's about time you two got home. Michelle's got homework she needs to get done tonight."

"I am sorry. . . . It's just such a beautiful starry night I didn't want to bring her home?"

"Yes," she responded with a radiant smile. "Aren't the stars unbelievable?"

"You know, Mrs. Schneider, I hope when Michelle is your age she's as beautiful as you are."

She laughed."Well, thank you, Stan."

I wasn't putting her on. I was particularly amazed

since she was thirty-eight years old, had born and raised two children alone and still retained her youthful figure and vitality. It occurred to me that a team of doctors and psychiatrist needed to study her to find out the secret of her apparent immunity from old age.

"Okay. You can have five minutes and then Michelle has to come in," she said as she turned around and went back into the house.

"Thank you, Mrs. Schneider."

"Boy that was quite a line Stan," Michelle said.

"It wasn't a line. I meant it."

"Yeah, sure."

"Come here I only have four and half minutes left to kiss you good night."

She smiled. "Do I get to breathe?"

"No," I said as I pressed her lips to mine.

The next day was career day at Buena High School for all Juniors. Representatives from a variety of professions and businesses were on campus to make presentations and talk to students interested in their particular field. Several weeks earlier every junior had taken a battery of test designed to help them determine which occupations they were best suited. Michelle was only a sophomore so she didn't have to take the tests, however, we agreed to meet after school near the cafeteria.

"Stan, there you are," she said. "Where have you been?"

"I was at the Bar Association's presentation."

"Was it good?"

"Yeah, it was pretty interesting but . . . "

"But what?"

"My counselor says I don't have what it takes to be a lawyer."

"What?"

"She say's I'm not smart enough and I don't have

the right personality to be successful as a lawyer."

"How does she know that?"

"Oh, from the tests we took a few weeks ago. I guess I didn't do too well on them."

"You said you weren't good at taking test."

"I hate tests. They don't prove anything."

"So what are you going to do?"

"She says I should become a plumber, a carpenter or a bookkeeper, something that doesn't require social skills. She says I'm shy and introverted and wouldn't be good dealing with people. She says I'm not smart enough to be an attorney."

"That's crazy. I wish I was as smart as you are."

"I don't know how smart I am, but one thing I do know is that some stupid counselor's not going to tell me what to do with my life!"

"That's right. Forget about her. She doesn't know what she's talking about."

"I've always wanted to be a lawyer and that's what I am going to do."

"Good. Now, forget about her. Let's get the hell out of this place, let's go for a ride."

"A ride?"

"Yeah. I thought maybe you'd let me drive your Dad's car."

"Yeah, sure. Right after the Dodgers move back to Brooklyn."

"Come on. I'm more experienced now."

"No way. I'll do the driving, thank you."

After I drove Michelle to her house I went home. Mom was cooking supper and Dad was on the couch reading the newspaper.

"Hi, Mom. . . . Hi, Dad."

"There you are?" Mom said. "Where have you been? Supper's been ready for twenty minutes."

"Guess."

"Michelle's house."

"You're so perceptive."

"You need to get home in time for supper," Dad said. "You know we eat at five."

"I'm sorry, I just lost track of time."

"You need to be considerate of others. Your Mom works hard making supper and then you don't ever bother to show up to eat it?"

"I'm sorry, it won't happen again."

"It better not," Dad said.

"Okay. Supper's on the table. . . . Let's eat," Mom said.

"Good, I am starving," I said.

"So what happened today at school?" Mom asked.

"It was career day."

"Oh really. Did you get your test results?"

"Yeah."

"So. . . . How were they?"

"No so good."

"What do you mean?"

"My counselor says I'm not smart enough to be lawyer and I don't have the right personality for it."

"Oh no. What does she think you should be?"

"A carpenter or a plumber, . . . maybe a bookkeeper."

"Well those are good careers."

"Bullshit! I am not going to be some damn plumber who sticks his hands in toilet bowls all day long."

"Watch your language young man," Dad said. "Being a plumber wouldn't be so bad. It's a good, honest occupation."

"I'm going be a lawyer. I don't care what some dumb test says."

"I just don't want you to be hurt if you don't make

it as a lawyer," Mom said.

"You've got to face reality son. If you don't have what it takes to be a lawyer then you'll have to find something else more suitable," Dad said.

"Well, I am not going to end up in some boring, worthless job that doesn't pay worth beans. I want to make a decent living? I don't want to have to worry about money the way you and Mom do."

"Well you've got to do a lot of growing up Stan. There aren't that many good jobs out there. You've got to take what's offered to you and make the best of it."

"I don't mind working. Obviously I'll have to work hard to become a lawyer."

"You know you haven't done all that well in school. I don't know what makes you think you could be a lawyer."

"I'm doing a lot better this year, Dad."

"Okay. . . . That's enough," Mom said. "We'll support you Stan in whatever you want to do?"

"Thanks, Mom."

After dinner I went into my room and sulked. I was pissed off at my counselor, the tests, my parents and the world in general. This was America where everyone was supposed to be able to do whatever they wanted. But what if the tests were right. What if I didn't have what it took to be a lawyer. I just couldn't accept that. I wouldn't be happy doing anything else.

After a while I started rummaging through some of my old memorabilia that I kept in an old shoe box. There was a baseball autographed by Duke Snider, some old political buttons, a few Canadian coins and a uranium sample from my grandfather who was a miner in Nevada. At the bottom of the box I came across a piece of paper folded up neatly in a four inch square.

Since I didn't remember the paper being there I was naturally curious as to what it was. I unfolded it and observed its curious content.

     '*UNIVAC HANDWRITING ANALYSIS*
     Struggling in a hostile world,
     Pursuing your destiny.
     You will stand resolute against adversity,
     Undaunted.'

     I read the poem over and over again wondering what it meant. Then it occurred to me that this poem wasn't given to me by accident. It was a message specifically for me. Who sent it and why? I didn't know, but I vowed to keep it with me from that day forward to give me strength and resolve in the battles that I knew must lie ahead.

Chapter Three
Love, War and Politics
Fall 1967

After graduating from Buena High School in 1965 I went to UCLA. It was at UCLA that I met my wife, Rebekah James. It was my Junior year, and I needed to take a fine arts course for my political science degree. I decided *the History of Art* was my best bet. I had absolutely no interest in art but after a while I actually began to enjoy the class.

It was a Friday afternoon in October when I strolled into the large auditorium in which the 350 students met twice a week for class. I walked down the aisle toward the front of the auditorium looking for a seat. I liked to be close to the stage so I could hear better and get a good look at the slides that were usually projected on a large screen behind the professor. As I scanned the available seats, I noticed an empty one next to a cute brunette wearing an orange blouse and brown skirt. She was diligently studying some handwritten notes. Immediately I claimed the seat and sat down.

"Hi, how's it going?" I said.

She glanced over at me and smiled. She had big brown eyes that where enhanced by a slender face.

"Hello, not too bad," she replied.

"I'm Stan."

"Nice to meet you, Stan. I am Rebekah."

"So are you an art major? I said.

"Yes, how did you know?"

I looked into her eyes and a rush of excitement overcame me. I smiled and replied, "From the looks of your notebook it appears you're pretty serious about this course."

She laughed and replied, "Oh, . . . well . . . actually these are my roommate's notes. She took the course last semester. I like to get a preview of what's going to be covered during each class. It makes it much easier to keep up. Dr. Breckenridge moves pretty fast."

"That's for sure. He lost me the first day."

She smiled and looked back at her notebook obviously hinting that I should leave her to her preparation. I didn't care, she was enchanting, I wanted to get to know her.

"I guess you must really like art?" I said.

She looked up and politely replied, "I love art."

"Huh. I never paid much attention to it before, but I am starting to like it."

As we continued to talk my initial excitement grew to exhilaration. Rebekah made me feel alive, better than I could ever remember. Suddenly I became keenly interested in this most remarkable young lady sitting next to me. She had beautiful soft skin, notable breasts and a firm muscular body. I wanted her phone number. I definitely wanted her phone number.

"What's your major? She asked.

"Poly Sci."

"What are you going to do with a degree in political science?"

"I am going to go to law school and become a lawyer."

"Oh really? That sounds exciting."

"Where are you from?" I asked.

"Portland, Oregon."

"You're a long way from home."

"Quite a ways."

"I'm from Ventura just 60 miles up the coast."

"Do you live at home?"

"No, I've got an apartment in Westwood with my friend Steve. Where are you staying?"

"In a dorm."

Just then the professor walked in and struck her pointer on the podium to get the students' attention. I smiled at Rebekah and then she turned to listen. If anyone had asked me what the professor had covered in class that day, I couldn't have told them. My concentration had been destroyed. After class we walked outside.

"Listen I'd like to see you again. Maybe I could buy you dinner?" I said.

"Well Stan, I appreciate the offer . . . but I've got a boy friend."

"Oh, no," I sighed. "How could you do that to me?"

Rebekah laughed, gave me a kindly smile and said, "We can still be friends. I'll see you Monday in class."

"Okay. . . . I'll see you later then."

I feared there was little hope of ever striking up a relationship with Rebekah since no man in his right mind would ever let a women like that go, but I sensed we had connected a little bit in that first conversation and I didn't want to just blow her off at this point. Every day for most of the semester I made a point of sitting with her. We got to know each other quite well and then I got lucky. One day as I was walking toward art class I saw Rebekah and her boyfriend engaged in a heated discussion. When they were done he stormed off and Rebekah was left crying incessantly. I went over to her to see what was wrong.

"Rebekah, what happened?" I said.

"That stupid son of bitch can rot in hell as far as

I am concerned!"

"What did he do?"

"I saw him last night kissing and fondling some slut on the drill team."

"Oh no!" I said as I silently thanked God for this miracle.

"And he has the nerve to think he can just come up to me and say he was sorry and that it didn't mean anything. Well I told him it meant something to me. It meant he and I were through."

"I don't blame you. When you make a commitment, it should be sacred."

Rebekah looked at me warmly and smiled, "I'm sorry Stan. You must think I am terrible carrying on this way."

"No. No. . . . It's good to get your emotions out. I only wish I could do something for you."

"Thank you but there's nothing you can do about a scum bag like that."

"Listen, you probably don't feel much like going to class I bet."

"Not really."

"I wouldn't mind skipping class today either. We can study your roommate's notes later."

Rebekah wiped the tears from her eyes and nodded approvingly.

"Why don't we go get a Coke? Maybe I can get your mind off what happened."

"That would be nice."

"Okay then, let's go."

That was it, the break I needed. Rebekah and I began seeing a lot of each other and I made the decision that I wanted to marry her. My only problem was money, I was absolutely broke. My parents were barely making a living and pretty much had told me once I graduated from high school I was on my own. Luckily

I was able to get a small scholarship from the Rotary Club, a couple student loans and was able to find two part time jobs to make ends meet while at UCLA. This was fine for me but hardly enough to support a wife so I decided not to divulge my intentions to Rebekah just yet.

My main job while I was in school was in the Varsity Bookstore in the Student Union. My hours were from three to seven Monday through Friday. It was a decent job but didn't pay enough for me to survive. After many trips to the job placement office, in the Spring of 1968, I found another part time job from six to eight every morning Monday through Saturday. It was a plush restaurant and sidewalk cafe in Westwood called "Micaela's Place." My job there was to hose down the patio and clean all the leaves and bird crap off the tables that invariably accumulated each night.

Micaela's Place was owned and operated by Miguel Sanchez and his wife, Micaela. They were wonderful people and I got to know them quite well. Each morning when I was about finished with my work Micaela would come out and talk to me. She would sometimes have additional tasks for me or offer me some constructive criticism about my work, but most of the time she just liked to talk.

She was the daughter of a farm worker who spent most of his life moving around Southern California from one harvest to another trying to scrape out a living for his large family. It was a cruel and bitter life but fortunately Micaela had been able to attend one public school or another and finally received a high school diploma. Armed with this education and the pride and confidence it provided her she was able to get a job as a waitress at the Ambassador Hotel in Los Angeles. Being an attractive, intelligent and ambitious woman she quickly earned the respect and admiration of the hotel management. They rewarded her with greater responsibility, longer hours but no significant increase in compensation.

When Micaela met Miguel she was depressed and frustrated with her life. She knew she was another victim of white racism. She saw her less talented Caucasian colleagues get pay raises and promotions while she struggled at minimum wage. She felt helpless and alone. She dreamed of owning her own restaurant. Then one day she was sent to pick up some linen from a local laundry company that had been inadvertently left off the regular delivery. The company was one of only a handful in L.A. owned by a Mexican American.

She entered the busy little enterprise not sure exactly where to go or whom to see. It was very noisy so her verbal attempts at getting help were ineffective. Seeing a young man with a clipboard giving instructions to a group of workers, she tapped him on the shoulder. The young man turned out to be the owner's son, Miguel Sanchez.

They fell in love and after several months of courtship, got married. Miguel loved Micaela very much and wanted to help her fulfill her dream of opening a restaurant so he convinced his father to back her. On July 4, 1951 she opened Micaela's Place in Hollywood. The restaurant was so successful Miguel had to quit his job and help Micaela's run it. About eighteen months later Micaela gave birth to a son, Thomas.

One day during one of our chats I told Micaela all about Rebekah. She insisted that I bring her over to meet them on one particular Saturday. We arrived at the appointed hour and were warmly greeted.

"Come sit down. Can I offer you some coffee or tea?" Micaela asked.

"Some coffee would be great," I said.

Micaela brought over coffee for everyone and sat

down."Stan has told me a lot about you."

"Oh really?"

"Yes, he says you love art."

"Yes, I do," Rebekah said.

"I love art too. I wish I could have studied it like you."

Rebekah smiled and replied, "It is fascinating, but you don't have to study it to enjoy it."

"That's definitely true."

Rebekah gazed at the ornately furnished room curiously.

"Did you decorate this place yourself?" Rebekah asked.

"Oh yes, Miguel and I did it many years ago."

"Well, you did a fine job. Your restaurant is absolutely charming, I love it."

"Thank you. Decorating is something I learned working at the Ambassador Hotel when I was very young."

"So, Stan says you have one son," Rebekah said.

"Yes, we have a eighteen year old son, Thomas," Micaela replied.

"Oh, does he still live at home?"

"No, he's in the Marine Corps at Khe Sahn, Vietnam right now."

"Oh, you must be very proud of him."

"Yes, he's a fine boy."

"What does he do in the Marines?"

"He's in the infantry."

"Did he want to go in the Marines or was he drafted?"

"He enlisted."

"Oh, I bet you must worry a lot about him."

"Yes, I pray for him every day. There is not an hour that passes that I don't think about him and wish that he were home with me."

"Maybe the war will be over soon and he'll be back home."

"I hope so."

"So, Miguel, were you a Marine?" I asked.

"Yes, during World War II I was stationed in the Philippines for a while and then the Canary Islands."

"So Thomas wanted to follow in his father's footsteps I guess?"

"Yes, he's always dreamed of being a Marine."

After glancing at my watch I noticed it was getting late.

"Well, it's been nice talking to both of you. Rebekah and I have to be going here pretty soon. I've got to go to a campaign strategy meeting and Rebekah has a term paper that's due tomorrow."

"Oh, what campaign?" Micaela asked.

"Nixon," I said hoping she wasn't a Democrat. "I'm his campus spokesman."

"Good, he's a fine man," Micaela said.

"That he is," I replied. "Well, thanks for inviting us over."

"You're welcome," Miguel said.

After leaving Micaela and Miguel I went to the Nixon meeting and Rebekah went back to her dorm. Ever since I was twelve years old, I had been intrigued with politics and thought that was ultimately the career I wanted to pursue. I knew most politicians were attorneys so I set my sights on that goal first, politics would come later. My first summer out of high school I was lucky enough to be selected as a congressional intern for Congressman Charles Harmon. During that summer I met a lot of influential people and got a real taste of politics. When I came to UCLA, I joined the Young Republicans and when Nixon announced he was running for President I was appointed chairman of UCLA Youth for Nixon.

In the Fall of 1968 the campus newspaper was sponsoring a *Candidate's Forum* designed to educate the students on the candidates and issues of the 1968 presidential campaign. I was invited to speak on behalf of the Nixon campaign. The forum was to be outdoors in front of the campus newspaper office. A large podium was erected with large speakers on both sides. In most years a crowd for this type of event would be small, but since the Vietnam War was not going well and antiwar protestors were focusing much of their activities on college campuses, I wasn't sure what to expect.

On the day of the event Rebekah and Steve came to watch my speech. I met them at the library twenty minutes before the forum was to start.

"Well are you ready, Mr. Politician?" Steve said.

"Ready as I'll ever be," I said.

"Do you think many people will show up?" Rebekah asked.

"Probably not. You know how apathetic people usually are."

As we reached the long descent that led from central campus down to the Student Union we were stunned by the mass of humanity that stood before us.

"What in the hell is this?" Steve said.

"Jesus Christ!" I exclaimed.

"What's going on, I wonder?" Rebekah asked.

"Beats me," I replied. "It must be some kind of political demonstration."

"What's that smell?" Rebecca said.

Steve took in a deep breath. "Umm. It smells like love weed."

"I wonder where all these people came from?" I said.

As we walked toward our destination we caught sight of the podium in front of the office of the Daily Bruin.

"Oh shit! This is the audience for the presidential forum," I said.

"Oh my God. And you forgot your bullet proof vest," Steve said with a half serious chuckle.

"I don't like this," Rebekah said. "These people are creepy."

"Well, I can't quit now. It would look pretty bad if the Nixon representative bailed out just because a few hippies showed up to debate presidential politics."

As we approached the podium Steve and Rebekah walked to the front of the crowd to listen to the presentations. I climbed up on the podium and looked around for a familiar face. A representative from the Daily Bruin saw me and walked over.

"Hi Stan. Quite a crowd isn't it?"

"Who are these people? Surely they're not students."

"No. I think they were bused in from Venice Beach. The antiwar movement decided our campaign forum was a good target for a protest."

"Do you think they will get violent?"

"No they are usually peaceful demonstrations, don't worry."

"Yeah. . . . That's easy for you to say. You're not going out on the podium to endorse an expansion of the Vietnam War to 10,000 antiwar protesters!"

"You wanted to be a politician, didn't you?"

I laughed "Well, until now I thought it would be fun."

"This is your chance to make a name for yourself. You've got 10,000 people who will be hanging on every word you say, plus national media coverage."

"National media coverage?"

"Yeah, right over there; NBC, ABC, CBS and UPI."

"Oh, my God!"

A sinking feeling quickly overcame me. Giving a speech before a small audience was bad enough, but this was overwhelming. I started to go over my speech in my mind, but I had a complete lapse of memory. My instincts told me to run, I'd say I got sick. The smell of marijuana made me nauseated.

"Okay, the Humphrey rep is on first then you're up. Good luck."

"Thanks a lot."

Linda Carmichael, a black activist, gave the remarks for the Humphrey Campaign which were warmly received by the left wing crowd. As her speech drew to a close I spotted a small contingent of Nixon supporters trying to work their way up toward the podium. They were waving their *Nixon Now* signs above their heads but were being jostled around by the beatniks and hippies around them. When Ms. Carmichael was done the crowd jumped to their feet and gave her a standing ovation. Now it was my turn.

As I looked out upon the vast sea of hostile faces my legs began to quiver. I looked over at Rebekah and saw her scrutinizing the crowd nervously. Then the Master of Ceremonies took the mike and began to introduce me.

"Ladies and gentlemen, the UCLA Daily Bruin is proud to introduce the spokesman for the Nixon campaign on campus, Stanley Turner, who will present the policies and platform of presidential candidate, Richard M. Nixon."

The crowd, which had not sat down from their standing ovation given to Ms. Carmichael, began to boo and then started chanting "Peace now! Peace now! Peace now!" I took the podium and waited for the crowd to quiet down but chanting just got louder. The master of ceremonies came over and asked the crowd for silence but to no avail. I began speaking anyway.

"You all claim to be the champions of freedom, liberty and the constitution yet you trample on the 1st Amendment. You want the citizens of this great nation to listen to your cries for peace but you turn your ears away from those seeking to engage in rational debate." The crowd began to quiet down except for a few hecklers.

"Two hundred and twenty-three American soldiers died yesterday," a heckler yelled.

"That is certainly a great tragedy and is the very reason that you should elect Richard M. Nixon president. As you will recall it was Democrat Lyndon Johnson's overreaction to the Gulf of Tonkin incident that got us into this war. But now that we are there, we should finish the job we started."

"Nixon is a fascist pig," another heckler yelled.

"What we need to do is turn the military loose to launch an all out effort to win the war. That's the only way we can get this war over quickly and bring our boys home."

The crowd went berserk."Murderer!"

"Go back to Germany you Nazis scum."

"Peace now! Peace now! Peace now!" the crowd chanted in unison.

The TV cameras zoomed in as the crowd began to dance to the chant of *peace now*. Two pretty young women in matching short skirts jumped on the stage and stood on each side of me. I looked over at the Master of Ceremonies and he shrugged his shoulders. The girls had matching blue and gold Bruin jackets which they were holding firmly over their breasts. When the noise of the crowd was about to subside the two girls pulled open their jackets exposing their naked breasts with the words *PEACE NOW* painted on them.

The crowd cheered and I couldn't help but laugh until the two girls moved in on both sides of me for the cameras. Before I could react the cameras were flashing. The demonstrators had managed to disrupt our debate, cut short my presentation and make it look like I was part of their protest. I was angry but I knew what had happened that day didn't matter much. Their efforts would do nothing but strengthen Nixon's resolve to bring the Viet Cong to their knees and show the American people that his policies had been correct all along.

The next day I was shocked and embarrassed to see myself on the front page of the Daily Bruin sandwiched between the two naked hippies. Steve thought the whole affair was hilarious and, I think, he was a little jealous. Rebekah, on the other hand, said it was a good thing she has been there to witness the entire spectacle because she never, in a million years, would have believed my explanation of what had happened.

Chapter Four
Marriage

Although both my part time jobs were relatively simple they put a major damper on my social life. Marriage, as much as I longed for it, was out of the question it seemed. But I loved Rebekah so much I didn't want to lose her. I wanted her to commit to me so I decided to ask her to marry me now even though we would probably have to have a long engagement. After saving every penny I could for several months I purchased a ring and invited Rebekah to dinner at an expensive restaurant in Beverly Hills.

It was a small quaint place with caricatures of Hollywood celebrities posted proudly on all the walls. The main dining area was illuminated primarily by candle light and soft music was playing in the background.

"This is a pretty ritzy place for us to be going to dinner, don't you think?" Rebekah said.

"It's nice, isn't it?"

"Did you get an inheritance you didn't tell me about?"

"No this is a special occasion."

"Well. . . . Let me see, your birthday is in August and mine's in February so it can't be a birthday."

"Do you know it has been six months since we first met?"

"Wow. I never thought you would keep track of something like that."

"I'm full of surprises."

"I like surprises."

"Good because I've got one for you tonight."

"You do? What is it?"

"You know I never met anyone like you before. When I'm with you I'm the happiest man alive and when we're apart, I can't keep my mind off of you."

"That's a sweet thing to say."

"I couldn't imagine life without you."

"Well, you don't have to. I'm here."

"We should make it official."

"What do you mean?"

I pulled out a small velvet box and placed it in front of Rebekah. "This is what I mean. Open it."

Rebekah gently picked up the box and cautiously opened it. As the candle light struck the diamond it sparkled magnificently.

"Will you marry me?"

Rebekah gazed at the diamond for a moment and then looked up at me with a gentle smile. "I thought you'd never ask."

"You mean you will?"

"Yes. Of course, I will."

"All right. Waiter! Champagne. . . . Champagne for everyone."

"Stan, that will cost a fortune."

"I can't help it. This is the happiest day of my life!"

On October 18, 1968 we were married in a small Catholic ceremony in Portland, Oregon. Once I proposed to Rebekah she insisted we get married right away. I protested due to my poverty but she pointed out if we lived together it would actually be cheaper. Rebekah had a part time job as an dance instructor and with what I was able to earn and borrow we decided we could make it. After our wedding we went to Lake Tahoe for a short honeymoon and then Rebekah moved into my apartment and Steve graciously moved out. We told him he could stay with us until summer break but he understandably declined.

On January 30, 1969 we had just got home from school, Rebekah was making supper and I was crashed on the sofa watching TV. At five o'clock George Putnam and the Channel Five News came on.

"Good Evening. In the small farming community of Liberal, Kansas authorities are perplexed by the third murder in two months of a prominent Negro leader. A spokesman for the Liberal Police Department said that the deaths appear to be the work of a single serial killer. Each of the three victims to date have been Negro males who were killed late on a Sunday night. All the killings were accomplished by a single slash to the throat and after each slaying the killer carefully carved the letter "t" on the victim's chest. Local law enforcement agencies have branded the killer the Sunday Night Slasher."

"In the war in Vietnam the communist today launched a massive offensive against thirty South Vietnamese cities. It is by far the largest offensive of the war and comes only months after the South Vietnamese people elected its first Democratic government under its new constitution. President Nguyen Van Thieu could not be reached for comment. Casualties are reported to be heavy as the U.S. and South Vietnamese troops attempt to repel the attacks."

"In related news antiwar protested staged another rally in Washington pointing out that the Vietnam War had now become the longest war in U.S. History. They called for the repeal of the Gulf of Tonkin Resolution and the immediate withdrawal of U.S. troops."

Rebekah interrupted her cooking to listen to the report. She had been concerned about the Vietnam war not only because of great loss of American lives but also because my student deferment would be up when I graduated in June 1969.

"Damn. I thought they were supposed to start

peace talks in Paris," Rebekah said.

"I guess someone forgot to tell the North Vietnamese generals."

"They've got to get this war over before you graduate."

"If Johnson and Nixon would have just let our generals handle the war by themselves, without constantly meddling, the war would over now."

"You think so?"

"Yeah, Washington is so worried about getting China in the war they won't turn the military loose on North Vietnam to cut off the supply lines to the south."

"What will you do if they draft you?"

"I don't mind serving my time in the military. I'd just like to do it after I get out of law school."

"I hope they'll let you do that."

"I'm just afraid if I don't go to law school immediately after college, I'll never go."

"I heard they weren't giving out graduate school deferments anymore."

"Who told you that?"

"I heard it on the radio. If it's true you won't be able to go to law school."

"Well. . . . No telling what will happen between now and then, let's not worry about it."

"But I am worried about it. I can't just turn off my concerns like a water faucet."

"There's nothing we can do about it anyway unless you want to move to Canada."

"I wouldn't mind that."

"Come on. . . . You'd leave the United States knowing you could never come back?"

"If we lived in Vancouver we wouldn't be that far from my parents."

"I couldn't do that. I'll fight if I have to. It's just too bad we're not fighting for something worthwhile."

"You mean you don't believe in the domino theory anymore?"

"No, it seems kind of ridiculous now."

"Well, dinner is ready, come and eat."

Later that year a controversy erupted over the fairness of the selective service system. Minority leaders complained that a disproportionate number of Negroes and Hispanics were being drafted due to unfair student deferments, biased draft boards and political intervention in the selective service system. As a response to that criticism Congress was considering a lottery system whereby draftees would be determined by a random drawing by birth dates. Each birth date would be assigned a number from 1 to 365 with all needed military personnel being drafted from the lowest birth dates until the needs of the military had been met.

In the Fall of 1968 I began to apply to various law schools around California and took the Law School Admissions Test. My grade point average at UCLA was only about a 2.8 so I knew getting into law school was not going to be easy. I applied to Berkeley, Hastings School of Law, UCLA and the University of San Diego. The first three were highly rated law schools any of which I would have loved to attend. The University of San Diego was included as a precaution in case I didn't do well on the LSAT. It was a much easier school to get in, yet still had a decent reputation.

One morning, about two weeks after the debacle at the candidates forum, I had got up early to go to work at Micaela's Place. When I arrived, I went to the storage bin and pulled out the long hoses that I used to hose down the patio. As I was connecting the hose to a faucet two U.S. Marines in dress uniforms walked into the patio area. One was a young enlisted man and the other an officer. They saw me and walked over.

"Sir, do you know where we can find Miguel

Sanchez?" the officer said.

"He should be inside; just ring the bell."

The officer rang the bell and waited. After a minute the door opened and Micaela appeared. She smiled at the two officers at first but then suddenly her face became pale as she realized the purpose of their visit.

"Oh, no! No! . . . Don't tell me my boy is dead."

"I'm sorry ma'am," the officer said.

Miguel came quickly to the front door after hearing his wife's cry out.

"What's wrong? What happened?"

"I'm sorry, Sir," the officer said. "Private Thomas Sanchez was killed by mortar fire eight miles North of Khe Sahn on November 3, 1968 at approximately 2:00 p.m."

"What? Oh my God," Miguel said. "Are you sure?"

"Yes, there was a positive ID. I'm sorry, Sir." the officer said.

"Miguel, it can't be," she said. "Thomas can't be dead. Oh God, no!"

Miguel turned to pull her into his arms and comfort her. She was pale, her breathing difficult and then she fainted. Miguel caught her before she hit the floor. I ran over and helped him put her on the sofa. Then Miguel leaned over her and began to weep.

"We don't have any additional information at this time but rest assured we will advise you as additional information is received about your son's death. Here's my card, call me if I can be of any assistance. I'm so sorry about your loss. Private Sanchez was an excellent Marine. You should be proud of him.

Chapter Five
The Draft Lottery

After hearing about Thomas I was sick and couldn't go to class. Although I didn't know Thomas, the pain I had just seen his parents go through overwhelmed me. When I got home, Rebekah was still there.

"Stan, what are you doing home?"

"Do you remember Miguel and Micaela? You met them a few months ago."

"Yes. . . . I remember them."

"Remember they told you they had a son in the Marine Corps."

"Right. What happened?"

"While I was there, this morning two Marine Corps officers came to tell them their son, Thomas, was dead."

"Oh my God!"

"It was horrible. Mrs. Sanchez collapsed from grief. Miguel was devastated."

"Oh no! How terrible. You can't get drafted Stan. . . . I won't let them draft you. Let's move to Canada."

"No, we can't do that. Maybe the war will be over before I graduate."

"It's got to be over, I couldn't handle you being drafted."

"Public opinion is turning against the war. It's just a matter of time until we'll be pulling out."

Thomas' death really jolted us. Up to that point the war seemed imaginary, more like a movie than real life. Sure we saw the television news reports and heard the endless commentaries about the war but it seemed so far away that it had little impact on our lives.

"Oh, there was a letter from Hastings in the mail today."

"Oh really, did you open it?"

"No, I thought you would want to."

"Let me see it."

"Rebekah handed me the letter and I held it up to the light trying to read what was inside."

"Open it," Rebekah said. "I've been dying to see what it says."

"I'm afraid. What if it says I wasn't accepted?"

"Well, whatever it says we'll just have to deal with it."

I slid my finger under the flap and gingerly opened the letter and began to read it.

We regret to inform you that your application for admission to Hastings School of Law has not been accepted. Thank you for your interest in Hastings. Best Wishes.

"Damn it! I didn't get accepted."

"Oh no! I thought for sure they would accept you."

"Shit! I really wanted to go to Hastings."

"I'm sorry Honey. You'll just have to go to Berkeley or the University of San Diego."

"What if neither of them accepts me? Berkeley is harder to get into than Hastings."

"You've got to get in one of them or you'll get drafted immediately."

In June of 1969 Rebekah and I graduated from UCLA which should have been a happy occasion except for the draft looming over our heads. Unfortunately the Hastings Law School rejection was quickly followed by Berkeley and UCLA. I was beginning to wonder if I had made a mistake in setting such a lofty goal. Maybe everyone was right, I didn't have what it took to be a lawyer. Rebekah and I fell into a deep depression worrying about the draft and what seemed to be a bleak future.

One day in late June I arrived home late from working on an inventory at the Student Union. The apartment was dark which I thought was unusual. When I walked in, I saw two candles lit on the kitchen table. The table was set with the China we had received as wedding gifts. Soft music was playing on the stereo. I was curious as to what was going on so I called out Rebekah's name. After a few moments Rebekah walked out of the bedroom in a slinky cocktail dress. She had obviously spent hours getting ready for me to come home.

"Rebekah. . . . My God, you look fabulous!"

"It's about time you got home."

"What's going on? What's with the candles and the music?"

"We have a lot of celebrating to do."

"What do you mean?"

"I've got a little piece of paper here you may want to see."

"What is it?"

"It's a letter?"

"Well I can see that. Whose it from?"

"The University of San Diego."

"You mean they accepted me?"

"Yes! You're in law school!"

Rebekah put her arms around me and gave me a passionate kiss. Then we embraced and I took a deep breath. What a relief I felt knowing I was one giant step closer to my dream.

"Oh my God! I can't believe it! This is incredible!" I said. "Where's the champagne?"

"Right over here. . . . I've already opened the bottle."

"Oh. I am so happy I could scream!"

I grabbed Rebekah and started swinging her around and around. We began to kiss and caress each other. I slid my hand under her blouse and began to squeeze her large sumptuous breasts. Her heart was beating rapidly. I broke away for a second and pulled off my shirt and pants. She removed her panties. We collapsed on the sofa and made love for over an hour. When we finally had worn each other out, Rebekah got up to finish fixing supper.

"I hope you're hungry," she said. "I've made filet mignon, baked potatoes and a salad."

"Oh, wow. . . . Bring it on I'm famished after wrestling with you for the last hour."

Rebekah gave me a naughty little wink and then walked naked into the kitchen. She picked up an apron, put it over her head and then tied it behind her back. I watched her intently.

"If you don't put some clothes on I won't be able to concentrate on all this great food," I said.

"I'm sorry. Don't look at me, just keep your eyes on your plate," she replied.

"Right. You know I can't resist that cute little ass of yours."

"Too bad."

With that comment I got up and began chasing Rebekah around the apartment. When I caught her I flung her on the bed and ripped off her apron. I pressed her warm body against mine and moaned in delight. She wrapped her legs around me and we made love again and again. It was after nine before we finally sat down to our candlelight dinner. After we ate we called everyone we knew to tell them the good news. All evening the champagne had been flowing so before long we had consumed several bottles. Shortly after midnight we succumbed to the effects of the alcohol and fell asleep on the sofa.

During the summer we located and moved into an apartment in San Diego. I applied for a student deferment but got no response. Rebekah found out she was pregnant. In all the excitement of my admission to law school we had forgotten to use a condom. I was a little upset because I had wanted to wait until I graduated from law school before we had kids. Rebekah, on the other hand, was delighted she was pregnant so her joy overshadowed by apprehension.

When I started law school in September, the much talked about Draft Lottery had been officially adopted. What this meant was that in December there would be a national drawing of birth dates to determine the order in which men would be drafted after January 1, 1970. If your birth date received a high number, it was unlikely you would be drafted. On the day of the national lottery Rebekah and I sat nervously in front of the TV set awaiting the results of the drawing.

"I'm so scared," Rebekah said.

"Don't be. . . . I feel good about this. I think we're going to be okay."

"Hey. . . . I feel the baby kicking, come feel."

I reached over and put my hand on Rebekah's stomach. There was a definite kick.

"Oh yeah," I said. "He's going to be a punter."

"How do you know it's going to be a he?"

"Oh. . . . I just know those kind of things."

"Oh no, they're starting."

The announcer introduced the persons who would be conducing the lottery and explained the procedure. Then the actual drawing began.

"The first date is October 21," the announcer said.

"The second number is July 7."

For thirty minutes we watched date after date picked. Rebekah trembled with fear as each date was pulled from the large wire bin. My birth date was August

22 so she was particularly alarmed when an August date was announced. But as the lottery continued and August 22 had not been pulled we began to feel a sense of relief. The commentators had said that those dates after 150 would probably not be drafted.

"Now we are picking for number 321. It is August 22."

"What do you think?" Rebekah said.

"I think we need to celebrate," I replied. "How about dinner, dancing and sex on the beach."

"I don't think I am in any condition for sex on the beach."

"Oh well then. . . . I'll settle for dinner, dancing and lots of champagne."

"Promise me you won't buy champagne for everyone in the restaurant. The last time you did that it cost us over $200."

"I know but it was worth every penny. It was the night you pledged to me your love."

"What a mistake."

"What?"

"Look at the condition you got me in."

"Hey. . . . You're the one who forgot to take the damn birth control pill."

"Yeah Yeah. . . . But it was your little spermatozoa that got me pregnant."

"Okay, forget it. . . . It's time to celebrate. Let's go."

The sense of relief that Rebekah and I felt after the draft lottery was overwhelming. Our lives had emerged from a dense cloud into the radiant sunshine. I was enjoying law school, Rebekah was working in an art gallery and we were both anxiously awaiting the arrival of our first child. The lingering fear that I wouldn't make it through law school all but vanished. Nothing could stop me now.

It was December 28, 1970. We were both on vacation for the Christmas holidays and had been busy buying baby furniture and fixing up the baby's room in the house we had rented. The baby was due in March and there was much to be done to get ready. Rebekah's doctor was in Westwood since that was where we lived when she got pregnant. Every month we had to drive all the way there, some 120 miles, for Rebekah's doctor's appointment. We had just returned and I went out to the mail box to bring in the mail.

"Did we get anything exiting Honey?"

"No. . . . Just a lot of bills."

"Nothing from my mother?"

"No. What's this?"

"What?"

"It's a letter from my draft board."

"Your draft board. Why would they be writing you?"

"I don't know," I said as I ripped open the letter.

"What does it say?"

"It says I've been drafted. . . . I've got to report to the U.S. Army medical facility in Los Angeles for a physical on March 2, 1970."

"How can that be? You were no 321. They can't have reached that number yet."

"It doesn't make any sense. I don't understand what's going on."

"Is there a number where you can call them?"

"Yeah. . . . Let me see, here it is. I am going to call them right now." I went over to the phone and called the number.

"Selective Service, may I help you," a male voice said.

"Yes, this is Stanley Turner and I need to talk to someone about this draft notice I just received."

"What's the problem?"

"It says I've been drafted and must report for a physical in March."

"So what's your question?"

"How can I be drafted? My birth date was number three hundred twenty-one."

"The lottery doesn't take effect until January 1, 1970."

"You mean you're drafting me two days before the lottery takes effect?"

"Apparently so."

"That's not fair! It's totally ridiculous! I can't believe you bastards can get away with that shit."

I slammed down the phone and fell back into an overstuffed chair next to the phone. Rebekah looked comatose. We sat silently for a few moments and then Rebekah began to weep.

"What about the baby?" she said.

"The baby will be all right. . . . We'll work this all out somehow."

"What if they send you to Vietnam?"

"Oh. . . . By the time they get me trained and everything the war will probably be over."

"How will we live on the pittance the Army pays you?"

"They have a commissary where you can get everything really cheap."

"What about law school?"

"The order says I can finish this year but I have to report for duty in November. That will give us time to figure things out."

"This isn't right, Stan.   Can't you call your Congressman friend?"

"Congressman Harmon?"

"Yes."

"I don't think he'll be able to do anything but I could try."

"Call him please. Maybe he can talk some sense in the draft board."

"Sure, I'll call him tomorrow."

Chapter Six
Enlistment

I called Congressman Harmon's office and talked to Mrs. Moody his executive assistant. She said she had been barraged with telephone calls all week from young men in the same situation as me. Unfortunately the draft boards could do what they wanted up until December 31, 1969 and Congressman Harmon couldn't do anything about it. She did say she was in the process of drafting a stern objection from the Congressman to the local draft board for their obvious attempt to subvert the intentions of Congress.

The baby came on March 8, 1970. It was a healthy boy, weighing in at 8 lbs. 6 oz. We named him Reginald Clayton Turner, Reggi for short. Clayton was my grandfather's name who I had loved very much before his death several years earlier. Reginald was Rebekah's grandfather's name. He lived in a senior citizen home in Phoenix, Arizona. At eighty-five years old he was still quite alert and active. We thought this was a nice way to honor our grandparents.

Ever since I was drafted, Rebekah had been in a melancholic state. When the baby came, however, she snapped out of her depression and began to return to her natural demeanor. She finally had resigned herself to the fact that I was going to have to go away to serve my country. One day after Rebekah had put the baby down for a nap I heard her singing a lullaby. The sweet sound of her voice lured me away from the newspaper. I crept up behind her and put my arms around her waist.

"I'm so glad to see you in a good mood for a change. It's been like a morgue around here lately."

"I'm sorry I just couldn't bear to think of you leaving me."

"You know its been a long time since we made love."

Rebekah turned around and put her arms around my neck.

"Too long. Let's go into the other room so we don't wake up the baby."

Rebekah grabbed my hand and pulled me into the bedroom. After she closed the door she began taking off her clothes.

"Let me do it," I said.

"Okay," she replied.

I began to unbutton her blouse exposing her milk swollen breasts. She wrapped her arms around my neck and thrust her pelvis against me. I began kissing and caressing her as I gently unzipped her skirt. Before long we had managed to fully undress and began to make love. It was different than in past, however, not a frenzied passionate encounter, but instead, a prolonged, harmonious blending of our bodies and our souls. It was an experience beyond sex, one that I had never realized was possible. When it was over, I felt a sense of calm assurance that no matter what fate had in store for us we would together persevere.

We decided while I was gone Rebekah and the baby should live with her parents in Portland. After three days in the hospital I brought Rebekah home. Her mother had flown in from Portland to help her with the baby. Steve drove down to visit and see the new arrival. While Rebekah and her mother were in the bedroom tending to Reggi, Steve and I were considering my military options.

"Are you going to just let them draft you?"

"What do you mean? Do I have a choice?"

"Well, you could enlist."

"Why would I want to do that?"

"If you enlist, you can choose where you want to go and what you will be doing. You can even join an officer program and get paid a hell of a lot more than a private."

"How do you know that?

"If they can draft you they can draft me, right? I've checked it out. Besides my cousin just enlisted. He joined the Navy. Now that's sweet duty, just cruising around the world from port to port."

"Did he join an officer program?"

"No. He didn't finish college so he wasn't eligible.

"You know I wouldn't mind being a pilot. I wonder if the Navy has an officer program for pilots?"

"Yes, they do. First you go to Marine Corps boot camp and then transfer into aviation training."

"I could see myself as a pilot."

"Why don't you check it out?"

"Maybe I will."

"Another option is the reserves."

"The reserves?"

"Yeah, you just go through basic training and then report for duty a few weeks each summer. It's the best deal around."

"That doesn't sound too bad."

"The next best deal is the Coast Guard."

"Really?"

"Yes. In the Coast Guard you just cruise up and down the coast looking for drug smugglers and illegal fishing operations. The problem is the Coast Guard has a waiting list so long you'd be on Social Security before they called you."

I laughed. "I'm thinking maybe I'll just be drafted and in two years be done."

"Oh no. You can't do that. After six weeks you'll be on your way to Vietnam."

"Really? . . . Shit. I don't know what to do."

Rebekah and her mother Sylvia walked into the room while we were talking. Rebekah had Reggi in her arms.

"What are you guys talking so intently about in here?" Rebekah asked.

"Oh, Steve is just giving me the benefit of his knowledge of military service options."

"How depressing," Rebekah said.

"Let Steve hold Reggi so he can see what he has to look forward to."

Rebekah handed Reggi to Steve and then said, "Watch out, he just ate."

Steve looked at Rebekah curiously and said, "Watch out for what?"

"Sometimes he burps up a little formula after he eats."

"Oh great."

"Steve thinks I should try to get into Navy aviation."

"That's too dangerous. What if you get shot down?"

"Well actually, not too may planes get shot down. Certainly it would be a lot safer up in the sky than wading through some swamp."

"I guess so."

"The only problem is I have to commit to three years service instead of two if I just let them draft me."

"Three years. That's too long."

"I'd get paid quite a bit more as a Navy officer."

"Your grandfather Clayton was a Navy officer," Sylvia said.

"Oh really?" I replied.

"Yes, he was a radio operator on a submarine."

"Wow, that must have been exciting."

"He loved the Navy," she said.

"Maybe that's what I will do."

The following week I went to see the Navy recruiter and enrolled in the Navy aviation program. Unfortunately there were two prerequisites, a qualification exam and a physical exam. Being a political science major did not prepare me for the qualification exam, none the less, I did pass it, barely. Unfortunately, I was not so lucky on the physical exam since it was discovered I had a depth perception problem. It wasn't one that would have any impact on me in my normal day to day life, but while flying a jet at supersonic speeds it could be a problem.

After a thorough investigation of all available officer programs the only thing open was the Marine Corps Officer Candidate School. Needless to say, neither Rebekah nor I were thrilled about this option. When Rebekah's father came down to San Diego to see the baby and bring Sylvia home we discussed our dilemma with him. I was bouncing Reggi on my knee.

"Well Dad, what do you think Stan should do?" Rebekah said.

"Neither option is too attractive. The Marine Corps boot camp is hell and the Marines are always sent on the most dangerous missions. You're almost sure to be put in combat immediately. But, at least you would be an officer."

"How bad could it be?" I said as I lifted Reggi up high over my head and began to bounce him around.

Reggi began to smile and laugh at my antics.

"I've heard it can be pretty rough. But if you're drafted it's not going to be too pleasant either."

"It would definitely be better for my political career to have served as an officer."

"That's true and if you're going to have to go

through hell anyway you might as well get paid as much money as possible."

"What do you think, Honey?" I said.

"Whatever you decide will be okay with me," Rebekah replied. "Give me the baby, you're going to make him throw up."

I gave Rebekah a hurt look and then handed him over to her.

"You can bring Rebekah and the baby up to our place whenever you need to Stan," Sylvia said.

"Thanks Ma. We really appreciate you helping us out."

The following week I reluctantly paid a visit to the local Marine Corps recruiter and signed up for Officer Candidate School. When I got my orders, I was instructed to report to Quantico Marine Base at Quantico, Virginia on December 2, 1970. After I finished my first year of law school we moved up to Portland to get Rebekah settled in before I had to leave. It was a very difficult time in our lives and Reggi apparently could feel the stress as he developed a bad case of colic. The doctor prescribed paregoric but it was not particularly effective. Every night Reggi would constantly cry for hours on end. Poor Rebekah got very little sleep and was worn out. Sylvia tried to help her but Rebekah couldn't sleep unless Reggi was quiet.

Since I knew I better be in good physical shape when I reported for duty and Rebekah needed to get back in shape after having the baby, I suggested we jog each night. I had always hated any kind of physical exercise, but running was the worst. Rebekah on the other hand loved to jog and she had always kept in good physical condition as an dance instructor. So when Rebekah agreed to jog with me I had mixed emotions. I enjoyed being out in the fresh air with Rebekah away from Reggi's relentless screaming, yet I hated the pain and agony of running. Somehow, however, I endured the pain and after starting at 1 mile we finally had worked up to 3 miles a day by the time I had to leave.

It was about a week before my scheduled departure for Quantico. We had gone to bed and were enjoying a rare moment of silence. I had fallen asleep when I vaguely heard Reggi begin to cry and Rebekah get up to comfort him. As the intensity of screaming increased I got up to see if I could help.

"What's wrong with that kid? He never sleeps," I said.

"I don't know I gave him the paregoric before he went to bed."

"What did the doctor say at your last visit?"

"He said there was nothing he could do. The colic was probably caused by stress and insecurity."

"It's funny how a little baby can feel the turmoil in our lives even though we try so hard to shield him from it."

"I'm so worried about you leaving. I'm not going to sleep as long as you're gone."

"You've got to take care of yourself and the baby. You've got to be strong. It's going to be tough enough for me just being in the Marine Corps without having to worry about you and the baby."

"Stan, I've got something to tell you."

"What?"

"You know when I went to the doctor last time?"

"Yeah. . . . Well he was checking me out and discovered that . . . that-"

"What?"

"I am pregnant again."

"You're what?"

"I'm pregnant again."

"Oh shit! Now what are we going to do? And I

thought you and the baby would be safe and sound here in Portland so I wouldn't have to worry about you."

"I'm sorry. I thought we'd always used protection but we must have screwed up some how."

"Oh God, I can't believe this."

"I'll be all right, Mom will take care of me."

"Sweetheart, any other time I would be ecstatic that you were pregnant, but your timing this time is so incredibly bad."

Rebekah started to cry. "I didn't want to get pregnant."

I put my arms around her and said,"I know. I know. Don't worry, it will all work out somehow. I love you. I'll always love you no matter what."

"Are you sure?"

"Yes, of course."

Chapter Seven
Reporting for Duty

The next week was spent preparing for my departure to Quantico, Virginia. The Marine Corps had sent detailed instructions on what items I would need to bring with me and what items were prohibited. By the eve of my departure we had obtained everything I required and I was fully packed. It was 10:00 p.m. and Rebekah and I were somberly watching the news prior to going to bed. The war in Vietnam was as usual the lead story.

"Administration officials reported today their frustration over the lack of progress in the Paris peace talks. The sides were reportedly far apart on issues of the release of prisoners of war and the make up of a post war South Vietnamese government. Talks have been suspended temporarily with no date set yet for them to reconvene."

"In a related story anti-Vietnam protestors broke into the Student Union at the University of California in Berkeley. Leaders of the group vowed to maintain control over the facility until President Nixon reversed his policy of widening the war. University officials announced they had no plans at this time to try to regain control of the Student Union."

"In Liberal, Kansas the Sunday Night Slasher struck again. Police say they have no clues as to who is responsible for the deaths of now nine prominent Negro leaders. Yesterday, Jefferson Alexander, was killed near his apartment as he returned from a church service late Sunday night. As in past attacks the killer carved the letter 't' in the victim's chest. Police for a while believed the Ku Klux Klan was responsible for these atrocities but now are convinced it was the work of a single perpetrator. The FBI has now been called in to assist in the investigation."

After the news, we shut off the TV and began preparations to go to bed as my flight was set to leave at 8:30 a.m. the following day. Before retiring we went in to check on Reggi. He had been sleeping soundly for some time which was rather unusual for him.

"I can't believe I'm not going to see him for six months," I said.

"He'll miss you."

"Do you think he'll even know I am gone?"

"Of course he will. Dr. Spock says babies are much more aware of what's going on than you would imagine."

I put my arm around Rebekah and stroked her pregnant belly. "I hope I'm back in time to be with you when you deliver."

"They've got to let you come home for that."

"Maybe, I guess it just depends what I'm doing when the time comes. If I've been shipped out to Vietnam there's no way I'll be able to come back."

"I don't even want to talk about Vietnam. You are not going there. Haven't you been watching the news? We're starting to pull our troops out of Vietnam and making the South Vietnamese fight their own battles."

"I hope you're right, but I am not as optimistic. The Marines will be the last ones out."

The following day, a Sunday, I said good bye to Rebekah and Reggi and boarded an American Airline flight to Washington, D.C. with a ticket graciously provided by the United States Marine Corps. It was a long flight and with the difference in time zones it was nearly 4:00 p.m. when I arrived. As I deplaned, I noticed two Marines holding up a sign that read, *Quantico OCS*. Six or eight young men were gathered around them. Seeing the Marines sent a cold chill down my spine. I slowly made my way over to the group of recruits. One of the Marines had a clip board and approached me.

"Welcome soldier."

"Hi."

"What's your name?"

"Stanley Turner."

"From San Diego?"

"Yes, Sir."

"Don't call me Sir, I am a corporal. You only call officers, Sir."

"Yes, Sir. . . . I mean corporal."

"Wait over with the rest of the recruits until everyone is off the plane and then we'll go pick up everyone's luggage."

"Yes, corporal."

I joined the other recruits and introduced myself. After a few minutes the corporal instructed us to go pick up our luggage and report to a big grey bus parked outside. We did as we were told and waited patiently to be transported to Quantico. I sat next to a tall, blond kid with blue green eyes. He had a flat top and was quite muscular.

"Hi, I'm Stanley Turner."

"Howdy. I am Brett Billings."

"Well, did you have a long flight?"

"Pretty long. . . . I came in from Lubbock."

"Lubbock huh? Do you live there?"

"No, I just graduated from Texas Tech. How about you? Where are you from?"

"All the way from San Diego, California. I was in law school at the University of San Diego when I got drafted."

"You got drafted into the Marines?"

"No. . . . I got drafted into the Army but enlisted into OCS to avoid being drafted."

"My Dad insisted I enlist. It's a family tradition."

"Then you might know what's going to happen to us tonight?"

"Well, my brother is a first lieutenant so he told me what to expect."

"Oh really? Do I want to know?"

"Well, I suppose not."

"That's what I was afraid you'd say. Does your brother like being a Marine?"

"Yeah, he says if you can make it trough boot camp it's not so bad."

"Where's your brother stationed?"

"Khe Sahn."

"He's in Vietnam?"

"Yeah, they shipped him over there about two weeks after he graduated from OCS."

"Oh shit," I said.

"Don't you want to go to Vietnam?" Brett asked genuinely surprised at my comment.

"Well, not really. I just want to serve my time and go back home to my wife and kids."

"You've got a wife and kids? You don't look old enough to be a father."

"Well I am, believe me, I've got one kid on the ground and one in the oven."

"Huh. I had a girl friend but we broke up."

"Really? That's too bad. So why did you enlist?"

"Every male in my family for the last 100 years has been a Marine Corps officer so I suppose I best go to OCS and then go to Vietnam," Brett said.

"Yeah, that's what your family wants but how do feel about it?"

"That's what I want too. I can't wait to knock off a few Cong."

"Really?"

"Yeah, I've been practicing for years."

"How do you practice killing Viet Cong?" I asked.

"You know, when you're hunting for deer or coyotes or even just target shooting you just imagine that you're aiming at one of those slimy yellow bastards running through the jungle."

"Interesting, you said your Dad was a Marine?"

"Colonial Samuel P. Billings, the biggest S.O.B. on the planet."

"S.O.B.?"

"My dad is the biggest asshole the Marine Corps has ever produced, and they produce a lot of them. He never cut me any slack when I was growing up. The lousy bastard used to beat up my mom too."

"Then why did you join the Marines? Why didn't you tell him to take a hike?"

"You don't tell my Dad to take a hike. If I crossed him he's liable to take it out on Mom. Someday he's going to kill her."

"Boy, there must be something you can do about him."

"I need to send her a dozen roses."

"What did you say?"

"That will make her happy, don't you think? She's all alone and she'll be missing me. I wonder if the base has a florist?"

"I don't know," I said wondering how we got on that subject.

"I hope they send me to Khe Sahn, that's where all the action is."

I thought of Thomas Sanchez and all the news stories of the death and destruction at Khe Sahn. How any human being could desire to be in a place like that was beyond my comprehension.

"Khe Sahn? That's where you want to go?"

"Of course."

"Huh. . . . Well, whatever turns you on."

After a couple of hours of travel through the cold Virginia countryside, we arrived at Quantico Marine Corps base at about 8:00 p.m. The Sentry waived us through the main gate and we continued on through a half dozen red brick buildings. We passed the base Headquarters, Commissary, Officers Club and Military Police. Two MP's were escorting a man in handcuffs to the brig. I watched them until they were out of view. Then looked to my right and saw the FBI Training Center.

We continued on until we got to a bridge. As we drove across the it I observed a large hanger and an airstrip. Wondering if we were ever going to get to our destination I took a deep breath and sank back in my seat. Finally, the bus stopped in front of a large gymnasium. As we got off I felt a cold north wind and noticed patches of snow on the ground. Our two marine escorts instructed us to go inside. Inside the gym were a half a dozen long tables staffed by two clerk typist at each table. We were directed to form a line at each table so our paperwork could be completed. When everyone had been processed a tall Negro drill sergeant and a Second Lieutenant made their appearance.

The drill sergeant spoke first. "All right girls when an officer enters the room you stand at attention! You see this man right here. This is Lieutenant Howard Littleton. When you see this officer or any other officer enter your room you stand at attention. Do you understand that?

The recruits did not respond.

"I said. Do you understand that?"

"Yes, Sir," the recruits yelled in unison.

"When you address an officer, you always say, Sir."

"My name is Sergeant Louis Foster. I am your drill sergeant. I'm not an officer. You do not stand up when I enter a room. You do not call me, Sir. Do you understand?"

"Yes, Si . . . Sergeant!" the recruits muttered.

"What was that you little scum bags?"

"Yes, Sergeant!"

"Now, Lieutenant Littleton has a few words to say to you."

Lt. Littleton was tall, thin and intense looking. It was obvious he was all business. I was beginning to feel sick inside.

"Men, welcome to Quantico. I know this is going to be a new experience for all of you and that you will be experiencing many things here at Quantico for the first time. Some of the things you will be asked to do will seem strange to you, many will be difficult and some will seem quite offensive. But I don't want you boys second guessing the United States Marine Corps. The Corps has successfully used these techniques for training its troops for decades. Listen to your drill sergeant and learn from him. He will be a hard taskmaster, but don't be discouraged because when he is done with you, you will be part of the finest fighting force on the face of the earth, the United States Marine Corps!

"Now tonight we're going to take it easy on you. Your going to go to the mess hall and have a quiet dinner. After dinner we're going to take you to your barracks and assign you bunks. Then you can unpack, get to know each other and go to bed. Tomorrow, however, your training will begin.

"Good luck men. I know you're going to make me proud."

Sergeant Foster then addressed the recruits. "Now everyone line up and follow me to the mess hall. From this point forward there will be no talking."

The recruits began to scramble into a single line. I was situated deep in the middle of the eighty to one hundred recruits directly behind Brett Billings. We filed outside and walked up the street toward a white and green frame building. As we got to the doorway the line stopped and Sergeant Foster addressed us again.

"Now everyone file into the mess hall quietly, grab a tray and silverware and get your supper. Once you have your food then find a place to sit and be quiet until everyone is seated. When I say *at ease*, then and only then may you talk."

Just as the Sergeant was winding up his remarks Brett turned around smiled and said, "Why do they let Niggers in the Marine Corps?"

Sergeant Foster saw Brett turn and talk to me. Luckily he was too far away to hear what Brett had said. He glared at Brett and me and then yelled,"You two little slime bags get over here!"

"Who me?" I said.

"Yeah you! And that little weasel in front of you. Get over here."

I reluctantly walked over to the drill sergeant with Brett at my side.

"Yes, Sir," I said.

"Yes, what?"

"Yes, Sir," I said.

"Do I look like a fucking lieutenant?"

"Oh, yes, Sergeant."

"Now, what were you love birds singing about?"

"Nothing, Sir . . . argeant. I didn't say a word."

The Sergeant looked at Brett and said, "What about you, soldier?"

"I just said. . . . Ah . . . I wondered if the food was going to be good," Brett replied.

"Didn't you hear me tell you not to talk?"

"Yes, Sergeant. I'm sorry," Brett said.

"You're sorry. Well are you going to be sorry when one of your buddies takes a bullet because you disobeyed an order."

"Yes, Sergeant. . . . No, Sergeant."

"Well, which is it?"

"Uh. . . . I won't let him take a bullet."

"The correct answer you little piece of shit is you will always obey orders!"

"Yes, Sergeant."

"Now I want both of you to report to me in my quarters after dinner tomorrow night."

"But Sergeant. . . . I didn't do anything," I protested.

"Are you questioning my orders? What's your name?"

"Stanley Turner, Sergeant."

"Well, congratulations Candidate Turner you just became *conspicuous*. Do you know what that means?"

"Not exactly, Sergeant."

"I know your name now. I'm going to be watching you. You better be careful soldier."

Sergeant Foster turned toward the other recruits. "Listen up ladies! You don't ever want to become *conspicuous* when you are in my platoon! Because if you are *conspicuous* then I am going to be all over your ass because I know you are a fuck-up and you need special attention!"

Chapter Eight
Honesty Is Not the Best Policy

After dinner we were taken to our new barracks. Sergeant Foster issued everyone blankets, sheets and pillows and gave us instructions on how to make our beds. He then split the platoon into four divisions, Alpha, Bravo, Charlie & Delta. Each division had a different assignment as to the day to day cleaning of the barracks. I was assigned to the Delta Group and given an upper bunk near the front door of the barracks. At 2130 hours everyone was given thirty minutes free time before bed. Brett immediately came over to talk to me.

"I'm sorry I got you in trouble, Stan."

"Why in hell did you have to talk to me. Didn't you hear Sgt. Foster say to be quiet."

"I was just excited . . . and hungry."

"You won't be so excited tomorrow evening."

"Maybe he'll forget to punish us."

"He said to come to his office after dinner."

"So, what if we didn't?"

"I don't know that could be pretty dangerous. Don't you think he keeps a log or something when he disciplines someone?"

"No. He didn't write anything down," Brett said.

"Shit. We better report like we're supposed to. I don't want to make matters worse."

"Well, if you report then I've got to."

"I guess you're stuck then."

"Damn you," Brett said.

"Hey. I'm sorry, but you're the one who got us in this mess."

As we were talking, I noticed Sergeant Foster come into the squad room. I looked at my watch and noticed that our thirty minutes were nearly up.

"I've got to go take a leak," I said.

"Okay. I'll talk to you later."

"Please don't!"

After I went to the bathroom Sergeant Foster walked to the center of the barracks and yelled. "Atten . . . tion! Okay, it's time for lights out, but before you go to sleep, I want to advise you of morning protocol. I know you girls are used to crawling out of bed in the morning whenever you damn well please. Well let me tell you something. While you're in the platoon when the lights come on in the morning I better hear you feet hit the floor immediately. If I come in here and catch anybody still asleep I'll take you to the commode and dunk your head in it until you wake up. Do you understand?"

"Yes, Sergeant!" the platoon replied.

"Now, tomorrow you'll have to wear your street clothes until we take you to the quartermaster to get outfitted. Don't forget to make your bunks in the morning and I better be able to bounce a quarter on them. And you probably noticed there's some construction going on in part of the showers. They're putting in new linoleum so stay away from that area, understand? Now get in bed and I don't want to hear a sound after lights are out."

The room suddenly became dark and very quiet. It was an eerie silence because you could feel the fear in the air. I couldn't sleep. My mind raced over the events of the day and I had a sickening feeling about what was going to happen tomorrow. How could I have got into such serious trouble so soon? What rotten luck. It was the longest night of my life. I tossed and turned but couldn't get comfortable. The sounds of my bunk mate snoring, an alarm clock ticking and a window shutter banging in the wind echoed in my head. I tried to look at my watch to see what time it was but it was too dark. What did Sergeant Foster have in mind for Brett and me after dinner, I wondered?   I worried about Rebekah and Reggi and the new baby. I cursed the draft board and wondered if I'd be sent to Vietnam after OCS.

Then I got up and went to the bathroom. It was dark and I could barely see where I was going. As I went by the shower I tripped on something. "Ouch. . . . What in the hell!" It was a tool box apparently left by the linoleum repairmen.   "Damn!"   Tools scattered everywhere. I looked back toward Sergeant Foster's office hoping I hadn't waked him. That's all I would need. I picked up the tools and quietly placed them back in the tool box. "Ouch! Shit," I whispered. I had nicked by finger on some kind of knife. The wound was not serious so I wrapped it in toilet paper until the bleeding stopped. As I was walking back to my bunk I nearly collided with Brett.

"Oh. Excuse me," I said.

"It's okay," Brett replied.

"It's so damn dark in here. I'm sorry. I didn't expect to run into anyone this time of night."

"What's wrong, can't you sleep?" Brett asked.

"No, as a matter of fact, I can't"

"Me either."

"See you in the morning."

"Good night."

When I returned I still couldn't sleep. I thought the night would never end. But it did, much to my horror, the lights finally came on.

Quickly, I got up, got dressed and proceeded to make my bed. Making the bed was not a big deal but getting it stretched out so tight a quarter would bounce on it was another story. No matter how hard I tried I couldn't get it as tight as Sergeant Foster wanted. What a waste of time, I thought.

Soon Sergeant Foster made his appearance. "Atten . . . tion!" he yelled. The men scrambled to the ends of their bunk and came to attention. He quickly strolled down the center of the barracks scanning each bunk. When he spotted a substandard bed he would grab the blanket and sheets and rip them off. He did this with nearly a third of the bunks including mine. When he was done, he said, "Now ladies you have five minutes to get these bunks properly made and lined up to go to the mess hall. At ease!"

We all leaped into action desperate to remake our beds and get in line to go to the breakfast. Somehow we managed to do it and at 0600 hours we entered the mess hall. After breakfast we were loaded into several big buses and driven across the base to see the quartermaster. When we arrived we were herded inside and Sergeant Foster then gave us instructions.

"Now girls you're going to get outfitted as Marines today. Each of you will get a duffle bag and two new uniforms. Alpha squad will start with pants, Bravo will get boots, Charlie will get underwear and Delta will start with shirts. Now we don't have all day so I want all of you to move it."

After we had received all of our gear Sergeant Foster lined us up to announce our next item of business. "Now I've got good news for all of you. You are now going to get a haircut compliments of the United States Marine Corps. Now you are probably wondering why all recruits have their head shaved when they start training. Let me explain the principle to you. When recruits come here to the Marine Corps, they are rough and uneven. They've picked up bad habits from their friends and families. They're spoiled and physically out of shape. So when you join the Marines we have to cut through all that crap and baggage you've brought with you. We have to tear you down so we can build you up into a model Marine. Because America depends on the Marine Corps to protect it and we're not going to let America down. Now when you go into the barber shop I don't want to see any cry babies. Get in there and get your haircut like a Marine!"

We were loaded into the buses and returned to our barracks so we could drop off our gear and get changed into our new uniforms. When we done, we marched to the barber shop. I was kind of fond of my hair but I had been warned about the Marine Corps ritual of shaving off recruits hair. Since I wouldn't be seeing anybody but Marines for the next six weeks I figured it would grow back before anyone important saw me. With that behind us we had lunch and then were scheduled to start physical training referred to by Sergeant Foster as PT. The Sergeant led us to the parade ground where we were to await instructions from Lieutenant Littleton.

"All right men, we're going to start your physical training with a little jog over the south part of the base. We'll be going over a few hills and some rough terrain but it shouldn't be too bad. The run will be approximately 4.1 miles. When we've completed the run, we'll have to march another 2 miles back to this location. Now I will lead the way and Sergeant Foster will bring up the rear. Some of you may not be in as good a shape as you should be and consequently may feel a little pain. I want you to act like men and not fall behind. Sergeant Foster does not like stragglers and if any of you lag he'll be there to deal with you. Okay, let's move out."

Lieutenant Littleton began to slowly jog out of the parade area with the platoon following close behind. I was midway in the pack and didn't have any problems until the Lieutenant quickened the pace about a mile and half out. The long line of Marines began to stretch out.

Lieutenant Littleton looked back at his troops, slowed down slightly and yelled. "All right let's tighten it up men. Don't lag behind. Keep up with the man in front of you."

A couple of the guys began to fall behind and I could hear them getting Sergeant Foster's wrath. "Get a move on you wimp! Don't you dare stop running! You're a damn sissy." It was cold out with patches of snow lingering on the north slopes of the hills we were traversing. Lieutenant Littleton made no effort to avoid these snow patches and several soldiers slipped and fell on their butts. When we had passed the three miles that I was trained to run I began to feel my body ache and I gasped for enough air to keep on running. Finally the Lieutenant slowed down and began to march. We hiked another 2 miles back to the parade ground and the Sergeant released us to go take a shower and report to class. As we walked to our barracks Brett caught up with me.

"You haven't changed your mind have you?" Brett said.

"No. If I could be sure he's forgot about it I'd forget it but I can't take a chance," I replied.

"He hasn't mentioned it all day. He hasn't even given us a dirty look or yelled at us."

"We were ordered to report to the Sergeant and I don't want to disobey a direct order. We'd be in serious trouble if we did that."

"Okay. So, how was the run?"

"It was tough but I had been running 3 miles a day before I came here so it wasn't too much farther."

"I heard tomorrow it will be 5 miles and eventually we'll be doing ten."

"Oh Jesus! I can hardly wait."

As we approached the barracks Sergeant Foster reminded us we had only thirty minutes until study hall. We all quickly took our showers and reported to the class room as instructed. Sergeant Foster was standing out front with a tall, lanky corporal. He began to address the platoon.

"Now listen up. This is Corporal Lance Smith. He is your combat tactics instructor. The class will meet Monday, Wednesday and Friday's at 1500 hours. Over the next few weeks you are not gonna be getting as much sleep as you may be used to. So there may be times when you might doze off in class, particularly a late class like this one. Let me advise you now we do not tolerate soldier's sleeping in class. If you begin to get drowsy stand up by your chair so you don't fall asleep. If we catch you sleeping, you'll be severely punished. Your training is only six weeks and we can't afford to waste one minute."

After class we reported to the mess hall for dinner. I was famished after such a grueling day of physical exercise and requested a large helping of everything. As I was devouring my food, I remembered I had to report to Sergeant Foster after I was through. Suddenly I wasn't so hungry. I looked around for Brett and spotted him at the other end of the mess hall. He was off in a corner all alone. I wondered if he was as terrified as I was of what was about to happen. After dinner we were dismissed at the barracks and each group began to do their assigned chores. After finding Brett, I advised him I was going to see Sergeant Foster.

"You're a god damn fool Turner. I know he's forgotten about this."

"He gave us a direct order. I can't disobey that order. It's too dangerous."

"Okay, I think you're wrong, but have it your way. Let's get it over with," Brett said.

We walked down the hall to Sergeant Foster's room and knocked on the door. He yelled for us to come in.

He looked up at us and frowned."What do you two want?"

"You ordered us to report to you tonight, Sergeant," I said.

He laughed and shook his head. "Oh, I had forgotten all about that. You dumb shits."

Brett turned and glared at me.

"Now I am going to have to punish you like I promised."

Sergeant Foster went to his closet and pulled out a long plastic stick.

"All right down on the ground and do a hundred push ups."

Unfortunately I could only do twenty or thirty pushup at best so I knew I was in trouble. I started strong, began to slow at 20 and when I got to 28 I could do no more.

"Twenty-eight? That's all you can do? You're a fucking weakling. Keep on going!"

I tried to continue but didn't have the strength. Finally I dropped on knew to the ground and just sat there, exhausted.

"Who said you could stop?" He said, and then smacked me on the my back with the plastic rod. I winced in pain. "You better start doing an extra fifty pushups every day Turner to get up to snuff. Now get up and start doing jumping jacks."

Jumping jacks didn't bother me. They were pretty easy so I didn't complain. The problem was anything, even something simple, becomes a chore if you do too much of it. The Sergeant started us on jumping jacks and then started reading a book totally ignoring us. After a half an hour we were both totally exhausted and ready to collapse. I began to slow down to almost slow motion. The Sergeant looked up and seeing my distress got up and grabbed his plastic rod. He smacked it on the ground a few times and then said. "Keep it going, nobody said you could stop." After a while I couldn't move my arms. Finally the Sergeant said. "All right, 100 sit-ups." I gave the Sergeant a cold stare but laid down anyway and proceeded to do sit-ups the best I could under the circumstances. After doing as many sit-ups as my stomach muscles would allow I fell back onto the floor. "Get your ass up Turner. You're not through yet. Let's see you two run in place for a while."

Sergeant Foster went back to reading his book. After we had jogged in place for twenty minutes he looked up at us and said, "Alright get the fuck out of my sight!"

I quickly got up and said. "Yes, Sergeant!" And then left the room. Brett stumbled out of the office right behind me. We staggered back to the squad room.

"I think I'm going to throw up," Brett exclaimed.

"My arms are killing me, I can hardly move them," I said.

"Me either. No human being should have to take that kind of punishment. I can't believe he did that to us."

"I didn't even do anything," I moaned. "What an asshole."

Brett said, "That's what happens when you give a Nigger a little power."

"He just assumed I was guilty," I said. "I'd smack him a few times with that stick and see how he likes it."

"Someday I'll met him on a dark street and he'll wish he hadn't fucked with me."

When we got back to our bunks, the other candidates crowded around us to ask us what happened. We explained what we had just been through and they all shook their heads in disbelief.

"Believe me guys, you don't want to ever go through what we just did. Kiss his butt if you have to but don't get sent to his office," I warned them.

Some of the guys helped me up onto the top bunk. My arms were swollen, I had a horrible headache and I had a dull pain in my back. I was so exhausted I fell right to sleep. After being out for twenty or thirty minutes I woke up with severe bladder pain. Thinking I had to take a leak, I got up and went to the bathroom. When I was done I looked into the urinal and it was full of blood. All of my life I had been very healthy so the blood scared me. I knew I had to report it to Sergeant Foster. I walked down to his room and knocked on his door.

"Who is it?" he said.

"It's Candidate Turner, Sergeant," I said.

"I thought I told you I didn't want to see your ugly face around here."

"Sergeant, I just went to the bathroom and, well, . . . I'm bleeding."

"You're what?"

"There's blood everywhere."

The door opened and Sgt. Foster gave me a hard look. "All right. Get dressed and report to the infirmary. Tell them to call me when they figure out what is wrong with you."

"Yes, Sergeant."

"Can you get there yourself or do need help?"

"I can manage alone."

"Okay then, get going."

I went back to my bunk, got dressed and started to leave.

"Where are you going?" Brett moaned from his bunk.

"I'm sick. . . . I'm going to the infirmary."

"So. . . . I feel like shit too but that's no reason to go to the infirmary?"

"No, you don't understand. I'm not just feeling like

shit. I'm pissing blood! The Sergeant told me to go to the infirmary."

"Pissing blood? Shit. What do you think's wrong with you?"

"I don't know, I hope it's not serious. I wonder what will happen if I miss a few days of training?"

"They'll wash you out and make you wait for the next OCS class."

"When in hell will that be?"

"Not for ten weeks."

"Ten weeks! Jesus Christ. I can't believe this."

Billings said nothing. He gave no apologies, accepted no responsibility for what had happened and showed no concern for my injury. I finally just shook my head and left hoping I'd never see him or Sgt. Foster again.

Chapter Nine
Quantico Naval Hospital

Sergeant Foster had told me the infirmary was behind the mess hall. When I arrived at about eleven hundred hours, the place was deserted except for a young, slim, dirty-blond haired nurse sitting behind the counter making notes on a clipboard. Her name plate read, "Miss Andrews, R.N." She was a pleasant sight. For a moment I forgot I was sick.

"Hello," I said.

"Yes, can I help you?"

"I'm Stanley Turner from C Company, OCS. Sergeant Foster sent me over."

"What wrong with you?"

"Well, I just went to the bathroom and . . . you know . . . my pee was dark brown."

"Oh really. . . . Huh. . . . Well, why don't you go in the can and give me a urine sample. The doctor will be back in a few minutes and he can take a look at it."

I watched her intently as she went over to a cabinet, reached up and retrieved a plastic cup. When she returned she smiled and handed it to me. She had gorgeous blue eyes and a kind face. I returned the smile, nodded and then went into the bathroom. When I returned with the cup she took it from me and said, "Okay, good. Now why don't you just have a seat? Dr. Chamberlain will be back in a minute. Oh, you'll need to fill out this paper work for me."

"All right."

"Are you a Marine?" I asked as I began filling out the form.

"No. I am in the Navy. Most of the medical

personnel for the Marine Corps is provided by the Navy.
Dr. Chamberlain is a First Lieutenant in the Navy."

"Do you like the Navy?"

"Sure, it's been interesting," she said as she
wrote something on a new chart she was making. "So
did anything happen today that might have caused you
this problem?"

"Well the drill sergeant ran us pretty hard today,
. . . and then he punished me and another guy for talking
in line."

"What kind of punishment?"

"Sit-ups, pushups, jumping jacks, running in place
and a few whacks on the back."

"He hit you?"

"Yeah, he whacked me on the back with a plastic
stick a few times."

"How many pushups did you have to do?"

"Well, I could only do fifty or sixty."

"I see."

"Then he made me do 200 sit-ups, I lost count of
the jumping jacks . . . maybe 3-400 and then we ran in
place until we dropped."

"Oh my God!" she said shaking her head. "It's a
wonder you could make it over here to the infirmary. I
can't believe some of the drill sergeants around here.
They must recruit them from penal institutions. It's a
disgrace."

"I know. . . . The second time he hit me I almost
took the stick and rammed it up his ass!"

The door then flew open and a tall, dark haired
man of about thirty years of age appeared. He had an
intense preoccupied look about him. He glanced at me
and took a deep breath. He didn't look pleased to see
me.

"Dr. Chamberlain," Nurse Andrews said.

"Yes, Miss Andrews."

"We've got candidate Turner here with possible blood in his urine."

He looked at me again, this time resigning himself to my presence. "Is that right? Did you take a specimen?"

"Yes, it's right here."

"All right. Let me have it and go ahead and put Mr. Turner in the treatment room. I'll need a blood pressure and temp."

"Yes, Sir."

Nurse Andrews escorted me to a small room and asked me to lie down on the table situated in the middle of the room. She stuck a thermometer in my mouth and took my blood pressure. After a minute Dr. Chamberlain poked his head in the door and said. "Nurse Andrews. Come here, I want to show you something."

Nurse Andrews left the room to follow the doctor. I wondered what it was that was so interesting. It must be something bad, I thought. I didn't panic though, in fact, I hoped there was something wrong as I had no desire to go back to C Company. After being left alone in suspense for five minutes Dr. Chamberlain and Nurse Andrews reappeared.

"Candidate Turner, you have what's called hematuria which in layman's terms means there is blood in your urine. Since your urine is smoky colored, it indicates that your kidney may be in distress. We're going to have to move you to Quantico Naval Hospital. We can't take any chances with something like this."

"Whatever you say, Sir," I said greatly relieved.

"Nurse Andrews tells me you had a pretty rough day."

"Yeah, it wasn't too pleasant."

"You could file a complaint against Sergeant Foster, you know."

"How would I do that?"

"I can have someone from the JAG office stop by to see you. They can advise you of your rights."

"Do you think it would do any good?"

"They would be required to have an inquiry."

"But would anything be done to Sergeant Foster?"

"Probably not."

"That's what I thought. No one would believe a new recruit. They would just think I was weak and didn't have what it took to be a Marine. No, I don't think I'll file a complaint. He'll get what's coming to him some day. Everyone does."

"Well, I am going to have a JAG officer come by and see you in the hospital anyway just so he can fully explain the procedure," Dr. Chamberlain replied.

"Okay, but I doubt if I'll change my mind."

Within an hour I was riding in the back of a jeep to Quantico Naval Hospital. The cold night air felt refreshing as it blew across my face. As we traveled along the narrow road past the big hanger, I thought how I had again been the victim of fate. Nothing I could have done or said could have spared me Sgt. Foster's wrath. It was something I had to endure for no apparent reason, but it was over and I was greatly relieved. At that moment my destiny seemed out of my control. It was almost a pleasant thought to be released from all responsibility for ones life. I needed only to sit back and wait for whatever was next. This was a contradiction to what my life had been up until now, but at that moment I didn't have the will to fight it.

After traveling several miles we left the base and turned into downtown Quantico. It was an old, ugly town consisting of five or six blocks of frame store fronts. Not a soul was on the street at that time of night. A half mile later the jeep turned left up a hill to the hospital entrance. It was a wooded area with enormous trees towering over the hospital. There were three red brick buildings surrounding a parking lot.

The driver took me inside to admitting. He gave the nurse on duty my file and then left. They put me in an eight-bed ward between a sergeant with gonorrhea and a sonar operator with hepatitis. They were both asleep. It was quiet and for the first time that day I thought of Rebekah. I missed her, I needed her.

Chapter Ten
Let Justice Be Done

The next day, which was a Monday, the doctors examined me, did several tests and then scheduled me for more testing at Walter Reed Army Hospital in Bethesda, Maryland. They indicated they could probably fit me in on Friday. In the mean time I was ordered to stay in bed and rest. I was greatly relieved to be in the hospital and away from Sergeant Foster but the thought that one day I would have to return to "C" Company haunted me. Since I wasn't in pain I figured I couldn't be terribly sick. It was just a matter of time before I would have to return.

How could all of this be happening? I could have killed that jerk, Brett, for getting me in this mess. At least now I was getting my revenge. I was here and he was still there in the clutches of that maniac. I laughed under my breath.

When I woke up on Tuesday I was surprised and delighted to see Nurse Andrews dispensing medication to some of the patients in the ward. After a few minutes she worked her way to my bed.

"Hello, Candidate Turner. How are you feeling today?" She said as she picked up my chart.

"Fine, what are you doing here?"

She looked into my eyes and smiled. "Oh, I work here most of the time. I just work in the infirmary one day a week."

I nodded. "That's great. . . . I'm glad I got to see you again. I wanted to thank you for being so nice and understanding the other night."

She shrugged. "That's my job."

"I know, but you really made me feel a lot better."

"Well I'm glad," she said as she stuck a thermometer in my mouth and then took my hand in hers to take my pulse. Her hand was warm and soft. "Dr. Chamberlain has prescribed some medication for you. You'll be taking two of these tablets after every meal."

"Okay."

"Get plenty of sleep now. . . . I'll be back to see you later." '

After Nurse Andrews left, the sergeant next to me introduced himself. Since I had been gone all day Monday seeing one doctor or another and he had been asleep when I returned, I hadn't actually met him yet.

"Hi there, mate. My name is Harry Matson."

"Oh, hello. . . . I'm Stanley Turner."

"Another victim of Sgt. Foster I see."

"What do you mean?"

"You're not the first Candidate that's ended up in the hospital after Sgt. Foster got through with him."

"Oh really?"

"Yes, I think there has been two or three others. One of them didn't make it."

"Didn't make it?"

"Yes, a wonderful young lad fresh out of college, so full of life. He died not two days after entering Sgt. Foster's company at OCS."

"You're kidding?"

"I wish I were," Sgt. Matson said. "The base commander convened a Court of Inquiry but everybody knew it was just a sham. There's no justice in the Marine Corps."

"I guess I am lucky then."

"Speaking of luck. That pretty little nurse really likes you."

"She does?"

"She doesn't treat any of the rest of us like she does you."

"Huh. . . . She has been awfully nice. I really like her."

"Better watch out, when a woman wants something she usually gets it."

"What? . . . Oh, no. . . . I'm married," I said. "I've got a kid at home and one on the way. I'm not interested in Nurse Andrews."

"That's not what your eyes say."

"Huh. . . . My eyes?"

"I know you've got a poker face, but I can see a man's emotions in his eyes."

"What are you some kind of psychic?"

"No, just a keen observer," Sgt. Matson said. "I'm a personnel specialist you see. It's my job to evaluate people and make sure they're assigned to the right job. I can give them personality or aptitude tests and interview them all day long, but the real test is to look them in the eyes and then peer deep into their souls."

"Aren't you the one in here for V.D.? I asked.

"No. Gonorrhea?"

"Oh, Gonorrhea. Well, . . . didn't you look into your pretty little wench's eyes before you screwed her."

"It was dark and I was drunk."

"Oh. . . . I see. Well I'm going back to sleep if you don't mind. My doctor says I've got to get a lot of rest if I want to quickly recover."

He nodded and replied, "Sweet dreams lad."

I quickly fell into a deep sleep and began to dream. I was young. There was someone with me. It was my friend Steve. We were walking our bikes across a railroad bridge. There was the shriek of a whistle. We looked behind us. The train was coming. We jumped onto the ledge. The bridge shook violently and we fell into the river. A big man in a coat and tie handed me a piece of paper. I read it. "Struggling in a hostile world, pursuing your destiny, you will stand resolute against adversity, undaunted . . . undaunted . . . undaunted. A tall man in a black robe suddenly appeared and pointed his finger at me menacingly and repeated over and over. "You're in big trouble young man. . . . You're in big trouble young man. . . . You're in big trouble young man." I broke into a cold sweat and began to toss and turn and moan.

"Candidate Turner. . . . Candidate Turner . . . wake up. You're dreaming," Nurse Andrews said.

"What? . . . Huh. . . . Oh, Miss Andrews."

"That must have been a terrible nightmare."

"Yeah. . . . I was just dreaming of some things that happened to me when I was a kid."

"You'll have to tell me about it sometime."

"Okay. . . . If you'd like."

Nurse Andrews looked at me and smiled. "I would, but never mind that now. You won't believe what happened."

"What?"

"Sergeant Foster was found dead."

"What? . . . Found dead?"

"Yes, I'm afraid so."

"You've got to be kidding?"

"Someone slit his throat last night."

"Oh, my God. Do they know who did it?"

"The killer got away. There were no witnesses."

"Shit."

"Well, I just thought you should know. Someone might come by asking questions about it. I wanted to give you time to think about what to say to them."

"What are you talking about?"

"Well, the other night you were pretty angry with Sergeant Foster."

"You think I killed him?"

"No, of course not, but the military police are going to be looking for suspects. . . . I am afraid you're going to be their first candidate."

"Oh Jesus. No. Please tell me this isn't happening."

"I wish I could, believe me, I wish I could."

Nurse Andrews sat on the edge of my bed and took my hand in hers to console me. Sergeant Matson looked on with great interest, as did everyone else in the ward. When Nurse Andrews turned away, he looked at me and winked. I gave him a scathing look and gently pulled my hand away from Nurse Andrews.

"Mind your own business, Sergeant," I said.

"Hey. I didn't say a thing."

"Thank you, Miss Andrews. The warning is appreciated, but I've got a good alibi. I was here all night, . . . wasn't I, Sergeant?"

Sergeant Matson sat up straight, folded his arms and replied, "How should I know? I'm a sound sleeper."

"Well, with six other people in this room and two nurses running around there's no way I could have got out of here unnoticed for several hours."

"That makes a lot of sense," Nurse Andrews said. "I'm sure the police won't consider you a suspect once they realize that."

"Hell, they may have already caught the bastard who killed Sergeant Foster anyway," I said.

"That's right, they may have indeed," Nurse Andrews replied.

That afternoon I thought it was time to call Rebekah and tell what was going on. I asked Nurse Andrews if there was a phone I could use and she directed me to a pay phone in one of the waiting rooms. There were several other people waiting to use the phone so I waited for my turn. After about thirty minutes I finally got the phone and called Rebekah collect.

"Hello," Sylvia said.

"Mom. This is Stan."

"Stan. . . . I wasn't expecting to hear from you for a couple of weeks."

"Yeah. I know. Is Rebekah around?"

"Sure, she's in with the baby."

"Please get her for me."

"Okay. Hold on."

"Hello Stan, what's wrong?"

"Oh, nothing ser-. . . . Well, I mean. . . . I'm okay."

"Where are you?"

"I'm in the hospital."

"What! Why? What happened?"

I gave her a brief explanation of what had occurred over the past few days. She was crying before I finished.

"I'm going to borrow money from Mom and fly out there immediately."

"No, no. . . . I'll be out of the hospital before you could even get here. They've just put me on a couple of days' bed rest. It's nothing really."

"Oh, Stan. Are you sure you're all right?"

"Yes, I've only got a few minutes to talk, but I wanted to call you to tell you that I was okay and that I missed you."

"I miss you too. I'm so worried about you."

"How's Reggi?"

"He seems to be sleeping better. He asks about you all the time."

"Good. How are you feeling?"

"I was feeling fine until you called but now I'm worried sick."

"I'm sorry, Honey but I just needed to hear your voice. I wish I were home with you."

"Oh, so do I," she said.

"I've got to go."

"Don't go. Talk to me some more."

"I can't, Honey, there are other people waiting to use the phone."

"Oh,. . . okay, call me soon."

"I will," I promise. "Goodbye. I love you."

"I love you too."

That evening when the Quantico Bulletin came out Sergeant Foster's murder was the front page headline. "QUANTICO DRILL SERGEANT SLAIN - Sergeant Foster's Throat Slashed By Unknown Assailant." The article identified Sergeant Foster as a highly decorated Korean War Veteran who was survived by a mother who lived in Washington, D.C. and a daughter who was in college in Chicago. The article went on to say that Sergeant Foster was coming back to the base around 11:30 p.m. on Sunday night from a weekly poker game in Woodbridge, Virginia. As he stepped out of his car the assailant apparently grabbed him from behind and slit his throat with a linoleum knife. Apparently Sergeant Foster, who is a black belt in Karate, put up a good fight as his shirt had been ripped from his body.

As I turned the newspaper over another story caught my eye. FORTY-FOUR MARINE RECRUITS HOSPITALIZED AT PARIS ISLAND. It was about a platoon of recruits at Paris Island, S.C. that had been over worked by their drill sergeant and a large portion of them had developed hematuria. The Drill Sergeant had been relieved of his duty pending an investigation into charges he was abusing his recruits. The article excited me because it appeared to be the exact same thing that happened to me. I made a mental note to show this to Dr. Chamberlin.

On Friday I was notified that my test at Walter Reed Army hospital had been delayed until the following Tuesday. Nurse Andrews brought me some books and magazines to read as I was beginning to get bored sitting around all day. In the afternoon I was visited by Second Lieutenant, Barney Burden from the JAG office.

"Hi. Mr. Turner?"

"Yes."

"I'm Barney Burden from the JAG office. Dr. Chamberlain asked me a couple of days ago to come by and see you about a possible complaint against your drill Sergeant."

"Oh, yeah, well you're too late."

"Too late?"

"My drill Sergeant is dead."

"What? Oh, your drill sergeant was Sergeant Foster."

"Yes, that's right."

"Wow. I guess I am too late."

"Pretty gruesome murder, wasn't it," I said.

"It's quite a coincidence that you had just, . . . just had a problem with Sergeant Foster the night of his murder."

"I know. . . . Nurse Andrews has already told me I am probably going to be a suspect."

"Were you here Wednesday night?"

"All night."

"Do you have any witnesses who can verify that?"

"Should I be talking to you? I have had one year of law school and if I learned anything in that year it's that you should keep your mouth shut when you're a suspect in a murder case."

"It's all right. I'm strictly a defense attorney."

"Even so, you haven't been assigned to me so there wouldn't be any attorney-client privilege."

"We can fix that."

"What do you mean?"

"Just say you want me to represent you."

"I can do that?"

"Yes, under the Uniform Code of Military Justice every soldier is entitled, almost required, to have legal representation when they are a suspect in any crime. Since I was coming to see you to ask you if you needed me to represent you, I could accept your request to represent you in this matter right now."

"Really? Are you good?"

He smiled. "Yes, very good."

"Well, I like your confidence. . . . Have you ever defended someone for murder?"

"No."

At least he was honest, I thought. I wondered if I shouldn't wait to see if there wasn't someone more experienced available. Lt. Burden wanted the job. I could tell by the eagerness in his voice. I didn't want to act impetuously but then I thought of how coincidentally he had shown up just when I needed him. Again I felt like my destiny was out of my hands. I decided not to fight it.

"Do you think you're ready?"

"Yes. I've been waiting for an opportunity like this. I'll do everything I can to protect your interests."

"Okay then. You're hired."

"Good," he said smiling broadly. . . . Now why don't you tell me everything that happened."

I explained the whole story to Lt. Burden. He said he would immediately start snooping around to see what was going on in the preliminary investigation. He promised to report back to me within twenty-four hours.

Chapter Eleven
Temptation

When the weekend arrived it got pretty boring around the hospital. Nurse Andrews was off and her replacement was an annoying old bitch who spent most of her time drinking coffee and smoking cigarettes. I had read all of the books and magazines that Nurse Andrews had provided me so I found my self counting ceiling tiles. I calculated there were approximately 1596 in our ward. Finally I broke down and started a conversation with Sergeant Matson.

"So. . . . When did you find out you had syphilis?"

"Gonorrhea."

"What?"

"Gonorrhea. . . . I had Gonorrhea."

"So how did you find out?"

"I had to piss every ten minutes and it hurt a lot."

"Have you ever had anything like that before?"

"I had crabs once in Singapore."

"Great."

"Can it be cured?"

"Sure. . . . They've been pumping me with antibiotics every day."

"Will there be any permanent damage?"

"The doctor said they got it before it infected my prostrate otherwise I would have been in serious trouble. Woman can become sterile from it you know."

"Damn. . . . Do you know who gave it to you?"

"Some broad I picked up in a bar in DC. I don't even know her name."

After I learned everything I didn't want to know about gonorrhea Sergeant Matson began telling me war stories. After a while I decided I needed rest and politely excused myself to take a nap. The weekend finally passed and I was happy to see Nurse Andrews on Monday morning. She advised me that I was scheduled for tests at Walter Reed Hospital in Bethesda, Maryland on Tuesday and that she had volunteered to drive me there.

The next day at 0800 she dropped by to pick me up. She was dressed in civilian clothes, a red crepe dress with a square neck, a flat silver chain necklace with matching bracelet and earrings. Her hair was pulled back into a pony tail. It was cold so she had on a thick white sweater. She looked like she was going to a party rather than to a military hospital. Once we had got off the base she said she needed to stop by her apartment in Woodbridge for a minute because she had forgotten something. When we got there she asked if I wanted to come up and see her place. I agreed and went up stairs to check it out. It was a nice, two bedroom apartment with one room turned into an artist studio.

"Gee. . . . I didn't know you were an artist."

"It's just a hobby."

"Can I take a look at your work."

"Sure. Go ahead. . . . I'll be right there."

I walked into the studio and pondered the many pieces of modern art that adorned the room. After a minute Nurse Andrews walked into the room. She had taken off her sweater and let her hair down.

"I never really understood Modern Art. My wife is the artistic one in the family. She would probably love this stuff," I said as I gazed at Nurse Andrews casual appearance. "Wow! Miss Andrews you have such beautiful long hair. I never realized it under that nurses cap you always wear."

"Thank you. You can call me Rita."

"Okay. . . . Did you find what you needed?"

Rita began to slowly wander toward me. "Well I have a confession to make."

"A confession?"

"I lied to you. . . . Your appointment isn't until 1400 hours," she said as she put her hands on my shoulders and shifted her body ever so close to mine.

"1400 hours? Why would-"

"I wanted us to spend a little time together, so we could get to know each other better," she said as she pushed her lips so close I could feel her warm breath. "There's no privacy in the hospital."

"That's really sweet Rita, . . . but I think I told you I was married."

"So. You're here and she's there and she'll never know what happens right now," she replied as she pressed her lips to mine ever so tenderly.

I tried to resist but her lips unleashed such excitement in me I nearly exploded into a sexual frenzy. Somehow, I don't know how, I managed to pull a few inches away and said. "You don't know my wife. We've got something special. If I go home to her and I've been unfaithful she'd know in less than thirty seconds."

"How could that be?" she said as she began to unbutton my shirt.

"She's very perceptive. Besides, she married me because I told her our commitment was sacred. I can't let her down. I can't let my children down."

Rita looked at me beckoning me with her eyes to take her. I didn't move. Suddenly she let me go, turned and walked a few feet away. "Well you're either one extraordinary man Mr. Turner or maybe I just don't turn you on."

I took a deep breath and then smiled at her. "If I wasn't married there's nothing I would rather due than ravish your, . . . your incredible body right now."

Rita turned around, frowned at me and said, "Are you for real?"

"I'm sorry, Rita. I really am."

"It's okay. I guess I misjudged you. I thought for sure we had something."

I didn't answer. I felt sick. I wanted her, but I knew it wasn't right. I just couldn't put Rebekah out of my mind long enough to let my passions go.

"Let's get the fuck out of here before I embarrass myself any further," she said and picked up her purse to leave.

"We can just forget this ever happened, okay?" I said. "We can still be friends can't we?"

On her way to the front door she said, "Sure, why not?"

Rita was angry and didn't speak to me for over an hour. Eventually she got over it and things got back to normal. Since we had plenty of time before my appointment she took me to a modern art studio where she hoped some day to sell her work. After we completed admiring the art on display at the studio we went to the hospital. It was very busy so we were advised we would have to wait at least forty-five minutes before the tests could be administered.

"So, what kind of test are they going to give me?"

"A cystoscopy," Rita replied.

"A what?"

"A cystoscopy. They're going to stick a tube with a light on the end of it up your penis to look around."

"What! You've got to be kidding."

Rita looked at me and smiled. She was getting her revenge.

"No. I would have told you sooner, but I didn't want you to worry about it."

"I wouldn't have worried about it. I just would have

stayed at Quantico. No one is sticking any damn tube up my penis!"

Rita tried to keep from laughing but with little success. "They have to see what's wrong with your urinary track."

"Can't they just take an X-ray?"

"No, X-rays only show up broken bones. They'll give you an anesthetic so you won't feel anything."

"It will hurt afterward, I bet."

"Come on, you're acting like a baby. Just take it like a Marine."

"That's easy for you to say."

"You want me to come in with you and hold your hand?"

"No, thank you. This is going to be humiliating enough without you watching."

The medical technician finally advised me that my time had come and I reluctantly followed him into the treatment room. Rita waved good bye and managed to suppress her laughter long enough to give me a sympathetic look. Somehow I survived the test although it was not pleasant. The results all turned out negative, so we returned to Quantico early in the evening. I thanked Rita for personally taking me to the hospital and went back to the ward. When I got there, two officers were waiting along with Lieutenant Burden.

"Candidate Turner," the older MP said.

"Yes, Sir," I said.

"I'm Lt. Martin Hooper with the JAG office. We have a few questions to ask you."

"Okay, Sir."

"We understand you have selected Lt. Burden to represent you in any interrogation that we might desire to conduct."

"That is correct, Sir."

Lt. Hooper pulled out an envelope from under his

arm. "These are your orders to report to the JAG office at O900 hours to be interrogated in conjunction with the murder of Sergeant Louis Foster."

I took the envelope from the lieutenant's hand, opened it up and began to read it. "Yes, Sir. I understand."

"Thank you, Candidate Turner. We'll see you tomorrow."

"Yes, Sir."

The two officers turned and left the room. Lt. Burden stayed behind.

"What's going on?" I asked.

"They found out about what happened to you on the day before the murder. Some of your fellow candidates have given statements detailing threatening statements you made regarding Sergeant Foster. Apparently someone has even stated that you threatened to kill Sergeant Foster."

"That's a lie! I never threatened him . . . at least not seriously."

"You may not have been serious but your colleagues think otherwise."

"Damn it! What am I going to do now?"

"Nothing. Just tell the truth. You'll be okay."

Lt. Burden continued to prep me for the interrogation for another hour or so. Then he brought up the Fifth Amendment.

"Did you study the Fifth Amendment in law school?"

"Yes, I had Con Law."

"You may want to take the Fifth Amendment and not answer any questions."

"Well, if I were guilty I'm sure I would do that, but I'm innocent."

"I know, but sometimes a good interrogator can put words in your mouth."

"Do you think I should take the Fifth?"

"Normally I would say yes, but with your legal training and your profession of innocence I think you should cooperate and allow yourself to be interrogated. It will make your position seem more credible."

"That makes sense."

"I'll see you tomorrow then, get a good nights sleep."

I guess I knew this was coming but I wasn't expecting it so soon. I thought, since I was innocent, my interrogation should be nothing but a routine formality. But Lt. Burden had me scared. What was all this about incriminating statements and threats? I didn't remember saying anything so bad. If I did, I didn't mean it seriously. Now they're going to try to pin this murder on me just because of a few casual, meaningless remarks. What else could go wrong?

At 2200 hours the lights went out and I went to bed. So much had happened that day I had trouble sleeping. My mind raced between my encounter with Rita, the tests and my conversations with Lt. Burden. I finally drifted off into a shallow sleep and began to dream.

Rita began to slowly wander toward me. "Well I have a confession to make," she said.

"A confession?"

"I lied to you. Your appointment isn't until 1400 hours." She said as she put her arms around me and shifted her body ever so close to mine.

"1400 hours? Why would-?"

"I wanted us to spend a little time together, you know, so we could get to know each other better," she said as she moved in closer and closer.

"That's really sweet Rita but I think I told you I was married."

"So, you're here and she's there and she'll never

know what happens right now," she replied as she pressed her lips to mine ever so tenderly.

I tried to resist but her lips unleashed such excitement in me I exploded into a sexual frenzy. I pulled her body next to mine so hard she let out a scream of joy. She opened her mouth and began caressing my lips with her tongue. I thrust my right hand down into her pants and stroked her firm buttocks for just a moment. Then I slid it up behind her waist and with my left hand swept her off her feet and headed for the bedroom.

We collapsed on the bed and ripped off each others clothes. I was overwhelmed by her magnificent body and thrust myself inside her. She moaned in ecstasy. I fondled her breasts gently as our bodies swayed in perfect harmony. After a while when our passion began to wane I grabbed her around the back of her neck and then rolled her over on top of me. As I turned over I suddenly saw a figure. Someone was watching us! I squinted to make out the face. It was Rebekah, she had a gun and she was pointing it at us. She pulled the trigger. Bang . . .

"Ah!"

I sat up in my bunk, perspiration was pouring down my face. I was terrified. Then I realized it was just a dream. Thank God.

Chapter Twelve
Interrogation

It had been a rough night. After the nightmare I tossed and turned unable to sleep. Rita came on duty at 7:00 a.m. and immediately came to wake me up. I was on my stomach and I felt her hands on my shoulders gently shaking me. I opened my eyes but didn't move. The touch of her hands felt so good I just moaned to acknowledge her presence.

"You better get up," she said sternly.

I rolled over and looked up at her. She was like an angel in her white nurses uniform. I wondered how I'd been so lucky to gain her favor. What would I have done without her.

I said, "Good morning, Rita."

"Nurse Andrews, please. Remember we're in the hospital now."

"Still mad at me over yesterday?"

"Who said I was mad?"

"I don't know you just seem a little cool."

"You ever heard of disappointment?"

"I'm sorry. I really wanted . . ."

"Shut up! We agreed to forget it ever happened remember."

"Right."

"Now you've got to get ready to go to the JAG office. You don't want to be late, you're the star attraction."

"Okay, I'm going to hit the shower."

"Come see me before you go."

"All right."

As I watched Rita leave the room for a moment I regretted the previous day. I could have had her, she could have been all mine. Worst of all I disappointed her, after she had been so wonderful to me. If it happened again could I resist her? Probably not. But would she try again? I almost hoped she would.

At 08:30 a driver showed up and indicated a car was outside to take me to the JAG office. On my way out I went by the nurses' station and said good bye to Rita. She wished me luck and said to come see her the moment I returned. I agreed.

When I got to the JAG office, Lt. Burden was sitting in the waiting room.

"Hello, Candidate Turner."

"Good morning, Lt. Burden."

"How are you feeling?"

"Fine."

"Ready to get this over with?"

"I guess so."

Lt. Burden pointed down a hallway to our left and said. "We'll be in the North conference room, right down this hallway."

"Thank you."

We walked down the long corridor until we came the conference room. The door was opened and inside I saw Lt. Hooper with another officer at his side. A court reporter was stationed at the end of the table and Lt. Hooper motioned for us to take a seat across from him.

"All right Mr. Turner. The court reporter will swear you in," Lt. Hooper said.

"Do you swear to tell the whole truth and nothing but the truth so help you God?"

"I do."

"Please state your name for the record."

"Candidate Stanley Turner, Sir."

"For the purpose of this deposition you do not

have to address me as Sir and I will refer to you just as Mr. Turner."

"Okay."

"Just relax Mr. Turner. All we want to do today is find out what you know, if anything, about the murder of Sergeant Louis Foster."

"I understand."

"Is it true that you are a member of *C* Company of OCS?"

"Yes."

"And is it correct that Sgt. Foster was your drill Sergeant?"

"That's correct."

"I understand that you and another candidate were recently disciplined for disobeying an order?" Lt. Hooper said.

"No." I replied.

"No?"

"I mean that may be what Sergeant Foster reported but I did not disobey his order."

"Didn't you talk in front of the mess hall after you were ordered not to?"

"No."

"So you were disciplined for something you didn't do, is that your position?"

"That's correct."

"You must have been upset?"

"I guess I was after what he did to us."

"Did you tell Candidate Billings that Sergeant Foster was a bastard?"

"I may have. The man had just beat the crap out of me."

"Why don't you tell us exactly what he did to you?" Lt. Hooper said.

"Okay," I said and proceeded to tell him the whole story. He listened intently seemingly quite interested but showing no emotion. When I was done he continued his questioning.

"After you left Sgt. Foster's office did you tell Candidate Billings that Sgt. Foster was an asshole?"

"Yes, I'm sure I did."

"So you were angry at him?"

"No, I was too scared to be angry."

"How do you mean?"

"Well, when you step into a rattlesnakes nest and get bit, you don't get angry, you get the hell out of there. All I wanted to do was get the hell out of C Company."

"Once you were out of C Company and thought about what Sgt. Foster had done to you, didn't you get angry then?"

"Not really."

"That's a little hard to belief, Candidate Turner. Didn't you, in fact, want to kill Sergeant Foster?"

"No. Not at all. I've never even thought about killing someone."

"But Mr. Turner you're in the Marines. Aren't you being trained to be a killer?"

"No, I thought I was being trained to defend my country."

"Alright do you remember talking to Dr. Chamberlain."

"I'm going to object to any questions regarding communications with Dr. Chamberlain as being privileged," Lt. Burden said. "I direct the witness not to answer the question."

"Okay. Let's go to last Wednesday night. Do you recall that night?"

"Yes."

"Where were you?"

"I was in Quantico Naval Hospital."

"Were you there all night?"

"Yes, Sir."

"What if I were to tell you that a member of the hospital staff checked on your ward and found your bed empty?"

"Ah. . . . That couldn't be unless, maybe I went to the can."

"What time would that have been?"

"I have no idea."

"Well this is important Mr. Turner. It would be wise for you to think about it and try to give us an answer."

I sighed and tried to think. "Probably about eleven or twelve, I don't know."

"Did anyone see you in the bathroom?"

"No, I don't think so. Most everyone's asleep at that time of night."

"Did you leave the hospital at any time during the night?"

"No."

"Did you kill Sergeant Foster?"

"No, absolutely not."

"Do you know who did kill him?"

"No. I have no idea whatsoever."

Lt. Hooper rubbed his chin and then conferred a moment with his co-counsel. I looked over at Lt. Burden to get his reaction as to how I was doing. He smiled.

Lt. Hooper said,"Okay then, that's all for now, Mr. Turner, but you are confined to the base until further notice."

"Is that really necessary?" Lt. Burden asked.

"Well right now Lt. Burden your client is our number one suspect so, yes, I think it is really necessary."

"All right Mr. Turner, do you understand you may not leave the base?" Lt. Burden said.

"Yes. I understand."

Lt. Hooper and his co-counsel left the room immediately. The court reporter packed up her things and left. When the room was empty I asked Lt. Burden, "How do think it went?"

"Well you did all right but I just wish you hadn't expressed your anger to your colleagues quite so vividly."

"Had I known Sergeant Foster was going to be murdered I wouldn't have."

"Overall I don't think they have enough to charge you."

"What do they need?"

"They have a motive; they have the right state of mind; but they can't prove opportunity. They need to prove you left the hospital. If they can prove that then they will probably charge you. That doesn't conclusively prove you did it, but it's definitely enough to justify an arrest and court martial."

"Well I never left the hospital so they are not going to be able to prove I did. Besides it's got to be at least three miles from the barracks to the hospital. I'd of been gone for hours and someone would have seen me if I'd of walked that far."

"Good then. You don't have anything to worry about."

I laughed. "Yeah, right."

Chapter Thirteen
Casual Platoon

After the interrogation I had lunch with Lt. Burden and then returned to the hospital. I stopped by the nurses' station to tell Rita I had returned but she was talking to Dr. Chamberlain so I didn't interrupt her. I knew she saw me so I went back to the ward, laid down on my bed and waited for her. Before long, the door opened and she walked in.

"Stan, how did it go?"

"Not good."

"Why, what happened?"

"I guess I said a few things in anger the night of the murder that might come back to haunt me,"

"I know. You said some things to me I wouldn't want to repeat."

I asked. "What are you going to do if they call you as a witness?"

"I've got a bad memory."

"That is noble of you, but I couldn't let you commit perjury."

"If I just conveniently forgot that wouldn't be perjury would it?"

"No that would be obstruction of justice. I can't drag you down with me on this. It wouldn't be right."

"Always doing what's right, haven't you ever heard of self preservation?"

"I'm innocent, Rita. They can't convict an innocent man."

"It's happened before."

"So what did Dr. Chamberlain have to say about

me today?"

"He says he's discharging you tomorrow. Whatever was wrong with you has disappeared."

"Shit. I wonder where they are going to send me."

"Casual Platoon."

"What's that?"

"That's kind of a transitional platoon where soldiers who are recovering from injuries or waiting for assignment stay until the brass can decide what to do with them."

"Hmm. Do you know what I will be doing there?"

"It's kind of a temporary labor pool."

"If anyone on base needs manpower they call over and get soldiers from the casual platoon."

"Great. . . . It sounds like I'll be breaking up rocks or loading lumber."

"Actually from what I've heard it's pretty much a vacation. Most of the time you sit around and play cards waiting for an assignment."

"Good, I can always use a vacation, but I'm just worried about what the brass is going to do with me once my vacation is over."

"Probably put you in the next OCS class."

"That will never work. You think my next Drill Sergeant isn't going to be watching me like a hawk?

Rita smiled. "He'll probably have a twenty-four hour guard assigned to him."

I took a deep breath. "Shit. . . . How did I get into this mess?"

"Oh, don't give up on me now, somehow you'll get through it."

"I'd surely like to know how."

After talking to Rita I called Rebekah to let her know what was going on and tell her the doctors had released me. She was glad to hear I was all right and told me that she and Reggi were doing fine. I didn't tell her about Sergeant Foster's murder and my involvement because I knew it would be too much for her. I might tell her later, but only if it was absolutely necessary.

I moved into casual platoon the next day. It was run by Corporal Robert E. Lemaster. He was a very laid back officer and pretty much left everyone alone as long as they didn't disobey orders or cause trouble. Rita was right, most of the time we sat around and talked or played cards. Occasionally we would get an exciting assignment like watching a coffee pot perk or painting speed bumps, but not too often luckily. During my free time I spent a couple hours each day jogging and lifting weights trying to get into shape for the inevitable return to OCS.

In the short time I was in casual platoon I only got to know a couple of the guys very well. One of them was Charlie Russell from Boise, Idaho. Charlie joined the Casual Platoon a couple days after me. I met him one day after I had returned to the barracks from jogging. He was laying on his bunk staring at the ceiling.

"Hi. . . . I haven't seen you around here before."

He didn't respond.

"Hello. . . . Are you awake?" I said. "Hello, are you okay?"

Finally he looked up. "Huh," he said.

"My name is Stan Turner. I haven't seen you around before."

"I just got here."

"Where from?"

"C Company."

"OCS."

"Yeah."

"That's where I came from. What's your name?"

"Charlie Russell."

"What happened to you?"

"They kicked me out."

"How come?"

"I couldn't pass the damn obstacle course."

"I've heard that's pretty tough. I never got that far."

"What happened to you?" Charlie said.

"I ended up in the hospital after the first day of training. Did you hear anything about it?"

"Yeah. . . . You're the guy who got the shit kicked out of him and landed in the hospital."

"That's me."

"Are you okay?"

"The doctor says I am."

"What are you doing in Casual Platoon?"

"I am waiting for the next OCS class."

"They're letting you back in?"

"Yeah. . . . It wasn't my fault that Sergeant Foster got a little over zealous."

"They say you killed him."

"Who told you that?"

"It's just a rumor but everyone in the company thinks you did it."

"Well, I didn't do it."

"I wonder who did then?"

"I have no idea. Who did they get to replace Sergeant Foster?"

"Some guy named Monroe."

"Is he an asshole like Sergeant Foster was?"

"No, he's was being really nice for a drill sergeant. I think he's afraid of us. They still haven't identified Sergeant Foster's killer and as far he knows it could be someone in C-Company."

"If he's so nice how come you got kicked out?"

"Completing the obstacle course satisfactorily is a mandatory requirement of OCS. I also flunked my tactics course."

"They were pretty tough, huh?"

"I'm just not an athlete, the obstacle course was impossible for me. They might have worked with me more on it but when I flunked the tactics exam they just said *sayonara*"

"What happens to you now?"

"They are sending me to Paris Island."

"Paris Island? You've go to be kidding. I was just reading about Paris Island. That's where forty-four Marines were just hospitalized for being abused by their drill sergeant. Did you see the article in the paper the other day?"

"No, but I heard about it on the radio and I've heard a lot of other things about Paris Island."

"Like what?"

"The drill sergeants love to get washouts from OCS."

"Oh really?"

"They love to pick on them and humiliate them in front of the rest of the platoon."

"Is that right? Shit. . . . I hope I don't end up at Paris Island."

Charlie stiffened up and said, "I am not going there."

"What choice do you have?"

"I don't care what they do to me. I am not going there."

"Do you have any idea when they will be shipping you out?"

"Sometime in the next two weeks."

"Maybe something will happen, maybe they'll give you another shot at OCS."

"No, once you're out you're out."

"Why did you join the Marines anyway?"

"My Dad was a twenty year veteran."

"So your Dad wanted you to join?"

"No. My Dad died when I was ten. My Mom

missed him terribly after he died and was always talking about what a great soldier he was. I wanted my Mom to be as proud of me as she was of Dad so I joined the Marines. I can remember Mom's reaction when I told her I'd joined. It was like she had been dying of a blood disease and suddenly got a transfusion. She got so excited you wouldn't believe it. She writes me every week and tells me how she's bragging about me all over the county."

"Oh. . . . I see.   Now you're worried about disappointing her?"

"Crushing her is more like it. I'd rather die than see her return to the state she was in before I enlisted."

"I'm sure she'll understand," I said.

I felt sorry for Charlie as he was a really nice kid and I certainly could understand what he had been through. I tried to spend a lot of time with him and become his friend. He seemed to be doing better until he got his orders directing him to report to Paris Island. The next day when I returned from an assignment, I noticed Charlie laying on the his bed apparently asleep. I thought it was kind of strange since it was midmorning. I didn't bother him since I figured he must be very tired or maybe he was sick. After a while though, I got concerned because he was so still. I finally went over to him and gently nudged his shoulder.

"Charlie, are you all right?"

There was no response.

"Charlie . . . are you all right?"

There was still no response so I turned him over. His face was pale and his eyes were wide open.

"Corporal Lemaster!   Corporal Lemaster!" I screamed. "Come here quick I think Charlie is dead."

Corporal Lemaster came running immediately. He stopped and starred at Charlie. "Oh my God! What happened to him?"

"I don't know I just found him like this."

"What's this?" Corporal Lemaster said as he held up an empty jar of pills.

"It looks like the medicine the doctor gave him to help him sleep," I said.

"Somehow I don't think the doctor intended him to take all of them at once," replied Corporal Lemaster.

"Look he has a piece of paper crumpled up in the palm of his hand."

"Pull it out. Let's see what it says."

I pulled the piece of paper from between his fingers. He had a firm grasp on it so it was difficult to remove without ripping. The note was printed in capital letters. "TO MOM. I'M SORRY YOU'RE HAVING TO READ THIS NOTE. I KNOW YOU HAD GREAT EXPECTATIONS OF ME. I TRIED TO BE A MAN AS GREAT AS DAD BUT IT JUST WASN'T MEANT TO BE. I TRIED SO HARD BUT IT'S NO USE. JUST TELL EVERYONE I DIED IN A CAR WRECK. I LOVE YOU. GOOD BYE." CHARLIE.

Charlie's body was taken away and a few days later shipped back to his mother. I wrote her a letter and told her I had been Charlie's friend and explained why I couldn't attend the funeral. I told her how much Charlie had loved her and how he talked about her all the time. She wrote me back and thanked me for my kind words and for being there for Charlie in his darkest hour.

After two weeks, Corporal Lemaster called me into his office and advised me that my new orders had finally come in. I was to report the next day to D-Company, a new OCS class that was already two weeks into training. So I called Rita at the hospital to tell her the news and see if we could get together for a cup of coffee. She said she had to work till 2300 hours. but if I would come by the hospital we could have dinner in the hospital cafeteria around 1900 hours. I agreed and met her there at the appointed hour.

"Hi, Rita."

"Hello, Stan."

"How's Casual platoon?"

"Like you predicted it's been a nice vacation."

"See. I told you it would be."

"Unfortunately, it's over."

"You got your orders?"

"Yesterday. I've been assigned to D-Company OCS."

"Well, that's good."

"Except they're already two weeks into training. I am going to start out way behind everyone else. Do you know how hard that's going to be?"

"Yes, but maybe they will cut you some slack."

"I doubt it."

"Hey I heard someone in your platoon took an overdose."

"Yeah, Charlie Russell. They were sending him to Paris Island and he couldn't handle it."

"Did you know him?"

"Yes, I really got to know him well. I think I was the only friend he had in the world."

"It must have been tough for you?"

"It was. I tried to cheer him up and make him look on the positive side of things but it didn't do any good obviously."

"Don't blame yourself. If it hadn't been for you he'd of probably done it sooner."

"Who knows? So, have you heard anything about the preliminary investigation?"

"I heard from one of the JAG officers that was in here last night that they found the murder weapon and it had several different fingerprints on it."

"What kind of weapon was it?"

"I don't know but apparently they are checking the

prints and hope to know the identity of the killer pretty soon.

"Oh man. I hope they find him really soon, like before tomorrow morning when I join D-Company. It would be nice to have my name cleared before I have to face my new drill sergeant."

"Maybe you'll get lucky and they will make the announcement tonight."

"Wouldn't that be nice?"

"So how are Rebekah and Reggi?"

"They're fine. I get a letter nearly every day."

"Every day?"

"Just about. I answer every one of them too."

"Wow, that's amazing."

"Well, there's not much else to do in casual platoon."

"You may not be writing quite as often after tomorrow."

"That's true. . . . So, how have you been doing?"

"Fine. I've had to work a lot of double shifts lately. The hospital has been short on staff with the flu epidemic and everything."

"What flu epidemic?"

"Didn't you hear? Thirty percent of the base has the flu."

"I didn't know anything about it."

"It must not have hit Casual Platoon yet."

"That's good. That's all I would need to get the flu my first week back in OCS."

Chapter Fourteen
D-Company

At 0800 hours I reported to Sergeant Washburn at D-Company. He was tall with red hair and a freckled face. When I arrived and knocked on his door he didn't seem pleased to see me.

"Hello, Sergeant Washburn, Stan Turner reporting as ordered."

"Come in. At ease. Well well, the infamous Stanley Turner. I've heard all about you, Mr. Turner."

"I hope you don't believe everything you hear."

"No, I don't and that's why I think we need to clear the air here. I don't know if you killed Sergeant Foster or not. Apparently the Military Police can't prove you did it or you'd be in the brig by now instead of here. So I am going to presume you're innocent. That doesn't mean you're going to get any special treatment. It means you're just as lowly as the other worms around here that we're trying to make into Marines. Do you understand?"

"Yes, Sergeant!"

"Now I guess you figured out you are two weeks behind the other candidates in this company. It's not going to be easy to catch up but I've heard you're a smart kid so I think you should be able to do it."

"I'm sure I can, Sergeant."

"Good. I've arranged for a special tutor to help you catch up. You'll meet with him for an hour after taps every night. That will mean you'll get an hour less sleep than everyone else, but you should be well rested coming from Casual Platoon."

"That will be fine, Sergeant."

Sergeant Washburn walked over to the doorway to his office and yelled, "Candidate Price, front and center!"

After a few seconds Candidate Randy Price entered the room and said,"Candidate Price reporting Sergeant."

"Take Candidate Turner to his bunk and see to it that he is properly oriented as to what is expected of him as a Marine in this Company."

"Yes, Sergeant."

I picked up my gear and followed Candidate Price into the barracks where he showed me an empty bunk.

"This is it," he said.

"Okay, thanks."

"You've got ten minutes to get your bunk made. Then I've got to get you issued a rifle because we've got a twelve mile forced march at 0930."

While I began making my bunk I continued to ask Candidate Price questions. "You said twelve miles?"

"Twelve miles over the hills."

"The hills?"

"Yes. The hills south of camp are similar to those found in Eastern Europe. Sergeant Washburn likes to train his troops on the hills because he says it's more like the terrain will be seeing if we get into combat."

"Great."

I made up my bunk and put away my gear and then reported to Candidate Price.

"Okay I'm done. You said I needed to get a rifle."

"Yes. Follow me."

I followed Candidate Price out the back door and across a parade field to the Armory. A corporal inside issued me a rifle and a cleaning kit. Other than shooting a twenty-two at Boy Scout camp for a few hours I had no experience with a rifle so I carried it awkwardly back to the barracks. When we arrived the Sergeant was calling the Company to assemble outside to start the march. Lieutenant Johnson, whom I had yet to meet, was addressing the men.

"Now a few reminders. During the march I want you to stay directly behind the soldier in front of you. Don't lag behind, keep your rifles tight and erect and no talking. All right? . . . Any questions? . . . Okay, forward, hut!"

Hiking I could handle. I had done plenty of it as a kid and even the fast pace set by Lt. Johnson didn't bother me. The hills were pretty steep and there wasn't a trail to follow but I was keeping up pretty well and was quite pleased. As we continued I began to tire, however, and my heavy rifle became a burden. It began to sag a little with the barrel dipping slightly in front of me. Suddenly the Company was ordered to halt. The candidate in front of me stopped quicker than I did and my rifle barrel smacked him in the back of the head. He let out a painful cry and fell to his knees. Immediately Lieutenant Johnson came over to me screaming.

"I told you to keep your rifle tight. Now do you see why I told you that?"

"Yes, Sir."

"Let me see that wound Soldier," Lt. Johnson said as he examined the gash in the candidate's head. "You'll have to go get that taken care of when we get back to the barracks."

"What's your name soldier?"

"Candidate Turner, Sir."

"You're Candidate Turner?"

"Yes, Sir."

"Oh my God. All right! On the ground. Give me twenty-five pushups."

"Yes, Sir," I said as I hit the dirt.

Lt. Johnson's assessment of such a nominal punishment for my negligence surprised me. I cringed at the thought of what Sgt. Foster would have done. When we got back to the barracks, it was time for lunch. After lunch, classes began. I was two weeks behind in every class so I was totally lost all afternoon. That night when everyone else was going to bed, I was taken to a small room where I was shown how to take my rifle apart, clean it and then reassemble it. By the time I went to bed I was exhausted.

The rest of the week was equally as difficult. By this time the Platoon was up to about six or seven miles of running every other day. I wasn't in that good of shape and would lag behind after three or four miles. Sgt. Johnson was giving me a lot of flack over this but luckily I wasn't the only one not keeping up. During class I was having trouble staying awake. The five or six hours of sleep I was getting was insufficient to rejuvenate my body each night. I found myself standing through every class to make sure I stayed awake. When Friday came I was ecstatic to learn we were getting leave for the weekend. It was at morning briefing that I found out.

"Okay, we've been working you candidates pretty hard for the past three weeks now so we're going to give you the weekend off. I've arranged for everyone to get a pass starting at 1800 hours tonight until 1800 hours on Sunday. Now I want everyone to leave the base and get the hell out of her. Go to DC or somewhere and get drunk, let off some steam and get some pussy, all right?"

"Yes, Sergeant Washburn!" the platoon replied in unison.

"So right after class this afternoon you can take off except whoever is on guard duty will have to stay on base. Okay. . . . Any questions? All right then, dismissed!"

I was very pleased at the thought of leaving the base for the weekend. Finally I would get a chance to relax. Then I remembered I had been instructed not to leave the base by Lt. Hooper of the JAG office. I decided I better go advise Sergeant Washburn of my problem. I went to his office and knocked on his door.

"Come in."

"Sgt. Washburn, I need to speak with you please."

"Yes, what is it?"

"Unfortunately, I can't leave the base this weekend."

"And why is that?"

"Lt. Hooper from the JAG office instructed me not to leave the base pending the results of the preliminary investigation of Sergeant Foster's murder."

"Is that right? Well let me give Lt. Hooper a call and see if that order still stands."

"Thank you, Sergeant."

Sergeant Washburn picked up the phone and called Lt. Hooper. After they talked, he advised me that I could leave the base as long as I was accompanied by another Marine and didn't leave his sight the entire weekend. He called in Candidate Price and advised him of my dilemma and Candidate Price volunteered to keep an eye on me over the weekend. I was embarrassed having to be chaperoned but anything was better than staying on base.

Chapter Fifteen
DC Caper

That night we all hopped on the Greyhound to DC. Although I had been in D-Company for five days I hadn't had much opportunity to get to know the rest of the guys. Before we got to DC I thought it would be a good idea to get better acquainted with my companions.

"Thanks a lot Randy for sticking your neck out for me," I said. "I would have gone crazy having to hang around the barracks all weekend."

"It's okay. Just promise me you'll stick close by me," Randy said.

"You've got my word on it."

"Good."

I smiled at Randy's friend and said, "I don't think I've met your friend yet. I've seen him around the barracks but- "

"Oh, I am sorry Stan this is Paul Jones."

"Glad to meet you Paul," I said.

"Hi," Paul said as we shook hands.

"So where are you guys from?"

"I'm from San Diego, California and Paul is, I think, from St. Petersburg, Florida, right?"

"Right," Paul said.

"Is that right? I lived in San Diego for a year while I was in law school."

"Really?" Randy said. "You must have gone to the University of San Diego then."

"Yeah, that's right. How did you know?"

"I used to drive by there every day on my way to

UC San Diego."

"Oh, yeah. UC San Diego. Everybody gets our two schools confused with each other."

"I know."

"What kind of degree did you get?"

"Engineering."

"What about you, Paul?"

Paul said,"I graduated from Rice with a major in mathematics."

"Huh. A couple of scientist," I said. "Do you think you'll be able to use all that scientific training in the Marines?"

"I'm going to Navy Flight School as soon as I graduate," Paul said.

"Oh, I didn't know you could do that," I replied. "I wanted to be a pilot but I found out I had lousy depth perception."

Paul leaned forward, gave me an intent look and said,"Stan, there's something I'd like to ask you."

"What's that?"

"There's a rumor around the company that your last drill sergeant beat you up pretty bad and you ended up in the hospital."

"That's true."

"And, of course, now he's dead."

"So what's your question? Did I kill him?"

Paul shrugged. "Well, yeah. I guess that's the question."

"No. I couldn't even conceive of killing someone. I promise you I'm not a murderer."

Paul shook his head. "That's too bad. That would have been pretty neat if you had done it."

I laughed. "How do you mean?"

"We'd love to rub out our drill sergeant, huh Randy?"

I said, "Come on, you're not serious?"

"No he's not," Randy said in a serious tone. "But he does hate Sergeant Washburn."

"Anyway, we owe you a debt of gratitude," Paul continued.

"Why is that?"

"After Sgt. Washburn heard about Sgt. Foster being murdered he totally changed his attitude toward us candidates."

"Yeah, these last two weeks have been a piece of cake compared to the first week," Randy said.

"Well, I am glad some good came out of my fiasco."

"Anyway, tonight we're going to forget about the United States Marine Corps and concentrate on beer and pussy, right?" Paul said.

"Damn straight?" Randy replied looking at me for a confirmation of the game plan.

"Yeah, you got it," I said wondering if they were serious about getting laid. "Are either of you married?"

"What's that got to do with anything?" Paul said. "We're under orders to get pussy tonight. We can't disobey our drill sergeant!"

"I guess not," I said.

When we got to the DC bus station, I discovered that my companions had no idea what they were going to do or where they were going to stay. We asked the ticket clerk where the closest decent hotel was and he directed us to a Howard Johnson down the street. We thanked him, walked a few blocks and entered the Howard Johnson Hotel.

"Are we sleeping together or getting separate rooms?" I asked.

"Separate, I don't want an audience when me and my girl start doing it," Paul said.

"You're really serious about getting laid tonight, huh?"

"I told you I was, aren't you?" Paul replied.

"Well, I don't know. I hadn't really given it much thought. I'm married with one kid and one on the way."

"Shit, you're not going to be a party pooper are you?"

"No. Don't worry about me I won't hold you back. But aren't you worried about getting gonorrhea?"

"Gonorrhea?" Paul said.

"Yeah, one of the guys in the hospital had it. He said he picked it up from a hooker in DC"

"So what happened to him?" Paul asked.

"His Dick swelled up and he had trouble peeing."

"Oh, gross," Paul said.

"Then it spread to his balls and when he ejaculated his sperm was full of blood."

"Oh shut up!" Randy said."I don't want to hear any more of this crap!"

"I'm not sleeping with a whore. I am going to find some nice girl whose looking for companionship. Anyway, Sgt. Washburn said that if you take a leak right after having sex you can't get V.D. or gonorrhea. He says piss is sterile and it will wash away any bad bacteria," Randy said.

"He told you that?" I asked.

"Yeah he said a doctor friend gave him that advice."

"I hope it works," I said.

We all got checked into separate rooms and then took off down the street to find a place to eat dinner. It was 9:30 when we finished and started looking for a good nightclub. Most of the clubs we passed looked pretty sleazy so we kept on walking. Finally as we got closer to Capitol Hill we found an interesting looking place called *the Senate Gallery Club*.

"Hey this place looks cool," Paul said.

"Yeah, let's check it out," Randy replied.

We opened the door and entered the noisy, smoked filled bar packed with, what appeared to be, college kids and young professionals. In the distance was a dance stage with a topless dancer performing to a rowdy crowd of young men. To our right was a long oak bar staffed by three young, muscular male bartenders who were flirting with a flock of female patrons. To our left was a long row of heavy maroon booths and in the center were dozens of oak tables being served by numerous scantily clad young waitresses. There seemed to be many more woman in the Senate Gallery Club than men.

"Where should we sit?" Randy said.

"I say we go check out the stripper," Paul said.

"No, there won't be any woman looking to be picked up over there. We should go to the bar or get a booth," Randy replied.

"I vote for a booth," I said. "The competition at the bar looks pretty intense."

"You're right. Let's get a booth," Randy said.

We flagged down a waitress who seated us at a cozy little spot not to far from the strip show in which Paul seemed quite interested. We each ordered a beer.

"There are some pretty hot chicks in here," Randy said.

"Yeah, this is going to be a fun evening," Paul said.

Before we could finish our first beer, the waitress brought us another round.

"We didn't order another round yet ma'am," I said.

"I know, these are compliments of the three ladies over there," she said as she pointed to three women sitting together at a table across the room smiling and giggling at us.

"Oh my God, I can't believe it!" Paul said.

"They look pretty damn hot," Randy noted. "They

must want some action."

"They look pretty old don't they?" I said.

"No, they couldn't be over thirty," Paul replied.

"What do you think we should do now?" Randy said.

"Let's go say hello," Paul replied.

"Okay," Randy said as he stood up. "Come on Stan."

Reluctantly I followed Randy and Paul to the table the girls were occupying. They welcomed us warmly and invited us to sit down. After an hour and forty-five minutes of trivial conversation and six rounds of beer Paul suggested we have a private party back at the Howard Johnson. I didn't want to ruin the evening so I didn't object. I wanted to make an exit and leave Randy and Paul to their women but the Sergeant had instructed me not to leave Randy's sight. There was nothing I could do, I was sunk. How was I going to remain faithful to Rebekah without offending my new found friends and disobeying a direct order? When we arrived at Howard Johnsons we were all pretty soused. Randy and Paul each grabbed one of the women and took them into their respective rooms. I was left with a short brunette named Nicole. She was pretty but no match for Rebekah, at least from my perspective. I felt sick with guilt just being there with her. I racked my brain for a polite way to extricate myself from the delicate situation.

"Well, I'm really tired," I said.

"Take me into your room and I'll rub your back," she said.

"Oh, okay," I said. "Let me find my key. Gee I can't find it."

"Don't worry, the desk clerk will have another one," she replied.

"Oh, here it is," I said as I fumbled to open the door.

"Come on, open the door. It's cold out here in the hall," she said.

"Okay. Here we go."

She followed me closely into the room and took off her coat. She wore a knee length, red linen dress, a long white pearl necklace and matching earrings. After taking off her necklace and kicking off her shoes she said, "Now just lay on the bed, take your shirt off and I'll give you a back rub you'll never forget."

"Oh you don't have to."

"It's all right . . . just take off your shirt," she said.

While I was taking off my shirt she pulled her dress off over her head. She was wearing black underwear and dark brown stockings. Her body was firm and sexy. When she looked up and saw me staring at her, she gave me a shove onto the bed. I laid face down as she commanded. She climbed on top of me, sat on my ass and began to rub my back. It really felt good my body became limp. I moaned a few times and that's all I remember. When I woke up it was dark and Nicole was fast asleep beside me. I still had my pants on and she was wearing her bra, so I assumed I hadn't been unfaithful. I covered her up and went to the window to get enough light to see what time it was. My watch read 3:45. After I went to the bathroom, I got under the covers and just laid there wide awake. The temptation to awake Nicole and make love to her was weighing heavy on my mind but somehow I restrained myself. In the morning I was awakened by Nicole running the water in the sink. I looked into the bathroom and saw her, naked from the waist up, brushing her teeth. I starred at her cute little breasts for a moment and then turned away.

"You awake?" She asked.

"Yeah."

"How you feeling?"

"Okay, I guess. So what happened last night? I

don't remember anything after you starting rubbing my back."

"Am I good, or what?"

"Yeah, you've got magical fingers. I don't think I've ever had a back rub like that before."

"Well, I'll have to confess I am a massage therapist by trade."

"You're kidding?"

"No, it's true. I could tell you were pretty stressed out last night so I thought I would put you out of your misery."

"Oh, God. I feel like shit. You're such a nice girl. I really wanted to make love to you but, frankly, I'm married and I was feeling so guilty I didn't know what to do."

"Yeah, I saw the ring and figured as much. Don't worry about it. I had a good time just being with you last night."

"Well, you're a very nice person and I feel terrible. Will you let me buy you breakfast so I can relieve some of my guilt?"

"Sure."

"I better tell Randy where we're going so he doesn't think I went AWOL."

"Why would he think that?"

"It's a long story. I'll tell you about it at breakfast."

I called Randy's room and the phone rang and rang with no answer. Finally after eight or nine rings Randy answered. "Yeah."

"Randy, I am taking Nicole to breakfast. We'll be back in forty-five minutes."

"Yeah, okay," Randy replied and then the phone went dead.

"He said that was fine. Let's go."

We went downstairs to the restaurant and were seated in a booth. The waitress brought us some coffee and then we ordered.

"So why do you have to tell Randy every move you make?"

"He's responsible for me. I was restricted to the base but my Sergeant got permission for me to leave if I were with another Marine at all times."

"Why were you restricted to base?"

"I'm murder suspect."

"What? That's ridiculous."

"Why is it so ridiculous?"

"You couldn't murder anyone."

"How do know that? You've only known me twelve hours?"

"Because in the short time I've been with you I've learned that you are kind, considerate and faithful, hardly the characteristics of a murderer."

"Well, I could have a split personality or an uncontrollable temper."

"I haven't seen any signs of either."

"What about you? Why is a pretty professional women like you and your friends picking up strange men at bars?"

"It wasn't my idea. Sandy and Sharon talked me into it. They've been trying to get me to date for over a year."

"You haven't dated for a year?"

"My husband was killed in Vietnam."

"Oh no. . . . I'm sorry."

"He died at Khe Sahn."

"Khe Sahn? That's weird, my boss' son died at Khe Sahn too."

"Really?"

"I was there when he and his wife were informed of his death. It was terrible. I can imagine how horrible it was for you."

"It was very difficult. So you can see I was kind of

relieved when it was obvious you didn't want sex."

"Yeah. I guess everything worked out for the best," I said. "But, you know, we shouldn't let our friends know what really happened."

"No, no. We'll tell them we fucked all night."

"Yeah. It was incredible, nuclear sex."

She smiled. "Right. I can hardly walk this morning."

"Exactly."

As we were finishing our breakfast Randy showed up with Sandy. Randy sat down and Sandy and Nicole excused themselves to go to the ladies room.

"Well look who finally got up," I said.

"It wasn't easy," Randy replied "I've got a splitting head ache."

"It must have been quite an evening."

"I don't know. I was so drunk I don't remember anything."

"You don't remember anything?"

"No, nothing."

"Wow. You must have killed a lot of brain cells last night."

"So how did you and Nicole do?"

"It was great. She's got magical fingers."

"Oh really."

"And a body that won't quit. I've never been with a girl that's got as much energy. She wore me out."

"Shit, and you didn't even want to get laid."

"Well, I am glad you twisted my arm."

The girls came back smiling and giggling. Nicole groaned as she sat down.

"Nicole told me all about you, Stan," Sandy said."You little devil."

Before I could reply I spotted Paul and Sharon coming out of the elevator.

"Look who's coming," I said. "Sharon doesn't look

so good."

"Morning," Paul said.

"What's wrong, Sharon? You look kind of pale," I said.

"She's been sick. Just as soon as we got into our room last night she started hurling.

"That's too bad," I said. "Sit down and have some breakfast, Sharon. You need to get some food in your stomach."

The waitress pulled two tables together so we could all sit together. Nicole and I drank coffee while the others ordered breakfast. After breakfast the girls had to leave so we decided to spend the rest of the day seeing the sights of Washington, D.C. Nicole handed me a note as she said goodbye. I opened it up and read it.

'Stan,

Here's my phone number (555-2241) in case you ever need a good massage again or just someone to talk to. I had a great time. I'll be praying that your trial goes well. Nicole.'

We toured the White House, Capitol Hill, FBI Headquarters and part of the Smithsonian. That night Randy and Paul insisted on going back to the Senate Gallery Club. I didn't think it was a good idea but I got overruled. When we arrived, Paul insisted we sit in the same booth as before. He said it was a lucky booth. We ordered a round of beers and waited.

"If you think some hot chicks are going to buy us drinks tonight you're crazy," I said.

"Well it happened last night," Paul replied.

"That was a fluke, believe me."

"If nothing happens we'll have to go on the offensive."

"What's this?" Randy said. "Here comes the waitress again with a round of beers."

"Fantastic!" Paul said. "I knew this was our lucky

table."

"Hello gentlemen. These drinks are compliments of some of your admirers," the waitress said.

Paul sat up straight, peered out over the crowded bar and pointed to a table with three unattached females. "Let me guess, it's those girls over there."

"No, I afraid not," she said.

Paul looked out over the crowd once more and said. "Okay, it must those three girls sitting at the bar."

"No, wrong again," she said.

"Okay, quit the games," Randy said. "Just tell us who our secret admirers are."

She smiled as she pointed out our benefactors. "It's those three guys over there."

The three guys raised their mugs and smiled at us. Randy frowned.

"Oh, sick!" he said.

Paul's mouth dropped open. "Jesus, let's get the hell out of here?"

I laughed. "I told you we shouldn't have come here again."

After escaping from the Senate Gallery Club we decided not to risk another DC bar and instead went to a late movie. On Sunday we went to all the DC monuments and Arlington Cemetery. That afternoon we caught the bus back to Quantico. DC hadn't been what Randy and Paul had hoped for, but I couldn't have had a better weekend, at least without Rebekah.

Chapter Sixteen
Incriminating Evidence

On Monday afternoon, after my arrest, I was escorted to a visiting cell to meet with Lt. Burden.

"Hi, Stan. How are you holding up?"

"I'm okay. This place is a little scary but no one has hassled me."

"You just let me know if you have any problems in here."

"Sure. Now what's this crap about my fingerprints being on the murder weapon?"

The lab did some test on the linoleum knife that was used to kill Sgt. Foster.

"Linoleum knife?"

"Yeah. They compared your fingerprints from when you first checked into the base with those on the knife and they got a match. They even found two different blood types on the knife. One of those blood types matches yours."

"Oh shit. The murder weapon was a linoleum knife? Sgt. Foster had told us that workmen were repairing the linoleum in the bathroom but I had forgotten about it. The night before Sgt. Foster was killed I went to the bathroom, it was dark and I tripped over a tool box left by one of the workmen. All of the tools fell out onto the floor. When I was putting the tools back in the box, I cut my finger on the linoleum knife. After I put the knife back in the tool box the killer must have taken that same knife and used it to kill Sgt. Foster."

"That story is not going to be easy to sell unless

you have a witness."

"Well, I did bump into Brett Billings. He was on his way to the can when I was going back to my bunk. We almost ran into each other."

"Good. He can corroborate your story. I'll go pay him a visit tomorrow."

"Okay. What about getting me out of here?"

"I don't know. They've set your bond at $100,000. Do you know anybody who will put up that kind of money?"

"No. My parents are living on Social Security and my wife's parents have maybe ten or twenty thousand dollars in savings but that's it."

"Well, I am sorry Stan. I tried to get the colonel to lower the bond but with your finger prints on the murder weapon he wasn't too sympathetic. Anyway, it will only be six weeks until your trial. The time will go fast, which reminds me, we need to get started immediately on your defense. If you have any ideas on how we are going to prove that you're innocent I would sure like to hear them."

"I have no idea other than to somehow find the real killer."

"You hit the nail on the head. But how do we do that?"

"I don't know, you're the lawyer."

"Who else would have a motive to kill Sergeant Foster?"

"How about every other member of C-Company. And those are just the obvious suspects. There could be other people in his life who might want to kill him," I said.

"Well, then the first thing we need to do is find out everything there is to know about Sgt. Foster. I'll get a copy of his military file. We need to get someone to start talking to his friends. Can you afford a private investigator?"

"Are you kidding? I'm broke."

"Well, then you'll have to get your friends or someone else to do it."

"All my friends are in the middle of OCS. They would never have the time to start snooping around plus they could get into a lot of trouble trying to help me. Wait. . . . I know who might help us."

"There's a guy I met in the hospital, Sgt. Harry Matson. He's kind of an eccentric guy but I kind of like him, and although he wouldn't admit it, I think he likes me. Anyway he's been around for a long time and knows everybody. Maybe you can find him and tell him I'd like him to come visit me."

"Sure. You said Harry who?"

"Matson, he was in the hospital with me a couple of weeks ago."

"Okay, what else?" Lt. Burden said.

"We need to investigate every member of C-company," I said. "Can you get all of their files?"

"Yes, but that's going to be a lot of work going through every candidate's file."

"I know just the person to help us with that."

"Who's that?"

"Rita Andrews."

"Boy you know a lot of people for a man whose been here just three weeks. Who is Rita Andrews?"

"She's a nurse at the hospital. I know she would like to help. She's already been a great comfort to me."

"All right, that should keep us busy for a while."

"Is there anything I can do here in my jail cell to help out?"

"Nothing comes to mind except maybe to rack your brain to see if you can recall something, anything that might give us a clue to who murdered Sgt. Foster."

"Okay, I will certainly do that. Hey, will I be allowed to make any phone calls while I am in here? I need to call Rebekah and tell her what's happened."

"Yes, I think they'll allow you a couple of calls each week. Just tell the jailer if you need to make one."

"Okay, thanks."

After Lt. Burden had left, I summoned the jailer and asked if I could make a phone call. He said he would check into it. Several minutes later he came back, unlocked my cell and led me to a small room with a telephone attached to the wall. He said I'd have to call collect and I would have just ten minutes. I thanked him and immediately dialed the number.

"Stan, is that you?"

"Yes."

"What is going on I've been so worried about you?"

"You won't believe where I'm call you from?"

"Where?"

"Are you sitting down?"

"Yes, where are you?"

"I'm in the brig."

"What?!"

"I am in the brig. They think I killed my drill sergeant."

"Oh, my God! Why would they think such a thing?"

"Oh, it's just a bunch of circumstantial evidence."

"What circumstantial evidence?"

"Well, I didn't tell you because I didn't want you to worry, but I had a little run in with my drill sergeant the first day I got here?"

"Oh no."

"He was pretty rough on me so I said some things that I shouldn't have said. Then when he was murdered everyone pointed the finger at me."

"I'm getting on a plane tomorrow and coming out there."

"No, I'm in the brig. There's nothing you could do."

"But I want to be with you."

"Wait until the trial. I want you to be with me when the trial starts. There's nothing you could do for me now. I'm only allowed visitors once a week."

"Stan, I'm scared. What if you can't prove you're innocent."

"That won't happen honey. I'm innocent. I'll figure out something. You know I can't live without you."

"What about your lawyer? Is he any good?"

"I think so. He's been really good to me so far. I think he knows what he is doing."

"I hope so. . . . I certainly hope so."

"Well, my ten minutes are about up, honey. How are Reggi and the baby?"

"Reggi is fine and the baby has been kicking up a storm inside me. He's trying to break out I think."

"I wish I were there with you so I could feel him kick, but I'll see you in a few weeks when the trial starts."

Rebekah began to cry. "Oh God, I can't believe you're going on trial for murder. This can't be happening."

"I'm sorry, Honey. I never dreamed something like this would happen. I gotta go."

"Okay, call me again soon. I love you. . . . I'll pray for you."

"I love you too, Honey. Bye."

Chapter Seventeen
To the End

It was late and I felt drained after recounting my life story to Mrs. Stone. For over two and a half days I had told her every detail of my life. She had listened intently and taken copious notes. I sat back in my chair and took a deep breath.

"That's it. That brings us to when you came to see me."

"Well, I believe you were concerned that I might be disappointed."

"Yes. Are you?"

"No, I'm not. Believe me. I'm quite pleased actually. I got more, much more than I expected. This story is going to be dynamite. It's going to be worth every penny of the hundred grand I had to fork out."

"Where did you get a hundred grand anyway?"

"I have an editor who I convinced to front the money for me. He owed me a favor."

"So, now what?"

"Now you better do whatever it takes to prove you're innocent. I want my story to have a happy ending."

"If only I knew how to do that."

"Well, if there is anything I can do to help let me know."

"You've already done a lot by getting me out of that hell hole."

"Where are you going to be staying now that you're out?"

"I've got to go back in casual platoon. They won't let me back in my OCS class."

"Well, then you'll have plenty of time to work on your case."

"Yeah, I should."

"Keep me posted if anything else develops. I'll be here for the trial."

"Good, I am going to need all the moral support I can get."

Mrs. Stone packed up her briefcase and said good bye. I waved to her as she drove off and then headed back to casual platoon. When I arrived, I was surprised to see Brett Billings with his leg in a cast.

"Brett. What happened to you?"

He shook his head. "You won't believe it. The other day I hitched a ride on a jeep to the firing range. The asshole who was driving decided to race one of his friends in another jeep. He was passing when suddenly an oncoming car appeared. In order to avoid the car he ran the jeep into the ditch and it rolled. As you can see my ankle was broken when I was thrown from the jeep."

"Oh, shit, that must have been painful."

"Pain I could handle. The worst think is waiting around here for it to heal."

"That's too bad. You were almost ready to graduate, weren't you?"

"Un huh."

"What a lousy break."

"Speaking of lousy breaks, I saw them arrest you."

"You saw that, huh?"

"Yeah, it was pretty pitiful."

"What do you mean?"

"Arresting someone for killing a Nigger."

"What?"

"You just did everybody a big favor knocking off

that no good commie piece of slime."

Brett's blatant racist remark sent a chill down my spine. I had let similar comments slide in the past but this was too much.

"Wait a minute. First of all I didn't knock Sgt. Foster off and secondly I don't share your sentiments about Negroes, in fact, I find your attitude very offensive."

"Huh," he said as if he hadn't heard a word I had said. He gave me a confused look and then replied, "Offensive? I wish President Nixon would go on the offensive in Vietnam. His wishy washy policy stinks. My brother says the war would be over already if Nixon would just let General Westmoreland run it."

"Well, he's probably right about that."

"Did you know my brother lives in San Francisco? I went to San Francisco once last summer to see he and his new wife. Did you know there is a military base right in the middle of San Francisco?"

"Yeah, I visited it once. Anyway, I've got to go check in. I'll catch you later."

I didn't have time to listen to Brett's rambling as Lt. Burden had set up a meeting with Sgt. Matson. We had agreed to meet at the coffee shop in the commissary. I arrived a few minutes late and Lt. Burden and Harry were already engaged in intense conversation.

"Why should I help Stan, what did he ever do for me?" Harry said.

"Well, Stan here seems to think maybe you would be willing to help him just because it's the right thing to do," Lt. Burden replied.

"When does right and wrong have to do with anything? The name of the game is help someone who can return the favor, otherwise you're wasting your time," Harry said.

"I don't believe that's what you really think Harry," I said.

"Oh yeah, what do you know?"

"I know that down deep, beneath that craggy facade of yours is a man that cares deeply about other people, about right and wrong and most of all, justice," I said.

"You're full shit," he replied.

"Listen Harry, I lived next to you for seven days. I heard all of your war stories. You bared your soul to me Harry whether you meant to or not. You're a good guy and you know it."

He looked at me a moment, thinking, and then replied. "Oh, what the fuck! What do you want me to do?"

"That's better. We need someone to do a little checking around, you know, talk to Sgt. Foster's friends and see if he had any enemies or if anyone knows anything about what happened the night he was murdered.

"Do you have a list of his friends?"

"Yeah, Lt. Burden does I think," I said as I looked over at Lt. Burden.

"Yes, right here," Lt. Burden said as he ripped a page from his yellow legal pad and handed it to Harry. Harry looked over the eleven names that had been neatly printed on the page.

"I know, most of these guys. I'll go talk to them."

"Excellent," Lt. Burden said.

"Thanks a lot, Harry. You don't know how much I appreciate this."

"How are you and Nurse Andrews getting along?" Harry said.

"We're doing fine."

"Watch out for her. She's got her sights on you."

"I know you told me that already. We're just

friends."

"Friends. Hah! When you two get in the same room together the temperature goes up ten degrees."

"Oh, you're a real comedian. Why do you care anyway?"

"Well, I lived next to you for seven days. I heard all your gushy stories about Rebekah and Reggi. You bared your soul to me Stan whether you wanted to or not. Now I don't want to see Rebekah and Reggi get hurt."

"Touche. Well I'd love to continue our verbal fencing but I've got to get back to casual platoon. I promised Corporal Lemaster I'd only be gone an hour. Thanks again, Harry."

I didn't really have to go back to the barracks. My intention was to see Rita. Obviously, I didn't want to tell Harry that since he had suddenly become the Rebekah's guardian angel.

The thought of seeing Rita excited me. So much had happened since I had seen her last. She promised we could go to dinner after her shift ended at 1500 hours. I got there fifteen minutes early and eagerly waited. When the shift was over, I watched intently expecting to see her pretty face emerge from the revolving door in front of the hospital. She didn't disappoint me.

"Hi, Stan."

"Hello, Rita."

"It so good to see you out of the brig. I was so worried about you."

"You don't know how happy I am to be out of that rat hole."

"So tell me about this Stone lady. How did she hear about your case?"

"She's been keeping pretty close tabs on the Marine Corps for personal reasons. When she saw that

I had been arrested for killing a drill sergeant she was intrigued to say the least. She flew here immediately. She thinks my trial is going to be a big story."

"Well, I am sure glad she showed up. Now at least you have a few weeks to track down the real killer."

"Let's go get some dinner."

"Okay, I know a nice little place in Woodbridge."

"Good, I didn't eat lunch today."

After a thirty minute drive we arrived at the Wildbriar Restaurant and Pub. It was a quaint little steak house furnished in an old English motif. We were seated at a cozy little booth in the far corner of the restaurant. The waitress brought us drinks and took our order.

"So what are you going to do now?" Rita said.

"Sgt. Matson agreed to talk to Sgt. Foster's friends to see if they know anything, particularly if he had any enemies."

"That's nice of him to help."

"Yeah, we had to twist his arm a little but he came around."

"What else?"

"Well, Lt. Burden is getting all of the candidate files for us to review."

"What do you mean, *us*?"

"Well, I thought maybe you might want to help me out. There are a lot of candidate files and each one needs to be studied carefully. Besides I've missed you and it would be a good excuse for us to be together."

"I thought you were the faithful family man?"

"I am, but I just need your company right now."

"What am I going to do when you don't need my company?"

I sighed. "Your right. It's not fair. I'm sorry, I'm being selfish."

"No, I want to help you. It's just hard to be around you because, . . . because I've fallen in love with you but

I know you'll never be mine."

Her words sent a flurry of excitement through me. She loved me, she really loved me and it felt good to be loved, but the feeling quickly left as I was swept away by a wave of guilt.

"I know, I've felt your love from the moment we met. It's wonderful. You make me feel so peaceful and secure when I am around you. But I still love Rebekah and I can't betray her,"

"I can accept that, but I need to know. Do you love me?"

I hesitated, was it fair to say it. Should I lie to protect her, to soften the blow? I figured the least I could do was to be honest.

"Yes, I've loved you from the very beginning,"

Rita took her napkin and wiped a tear from her eye and said. "Well then, when do we get started?"

"In the morning. We're supposed to meet Lt. Burden at 0900 if that's convenient. Do you have to work in the morning?"

"No, I don't go on duty until 1500 hours."

"Good, that will give us plenty of time."

The next day we met at Lt. Burden's office as scheduled. He had arranged the sixty-six candidate files on his conference table in alphabetical order.

"Let me see. I'll start with "A" and you can start with "M," I said.

"Okay, what are we looking for?" Rita asked.

"I don't know exactly, just something unusual. Hopefully something will stick out and slap us across the face."

"Somehow I don't think it will be that easy."

After twenty minutes of silence Rita's face lit up and she exclaimed. "Look at this. Robert T. Hamilton was arrested for assault and battery in Memphis, Tennessee in 1968."

"Hmm, who did he assault?"

"A black team mate on his college football team?"

"Well, put that one aside for further study."

"Okay."

Another hour passed when I came across an interesting file. "How about this. Paul Sheffield of Miami, Florida once admitted being a member of the Ku Klux Klan."

"That's pretty good, don't you think?"

"Well, he probably didn't like being pushed around by Sgt. Foster. You know, that reminds me, I didn't see the file for Brett Billings. He doesn't like Negroes much either."

"How do you know that?"

"By some comments he's made to me. You know, like the night I got in trouble his comment was something like, 'I don't know why they let Niggers in the Marine Corps.' And then the other day he says something like, 'I don't know why anyone cares about a Nigger getting killed.'"

"Well, he obviously didn't like Sgt. Foster then."

"Yeah. He didn't like Sgt. Foster because he was black and then Sgt. Foster beats him up. He had motive but we can't prove opportunity."

"So how do we get the proof?"

"I don't know, maybe Sgt. Matson will come up with something. In the mean time we need to find Brett's file. I wonder where the hell it is."

"It should be in your stack."

"I know, but it's not here. I'll tell Lt. Burden when we leave that it's missing and maybe he can track it down."

"Okay, I've got about a half dozen files left to go through and then I've got to leave to get ready for work."

"Yeah, take off just as soon as you need to. You've been a big help and I appreciate all you've done."

After a few minutes' Rita finished and left. A little while later I completed my files and then went to see Lt. Burden. I knocked on his door and he invited me in."

"Well, how did you make out?"

"We found a couple of possibilities, a candidate arrested for assault and battery and a former KKK member."

"Interesting, do you have the files with you?"

"No, I just put them in a separate pile for you in the conference room."

"Okay, I'll go by and get them later."

"You know there's one file missing"

"Really? How would you know that?"

"Well, Brett Billings' file isn't there."

"Who's he?"

"He's the jerk who started this whole mess."

"You mean the one in the mess line."

"Yeah. I'd like to see his file because he certainly had a motive to kill Sgt. Foster and he obviously isn't fond of Negroes."

"That's true, but Lt. Hooper has already checked him out. He was their number two suspect after you."

"Really, and they didn't find anything."

"No. Other than a motive they have nothing on him. Their investigators found no evidence that he left the barracks on the night of murder."

"Well, I don't want to give up on him quite yet."

"Okay. I'll see if I can track it down for you. Lt. Hooper may still have it."

"I hope you can find it soon . . . we've got less than thirty days to trial."

"I am painfully aware of that fact, Stan. I'll get right on it."

"All right. I've got to get back to Casual Platoon. Let me know if anything develops."

"I will. See you later."

When I got back to the Casual Platoon I had a message from Sgt. Matson. It said he had some interesting information for me and to meet him the next morning at 0900 hours in the parking lot where Sgt. Foster was killed. That night I could hardly sleep. What had Sgt. Matson found, I wondered? The next day I woke up early, got dressed and was about to leave when Corporal Lemaster stopped me.

"Candidate Turner. Colonel Swift needs you this afternoon for coffee duty."

"Oh, no."

"Sorry, but you'll have to report at 1400 hours."

"Yes, Corporal."

I immediately left before Corporal Lemaster could come up with some other menial assignment for me. Since it was only 0730, I went to the mess hall for breakfast where I ran into Candidate Price.

"Hey Randy, how are you doing?"

"Hanging in there. What about you. How's your defense coming?"

"Not so good. We've got a couple of leads but we haven't found anything earth shattering."

"That's too bad."

"I'm supposed to meet Sgt. Matson at 0900. He left me a note saying he had found some interesting information."

"Well, I hope whatever it is it will be helpful."

"Hey, I heard Brett Billings broke his leg in a jeep accident?"

"I didn't know him. He was in C-Company wasn't he."

"Yeah."

"I heard something about the jeep accident. So Billings must have been the lunatic that was riding in the jeep."

"Lunatic?"

"Yeah, after the accident he got so angry with the driver of the jeep he nearly killed him. It took three Marines to subdue him."

"Did they press charges? No they just figured he freaked out from the trauma of the accident."

"Pretty bizarre, but I can't say I'm surprised. The guy has to have a screw loose the way he acts."

After breakfast I looked at my watch and saw it was 0855. I immediately set out for my much anticipated rendezvous with Sgt. Matson. The note he had left me had greatly lifted my spirits and I sincerely hoped I would be feeling as good after the meeting as I did now. As I approached the parking lot, I saw Sgt. Matson talking to another Candidate.

"Sgt. Matson, hi," I said.

"Hello Turner. It's about time you showed up."

"I'm sorry. I ran into an old friend in the mess hall."

"How exciting. Now let's get this over with. I've got other things to do today."

"Okay. Please forgive me for being five minutes late."

"This is Candidate Peter Wallace."

"Glad to meet you. You can call me Stan."

"Nice to meet you, Stan."

"I was talking to Lt. Littleton over at C-Company and he told me about Peter here. Apparently Peter was assigned guard duty the night of the murder. I don't know if you're familiar with guard duty or not."

"Not really. . . . I know someone got assigned guard duty in D-company but I really never knew what they were guarding."

"Well, there has been a lot of vandalism of the cars in the OCS parking lot so the brass instructed each Company on a rotating basis to provide a guard from sunset to sunrise every day. The OCS parking lot is not far from the staff parking lot. Candidate Wallace was on guard duty the night of the murder."

"Is that right?"

"Yeah. Tell Stan what you saw."

"Well, it was about 2300 hours on Sunday night when a Marine walked by heading toward the Staff Parking Lot. It was dark so I couldn't tell you what he looked like other than he was medium height. About thirty minutes later a man who I believe was the same man, who I had seen earlier, came back the other direction. This time he was in a hurry."

"That's all you saw? An unidentified man coming and going from the staff parking lot," I said.

"Well, there is one more thing."

"What?"

"On the way back the man threw something in the dumpster over there by that building."

"Did you go see what he threw in the dumpster?"

"No. He was too far away and it was dark."

"Shit."

"Now wait a minute," Sgt. Matson said. "Don't be too hard on us volunteers."

"I'm sorry. . . . I'm just disappointed."

"Well Candidate Wallace didn't check out the dumpster then. He couldn't leave his post. But later he did check it out and I found two rubber gloves."

"So you think the killer wore a rubber glove so he wouldn't get his finger prints on the murder weapon."

"That's my guess."

"You're probably right but we can't prove the rubber glove belonged to the killer."

"Well, this is all I could come up with. Nobody else on your list knew anything."

"I know you did your best Sgt. Matson. I really appreciate what you did. Maybe this rubber glove thing will prove to be important."

"I hope so."

"I'll keep you posted on anything else that develops."

"Good. Let me know if I can help with anything else."

"Okay . . . I will."

"Thanks Peter for your help," I said.

"If I can think of anything else where can I find you?" Peter said.

"Casual Platoon."

"Okay, good luck. I hope you can find the evidence you need to prove your innocence."

"Me too."

Chapter Eighteen
The Morgue

After meeting with Sgt. Matson I was very disappointed. His note had given me false hope. Now I was faced with calling Lt. Burden and telling him Sgt. Matson had come up almost empty-handed. It was late in the afternoon and I was relieved when I found him still in his office.

"I just got through meeting with Sgt. Matson."

"Did he come up with anything?" Lt. Burden asked.

"Not really, he found a witness, a candidate on guard duty, who saw an unidentified man walk toward the staff parking lot around 2330 hours. A few minutes later the same man came back in a hurry."

"Was he sure it was the same man?"

"I believe so. He also may have tried to dispose of some rubber gloves that were found by a dumpster."

"Huh, not much to go on."

"Now what do we do?" I said.

"Well, do you want to go to the hospital with me tomorrow to review the autopsy report and take a look at Sgt. Foster's personal belongings?"

"Sure, but I imagine the autopsy report will be Greek to me."

"I don't know anything about medicine either. Why don't you get your nurse friend to come a long? She's not a doctor but she'll understand that autopsy report a hell of a lot better than we will."

"Sure. I'll call and ask her if she will come."

"Good. About 1000 hours tomorrow in the basement of the hospital."

"I'll see you then."

When I got back to Casual Platoon I immediately called Rita to see if she was available to meet the next day. She said she was on duty but could probably arrange to take her lunch break and come down to the basement records room to help us out. Talking to Rita made me feel a little guilty so I thought it was a good time to call Rebekah and arrange for her to come to the trial. I calculated in my mind that it was about 4:00 p.m. in Portland so it was a good time to call. I dialed the number and the long distance operator connected us.

"You sound tired," I said.

"Now how can I sound tired when I've only said two words to you?"

"I don't know. I guess it was the inflection of your voice."

"Well I am a little tired actually. The baby's getting pretty big and carrying him around all day in my belly is a chore."

"You poor kid. I wish I were there to help you out."

"It wouldn't be so bad if I didn't have to worry about Reggi."

"Isn't your Mom taking care of him?"

"Yeah, but I still have to get up with him in the middle of the night. I don't want Mom to have to get up after she's gone to bed. She's too old for that."

"Are you going to be strong enough to come out for the trial?"

"Yes. Nothing is going to stop me from being there. I don't care if they have to transport me by ambulance, I'll be there."

"Well, the trial starts June 23. I think you should come out about a week before it starts so we can get you settled."

"Okay. How's your defense coming?"

"Oh. We're making a little progress. We're going to take a look at the autopsy report tomorrow to see if it will give us any clues as to who is the actual killer. Nurse Andrews from the hospital is going to review the report with Lt. Burden and me to give us the benefit of her medical knowledge."

"That's nice of her. Why is she helping out?"

"Oh, I don't know. She's just a nice person."

"Hmm. You better be behaving yourself?"

"What do you mean?

"She may have ulterior motives in helping you?"

"Why would you say something like that? You've never even met her."

"I don't know. I'm just getting bad vibrations. I don't like being 3000 miles away from you."

"Me either, but we'll be together in just a couple of weeks."

"I wish it were tomorrow."

"Did you ask your Mom if she would watch Reggi for a few weeks?"

"No, but I am sure she will. It's going to be horrible leaving him."

"Well, you can't bring him here, not with a trial going on?"

"I know, but I am going to miss him."

"I know. . . . I've got to go, Babe. I'll call you in a few days. Go ahead and make your plane reservations okay? I'll find someone to go pick you up."

"I will. I love you."

"I love you too. Good bye."

"Why did I tell Rebekah about Rita?" Was I just trying to open and honest with Rebekah or was I feeling guilty? I don't why I did it but it damn near got me in big trouble and I vowed not to make that mistake again. I didn't sleep well that night between worrying about

Rebekah's subtle suspicions and what, if anything, we would find in the autopsy report. When I woke up, I had a splitting headache. I could feel the tension starting in my neck and shoulders and moving up into my head. I got up early, took some aspirin and decided to go jog hoping the cool morning air and exercise would relax my muscles. After I had returned and taken a very hot shower I was feeling better and went to the hospital. Rita spotted me as I walked into the reception area and immediately joined me as I headed toward the elevators.

"Hi, Stan."

"Good morning, Rita."

"How are you?"

"Not great. The stress of this trial is starting to get to me."

"Huh. You haven't looked stressed out. You've actually looked pretty calm and collected."

"Well, I made the mistake of mentioning your name to Rebekah last night."

"What did you tell her?"

"I just told her you were helping me out on the case and she immediately got suspicious."

"What did you expect her to do? Women don't like their men messing with other woman."

"Have you been messing with me?"

"No, . . . but Rebekah doesn't know that."

"Why can't guys just have a female friend without everyone thinking there is romance involved?"

"Because if a man is around an attractive woman you can rest assured it won't take him ten minutes to mentally fuck her, . . . except you of course who are not typical of the male species."

"I've done my share of mental fucking."

"You mean you are actually flesh and bone?"

"You can pinch me to find out if you promise not to do it too hard."

Accepting my invitation with alacrity, Rita pinched my arm.

"Ouch! I said not too hard."

As we reached the elevators I stopped, faced Rita and starred silently into her eyes. She smiled back at me nervously until the elevator bell rang. We entered the elevator along with and orderly and an elderly lady.

"Why were you looking at me like that?" Rita said.

"I just trying to figure out why you have such a soothing effect on me. No matter how bad I'm feeling as soon as I'm with you for five minutes I feel like I don't have a care in the world. I guess it's those bright blue eyes."

"Is that the way you talk to all of your friends?"

"No, forgive me, I'm from the male species and, you know, I was just mentally fucking you."

The orderly smiled and the old lady's eyes lit up.

"Listen Boy, I don't like mind games. If you want to fuck me you better take your pants off."

The orderly couldn't contain his laughter and the old lady let out a sigh of disgust. Luckily the elevator door opened and Rita and I escaped. After the elevator door closed we both started laughing uncontrollably. Lt. Burden who was already waiting for us starred at us in disbelief.

"Hi, Lt. Burden," I said in between episodes of laughter.

"Hello Stan, . . . Nurse Andrews."

"You're in a pretty good mood for a man on trial for murder."

"I can't help it. Nurse Andrews is so funny."

"I didn't know that. Well, I hate to break up the party, but they have the report ready for us inside."

"Good. Let's take a look," I said.

Lt. Burden took us into a small conference room with a round table and three chairs. We huddled around the table and began to review the report.

"Okay, this box here contains everything that was found on Sgt. Foster when he was murdered. As you see he had a wallet with various credit cards, identification, a few photographs and $82. In his pocket he had some keys, half a pack of life savers and forty-seven cents," Lt. Burden said.

"That doesn't help much," I replied.

"Now here are some photographs taken at the scene of the crime," Lt. Burden said as he began passing the photographs around to us.

"Pretty sick," I said.

"Lt. Burden. Why is there a chest wound? I thought Sgt. Foster's throat was cut," Rita said.

"Well, it apparently is just a flesh wound. I guess Sgt. Foster might have put up a fight and the linoleum knife grazed his chest."

"Can we look at Sgt. Foster's undershirt?"

"Sure, it's in the box here," Lt. Burden said as he handed the undershirt to Rita.

"There are no cuts in the undershirt," Rita said.

"Then the killer must have taken off Sgt. Foster's shirt after he killed him," I said.

"But why would he do that?" Lt. Burden asked.

"He obviously intended to make the wounds on Sgt. Foster's chest," Rita said. "Maybe he wanted to leave a signature."

"Huh, interesting idea," Lt. Burden said. "Can you make out anything out of those chest wounds?"

"The tissue is pretty swollen and discolored so it's difficult to characterize them," Rita said. "But it kind of looks like a 't' or maybe a cross."

"I wonder if Lt. Hooper or his investigators considered the significance of these chest wounds," I said.

"I seriously doubt it. Once they found your

fingerprints on the murder weapon they pretty much shut down the investigation. I'll discuss these chest wounds with Lt. Hooper and see if he'll have someone study them more carefully."

Rita began to read the autopsy report while Lt. Burden and I were talking.

"Can we do anything ourselves to follow up on them?"

"Not really. This type of thing needs to get sent to the state police or the FBI for computer analysis."

"So we're at another dead end?"

"Not necessarily, Hooper has a duty to fully investigate the crime. He may take the ball and run with it."

"Yeah, but we're running out of time. We have less than three weeks to the trial and we have absolutely nothing to prove I am innocent. Oh, by the way, did you find Brett Billings' file yet?"

"Yes, Lt. Hooper has it and he promised he would turn it over to me next Monday."

"Monday? Why so long?"

"I don't know, he just said he couldn't get it for me until Monday."

"Billings is our only decent suspect. We need to get that file so we can start digging into his past."

"You and he are both in Casual Platoon aren't you?"

"Yes."

"Maybe you should try to engage him in conversation. He might slip up and tell you something useful."

"I can try. Talking to him is kind of difficult, though, he tends to change the subject often and ramble on about anything that pops in his mind."

"It sounds like he's a schizo," Rita said.

"A what?" I replied.

"A schizophrenic. They have a brain misfunction that is characterized sometimes by short attention span, rambling speech and antisocial behavior. Is he a loner?"

"Huh? What do you mean?"

"Does he keep to himself, kind of antisocial?"

"Yeah. That's right. . . . I don't think he has any friends. At least I can't remember seeing him hang around with anybody."

"Stan, I think the more you can find out about this guy the better," Lt. Burden said.

"Okay, I'll sit down and have a long chat with Mr. Billings just as soon as possible."

"There's only one thing in this autopsy report that doesn't make sense," Rita interjected.

"What's that?" I said.

"You're right handed, aren't you?"

"Last time I checked."

"Well, the lacerations to the throat obviously were made by someone that was left handed."

"How's that?"

"If I came from behind you and wrapped by arm around your neck to slice it, the gash would begin high on the left side of the neck and angle downward toward the right side. Isn't that correct?"

"Ah . . . let me think about that a minute," I said. "Yeah, that's right."

"So if the wound starts on the high right side of the neck and angles downward toward the left side you would have to assume it was made by a left handed killer."

"Damn. You're good," I said smiling at Rita.

"Lt. Burden said. "That's good thinking, Rita, but it's not conclusive. It won't overcome finding Stan's fingerprints on the murder weapon. But it is does dull the edge on their sword a bit."

After our meeting I took Rita to lunch. I was in a

better mood than I had been in weeks. Rita was feeling pretty proud of herself too since she had turned detective. As she walked me out of the hospital we talked about Brett Billings.

"Since you're the expert on Schizophrenics how would you suggest I handle by conversation with Brett tomorrow," I asked her.

"Well, you must be very friendly and non-threatening. Don't insist he talk about anything in particular or do anything that he doesn't feel comfortable doing."

"So how am I going to get him to tell me what I need to know?"

"Just get him talking about anything and then plant suggestions in his mind."

"What do you mean?"

"If you want to talk about his childhood start telling him about your childhood. If you want to talk about his father tell him you wished your father had been a Marine."

"Okay, I guess I kind of got the drift."

"Call me tomorrow night and tell me how it went."

"I will."

Chapter Nineteen
The Liberal Connection

The following day I waited for an opportunity to start a conversation with Brett. I looked on the duty board to see what he had scheduled for the day. It appeared he was on mess hall duty all morning but had the afternoon free. Before he went to breakfast, I wandered over to his bunk and stood beside him. He was busy giving his boots a spit shine and didn't look up.

"Hi Brett," I said.

There was no response so I spoke a little louder. "So you've got mess hall duty today, huh?"

He looked up at me slowly. "Yeah, what's it to ya?"

"Well if you're not doing anything this afternoon I thought you might want to go to the Marine Corps Museum."

"The Marine Corps Museum?"

"Surely you've heard of it coming from a long line of Marines."

He looked at me and frowned. "Of course."

"Did you know it was located here at Quantico?"

"No."

"So, do you want to go?"

He shook his head and turned away. "I don't think so."

"They have the actual flag that the Marines planted on the top of Mt. Suribuchi at the battle of Iwo Jima displayed there."

He looked up. "Really? My father was in that

battle."

"You're kidding?"

"No. What else do they got?"

"They have some of the original artifacts of Captain Samuel Nicholas, the founder of the United States Marine Corps, from way back in 1765."

"Huh."

"Wouldn't your Dad be impressed if you spouted off to him about the Marine Corps Museum the next time you saw him?"

"Yeah, maybe. . . . I guess he would."

"It doesn't matter to me. I just thought I'd go see it and wondered if you wanted to go. It's no big deal, I can go alone."

"Well, it might be better than hangin' around here."

"Yeah, there's not much else to do."

"Okay, I'll go with you. What time?"

"How about thirteen hundred hours?"

"Okay, I'll meet you here."

"Good. See you then."

All morning I carefully thought out what I wanted to learn from Brett and how best to draw it out from him. It wasn't going to be easy but it was my only hope if I were to escape what was beginning to appear like a certain conviction for the murder of Sgt. Foster. This was an important encounter and I couldn't blow it. I met Brett at thirteen hundred hours and we hopped a bus to the museum.

"Well did you survive mess duty?" I said.

"Barely, I am so sick of potatoes. All I did was run damn potatoes through the potato peeling machine all morning."

"Oh, I know, I hate that too. That's as boring as watching Colonel Swift's coffee pot perk all day."

"Yeah, I'd like to stick that coffee pot up his ass."

"Really, let's see you went to Texas Tech right?"

"Un huh."

"I went to UCLA as an undergraduate and then the University of San Diego Law School for a year."

"I joined the Marines right out of college. My Dad made me go to college so I could go to OCS. It didn't really matter to me if I went to college or not. My Mom didn't want me to go. I think she was afraid to be home alone with Dad. Dad's a great guy but he has a bad temper. My brother left home because of that."

"I'm originally from Ventura, California," I said.

"I live in Liberal, Kansas. School was close enough that I could come home every weekend to check up on Mom. Liberal is not to far from Lubbock, just about 250 miles. I could make it home in three and a half hours."

"You must drive pretty fast to make it back that quickly."

"I've got a '67 Thunderbird. I love that car. I've got it up to ninety-five before."

"Damn, that's pretty fast," I said and then noticed the bus was stopping. "Oh, here we are, there's the museum."

We got off the bus and toured the Museum. Although he wouldn't admit it, it was obvious Brett was very interested in everything he saw. He even bought a booklet describing in detail each of the museum's displays. It was crowded and noisy in the Museum so I couldn't really talk with him effectively while we were there. While he was absorbing every word from the tour guides mouth I was calculating my line of questioning for the return trip. Finally after an hour or so he was ready to go. We caught the next bus back to the barracks.

I said, "Well, that was interesting. There's certainly a lot about the Marine Corps I didn't know."

"Really, I'm going to impress the hell out of my

Dad the next time I see him. I'm going to memorize this book. I can't wait to see his face when I start spouting off some of this stuff."

"He'll be surprised, I bet."

Brett frowned. "I just hope I get back into OCS and get my commission. If I don't, it won't matter how much I know about the Marine Corps."

"Yeah, if I don't find the person who killed Sgt. Foster pretty soon it won't matter what I know about anything."

"What will happen to you?"

"It's up to the three officers that are appointed to try my case."

"It could be life imprisonment or maybe even, God forbid, the firing squad."

"Jesus Christ, and all because of a lousy Nigger."

"I can't really blame it on Sgt. Foster. Whoever killed him must have had some good reason."

"If there's anything I can do to help you let me know."

"Thanks, but I don't know what that would be."

"I didn't know they still used the firing squad? My uncle had to serve on a firing squad one time. He didn't like it. Whenever he fell asleep he would dream of that poor bastard getting pulverized by a barrage of twenty-one bullets. I wouldn't mind being on-"

"Please! . . . I am trying to put that out of my mind. If I start worrying about the firing squad I won't be able to fully concentrate on solving this murder."

"Didn't they find your fingerprints on the knife that killed Sgt. Foster?"

"Yes, don't you remember how they got there?"

"How?"

"Remember I went to the can the night before Sgt. Foster's murder. It was dark and I knocked over the tool box."

"Yeah, I remember that."

"And I ran into you as I was coming back from the bathroom. You wondered what all the noise was about. I told you I had cut my finger on the knife."

"Oh, right. I remember."

"Well, that's how my fingerprints got on the knife."

"Whose prosecuting your case?"

"Lt. Hooper."

"What does he say about your explanation?"

"He thinks it pretty flimsy. He didn't talk to you about it did he."

"A couple of investigators questioned me. Sgt. Badger from the JAG office and Sgt. Matson from the personnel office."

"Sgt. Matson came to see you? Huh, I didn't know you were on his list. Oh well."

"Did Sgt. Badger ask you about my explanation?"

"I'm not sure. He may have."

"Huh . . . Well, here's our stop."

We got off the bus and went into the barracks. Since it was almost time for dinner I wasn't able to talk any more with Brett. I started to sift through my mind what I had learned. I didn't expect him to confess obviously, but I had hoped he would tell me something revealing, something that would let me begin to unravel the mystery. There was something there, but what was it? I went to the mess hall and saw Randy Price so I sat with him at dinner.

"So, how's your training coming," I said.

"Pretty good. Just a few more weeks to graduation."

"God, that is so great. I wish I were still in the Company with you."

"How's your defense coming along?"

"I don't know. We have less than three weeks to the trial and still don't have much. We did figure out that the killer was left handed."

"Really? Are you left handed?"

"No."

"Well, isn't that enough?"

"No, it's not impossible for a right handed person to slash someone's neck with his left hand, it's just not likely."

"Is that all you have?"

"Well, you know Brett Billings don't you?"

"Oh yes, I know that weirdo."

"Well, you remember he's the one that got me in trouble in the first place?"

"Yeah, what an asshole."

"He got disciplined like I did that night so he was probably pretty pissed off at Sgt. Foster. We think he might have done it. He has a motive, he doesn't like Negroes, he saw me knock over the tool box and knew I cut my finger. He could have gone and got the linoleum knife wearing rubber gloves so he wouldn't disturb my fingerprints and then slashed Sgt. Foster's throat knowing that they would pin the murder on me."

"Damn, that's a pretty impressive theory."

"Yeah, but how do we prove it. There's no witnesses and Brett's certainly not going to confess, although I've tried to pry information out of him that might lead to something."

"You've been talking to him?"

"Yeah, I took him to the Marine Corps Museum today, can you believe it. He really opened up to me?"

"So, what did you learn?"

"Well, he's from Liberal, Kansas, he graduated from Texas Tech, he drives a '68 Ford Thunderbird, he likes to drive fast, he's afraid of his father and he loves his mother."

"Wait, you said Liberal, Kansas?"

"Un-huh."

"That's where the Sunday Night Slasher used to operate."

"The Sunday Night Slasher?"

"Yeah, You must have heard about him on the news six or eight months ago. He killed something like nineteen black leaders in Liberal, Kansas between 1968 and 1969, all killed on a Sunday Night."

"You don't think-"

"If I were in your shoes I'd follow up every lead."

After dinner I called over to Lt. Burden's office to tell him about the "Sunday Night Slasher." He had already left so I told his secretary I had to speak with him immediately. I told her it was a matter of life or death. She said there was no way she could contact him as he was on his way home and she had to leave, but that she would give me his home telephone number if it was urgent. I repeated that it was a matter of life or death and she gave me his phone number. I called the number but there was no answer. After fifteen nervous minutes I tried again. This time he answered.

"I've got some great news. I had a long conversation with Brett Billings today and I found out he's from Liberal, Kansas."

"So what?"

"Do you know what's been going on in Liberal, Kansas?"

"No, not really."

"Well, have you heard of the Sunday Night Slasher?"

"The what?"

"The Sunday Night Slasher. He's a serial killer that operated in Liberal, Kansas during 1968 and 1969. He killed something like 19 Negro leaders all on a Sunday night."

"Huh, that's interesting, but-"

"We know Sgt. Foster was a Negro, he was a leader and he was killed on a Sunday night from a slash to his throat."

If you're thinking that Brett Billings is the Sunday Night Slasher, . . . I've got to say that's a little far fetched."

"I know it is, but it's possible and I can't afford to overlook any possibility. My life's at stake here."

"You're right. . . . We'll have to look into it. Let me see, we need someone to go to Liberal, Kansas and talk to the authorities or maybe Brett's family."

"I have a friend in California who would go if I called and asked him."

"Yeah, but we need an experienced investigator. We don't have much time here."

"You know who would do it?"

"Who?"

"Virginia Stone. . . . You know, the writer who put up my bail. . . . She'll go ballistic when I tell her a serial killer may be responsible for Sgt. Foster's murder."

"She'd be perfect. Call her right away. If she needs to talk to me, you can give her my home phone number. How did you get my home telephone number anyway?"

"I think I scared your secretary. I told her it was a matter of life or death so she gave it to me."

"Well, I am glad she did."

"Good luck finding Mrs. Stone."

"Thanks. I'll keep you posted."

Immediately I called the number Mrs. Stone had given me to reach her. The number had been forwarded to an answering service for the evening but the operator advised me that Mrs. Stone would be calling in for messages periodically. Finally at 2200 hours I got a call back. I told her the situation and as much as I knew about Brett Billings. She was excited about the possibility that the Sunday Night Slasher was responsible for Sgt. Foster death. She said she would take the first flight out to Kansas City and then rent a car and drive the rest of the way to Liberal. She said if she found anything interesting she would immediately fly to DC to tell me about it in person.

Chapter Twenty
The Sunday Night Slasher

Just as Mrs. Stone had promised I got a call from her a couple days later. She was at Dulles Airport and wanted to let me know she was on the way to see me. She said she had a lot to tell me. I met her at the Holiday Inn in Woodbridge where she planned to stay the night. We exchanged greetings and then she began to tell me what had transpired in Liberal.

When I got into Liberal I thought I would go to see Brett's mother first before I got the local police stirred up about a possible connection between the Sunday Night Slasher and her son.

I got a local map at a gas station and managed to find the Billings' house without too much trouble. It was a two story white frame house in a middle class neighborhood. I parked out front and then went to the front door and knocked. After a minute Mrs. Billings appeared."

"Hello," Mrs. Billings said.

"Hi Mrs. Billings, I'm Virginia Stone. I'm a writer on assignment for the Charlotte Gazette."

"Well nice to meet you. What brings you to Liberal?"

"I'm doing a story on the United States Marine Corps and heard that the Billings family has a rich tradition of service to the Marines."

"Well, that's true. My husband is a Marine as was his father and grandfather."

"I understand you also have two son's who are Marines."

"That's right. John who is stationed in San

Francisco and Brett whose going through OCS at Quantico."

"That's really wonderful. I wonder if you might give me an hour or so for an interview. You know it's always good to interject some human interest into a story. I want my readers to get a feel for the family behind the Marine."

"Well, I don't know, I probably should ask my husband."

"Oh, no there's no reason to bother him. It will just take a few minutes."

"Well, okay why don't you come in."

I went inside and sat on her green fabric sofa. She sat in a rocking chair across from me.

"Can I get you a cup of coffee?"

"Well, if you have some made, otherwise a glass of water will be fine."

"I've got a fresh pot all made."

"Fine. I take it black."

Mrs. Billings left to go get the coffee. While she was gone I snooped around the room looking at photographs and searching for anything that might give me some insight into Brett's life. When I heard her coming back I returned to where I had been sitting when she left.

I smiled and said, "Now Mrs. Billings, why don't you tell me first about your two sons who are Marines?"

"Okay. John is our eldest son. He's a Lieutenant stationed in San Francisco. He's married and has two wonderful children."

"How old was he when he joined the Marines?"

"He was just seventeen, fresh out of high school."

"Why did he join so young?"

"John was always very independent and didn't like to be under his father's thumb."

"How did he get to be an officer without a college

degree?"

"He managed to go to school while he was in the Marines and with the help of his grandfather, Colonel Howard Billings, he was able to get into OCS."

"That's amazing. You must have been very proud."

"Oh, yes."

"What about Brett? He graduated from Texas Tech didn't he?"

"Yes. He and I were very close. I don't think he really wanted to leave home. He just joined the Marines to please his father."

"What kind of a boy was he?"

"Oh he was kind of shy, kept to himself but he was very smart."

"I know this is kind of a strange request but I'd like to see his room. You know, just to get some insight into what makes a Marine tick."

"Well, I don't know."

"I won't disturb anything. It would really help me get an in depth understanding of what makes a Marine so special."

"Well, I guess it will be all right."

Mrs. Billings led me up a narrow flight of stairs and down a hallway to Brett's room. I followed her with great interest sipping my coffee as I went. As I walked into the room, an eerie feeling overcame me. The room was decorated with combat memorabilia from the Civil War to Vietnam. Of particular interest were a German Helmet and a saber that adorned one wall and a full sized Nazis Flag hanging from the other.

"Brett's really into military history as you can imagine," she said obviously trying to explain his bizarre decor. "Brett's father brought that flag back from the war. He took it off a school flag pole on the outskirts of Paris after his platoon liberated it. He got the helmet and saber off an enemy soldier he killed."

"Is that right?" I said amazed at what I was seeing. I wondered how I could get rid of Mrs. Billings for five minutes so I could give the room a thorough search.

"Gee, I wonder if I could have another cup of this wonderful coffee. It's so good."

"Why of course, let me have your cup. I'll be right back."

After she had disappeared, I quickly went to work opening drawers, peeking into the closet and looking under the bed. It was under the bed that I found something interesting, a stack of old newspapers. I looked toward the door and listened to see if I could hear Mrs. Billings returning. It was quiet. I pulled out the pile of newspapers and began to scan them. It didn't take but a second to see that each paper displayed a headline about the Sunday Night Slasher. Hearing Mrs. Billings walking up the stairs, I quickly returned the newspapers to their hiding place and stood up.

"Here's your coffee, Mrs. Stone."

"Thank you. What kind of coffee is this anyway?"

"It's a special blend that the officers get from Columbia."

"Is that so? Well I want to thank you for your hospitality. I can't wait to get this story written. You've been such a great help."

"Well it was my pleasure. Would you send me a copy of the story after you write it?"

"Why of course. I'd be happy to."

We walked back downstairs, I said good bye and left. I had seen enough now to warrant paying a visit to the local police department. It was almost lunch time so I stopped across the street from the police station at a little cafe to have lunch. I also wanted to do a little research on the local police department to enhance my chances of quickly getting the information I needed.

Police officers usually didn't like the press and a direct request for sensitive information coming from an East Coast reporter would probably be flatly rejected. A waitress wandered over to take my order.

"Hi, Ma'am. What can I get ya?"

"I'll take a Club Sandwich, potato chips and iced tea."

"All right. Comin' right up."

The waitress left and disappeared into the kitchen. While I waited I took a good look around and watched some of the customers eat. After about ten minutes the waitress came back with my lunch.

"Here you are."

"Thank you. This looks so good."

"It's our specialty."

"Oh."

"You're not from around here are you?"

"No. I am a writer. I am doing a story on small town police departments. I bet you get a lot of police officers over here eating since you're so close to the station house."

"Yeah, most everyone comes over here sooner or later."

"I bet you know a lot about the Liberal Police Department."

"Quite a bit, I suppose."

"Listen, maybe you could help me. If I want to really find out about what makes the department tick who should I talk to?"

"Well don't go to the Chief. He's paranoid as hell. He won't give you the time of day."

"Really?"

"Yeah, I'd go to Lt. Winston. He's been on the force for twenty-three years and loves to tell everybody all about it."

"Good, maybe you could give me a description of

him."

"No need. I'll just point him out to you. He's over there in the corner eating a bowl of chili."

"Oh really, thank you."

I ate my lunch quickly wanting to finish about the same time as Lt. Winston. Just as he was getting up to leave, I walked over to him and introduced myself.

"You must be Lt. Winston," I said.

"Yes, that's right."

"I'm Virginia Stone. I am writer for the Charlotte Gazette. I'm doing a story on the United States Marine Corps."

"So what are you doing in Liberal?"

"In the course of my story I've come across some information about a local criminal here in Liberal that may have joined the Marine Corps."

"Who is it?"

"The Sunday Night Slasher."

"What? The Slasher?"

"Well, it's just circumstantial evidence right now but there is local resident who recently joined the Marine Corps who may have committed a murder in Quantico, Virginia very similar to the ones committed here by the Sunday Night Slasher."

"Why don't you come across the street and talk to the chief?"

"I don't want to cause a big commotion. I'd rather just deal with you for right now until we're sure that there is some substance to my suspicions. I don't want anyone to get hurt if I am wrong."

"Okay. But if we find out anything concrete we'll have to go to the Chief."

"Do you know Brett Billings?"

"Sure, his family has lived in this county for over a 100 years."

"Well, I was just over at his house and did you

know under his bed he has a copy of every newspaper in which the Sunday Night Slasher made the headlines."

"How do you know what's under his bed?"

"His Mom let me take a look in his room."

"So that doesn't prove anything."

"True, but a few weeks ago Mr. Billings was severely disciplined by his Negro Drill Sargent and two nights later, Sunday Night, his throat was slashed."

"Huh."

"You don't seem too surprised?"

"Well the FBI was here about six months ago asking about Brett Billings?"

"They were?"

"Yes. They said he was a suspect. They wanted to know everything possible about him."

"Do you remember who was handling the investigation for the FBI?"

"Yes, I believe it was Agent Raul Sierra."

"What did the Chief think about the FBI's suspicions?"

"He didn't like it much on account of Brett's dad is one of his best friends."

"So no further investigation took place?"

"That's right."

"Is there anybody in town who knows Brett Billings pretty well who might talk to me?"

"You might want to talk to his old girl friend, Angela Mayberry. She knew him better than his own parents. About a year ago they broke up. Her parents say Brett beat her pretty badly, but she denies it. Whatever he did though, was enough to cause Angela to end the relationship."

"Where can I find her?"

"She works at the library downtown."

"Great, thanks for your help."

"I hope you can find out the truth. It's time the

Sunday Night Slasher is put out of business."

"Thank you. I am going to do everything in my power to make that happen."

I went immediately downtown to find the Liberal Library and hopefully Angela Mayberry. When I arrived, I asked the girl behind the information desk where I could find her. She said she was restocking shelves in the nonfiction section of the library. As I approached the nonfiction section I spotted her in one of the isles. For a moment I gazed at her, unsure how to approach her. If she knew something she may be too scared to talk. I needed to gain her trust before I started asking her provocative questions.

"Hello, Miss."

"Can I help you?"

"Are you Angela Mayberry?"

"Yes."

"I'm Virginia Stone of the Charlotte Gazette."

"Charlotte, North Carolina?"

"Why yes."

"What are you doing in Liberal, Kansas?"

"Well, I'm doing a story on a young Marine, Stan Turner, in OCS at Quantico, Virginia. He's been charged with murdering his drill sergeant but I think he's innocent."

"So why would you want to talk to me about that."

"Well, it kind of complicated, but I have been told that you used to date Brett Billings."

"Oh, that's what this is about. I'm sorry I am really busy right now. Maybe we can talk another time."

"But Miss Mayberry Stan Turner is just about out of time. His trial is less than two weeks off. I've got to find out the truth about Brett Billings."

"I'm sorry but I can't help you. Now I've got to get back to work."

"Okay. But if you change your mind I'll be at the

Best Western Motel near the police station until 8:00 a.m. tomorrow."

Angela nodded her head and then turned and went back to stacking the shelves. I was extremely disappointed because I could tell she was hiding something important. Did she know that Brett was the Sunday Night Slasher? I wondered. After checking into the Best Western Motel, I called the editor, Wally Slocum, at the Charlotte Gazette.

"Hello."

"Wally, this is Virginia."

"Oh hi. Where are you?"

"In Liberal, Kansas. I had to check out a lead on my Marine Corps case."

"So what were you looking for in Kansas?"

"The Sunday Night Slasher."

"What?"

"Would you believe Sergeant Foster was killed by the Sunday Night Slasher?"

"How could that be?"

"The Sunday Night Slasher is a kid named Brett Billings from Liberal, Kansas. Sgt. Foster was killed exactly like the nineteen victims in Liberal. The Liberal murders stopped when Brett Billings joined the Marine Corps and was sent to Quantico."

"Can you prove all of this?"

"I personally inspected his room and found nineteen newspapers under his bed each with one of the Sunday Night Slasher headlines on the front page."

"That doesn't prove anything."

"I know it doesn't prove it but it convinces me he's the one. I have a witness who I think knows he's the Slasher but she won't talk."

"You've got to get her to talk or we have nothing."

"Oh. . . . Did you know the FBI already has Brett Billings on their suspect list?"

"You're kidding?"

"Apparently Brett's dad is a friend of the Police Chief so the investigation into Brett hasn't been too diligent."

"So where do go from here?"

"You've got some contacts at the FBI, right?"

"Yes."

"Give them a call and tell them that one of your reporters is about to solve the Sunday Night Slasher case and make them look like a bunch of incompetents. Tell them about the newspapers under Brett's bed and you might say I even found some more incriminating things but that I wouldn't tell you what they were."

"You sure you want the FBI interfering with your story?"

"I don't give a shit about the story right now. I just want them to get down here and solve this case in time to save Stan."

"Do you know who was in charge of the FBI investigation down there?"

"Yes, an agent named Raul Sierra."

"Okay I'll get right on it. Be careful."

"I will, thanks. I'll call you in a couple of days."

After talking to Wally I turned on the TV and laid down to watch the evening news. I didn't realize how tired I was until my head hit the pillow. Before long I was fast asleep. Several hours later I was awakened by a gentle but persistent knocking at my door. I looked at my watch and saw that it was 10:32 p.m. I walked to the door, put my ear against it and said, "Who is it?"

"It's me, Angela," a voice said.

"Oh, . . . wait one minute," I said as I scrambled to take off the safety chain and unlock the door.

"Angela, come in."

"Thank you, Mrs. Stone."

"You can call me Virginia."

"Oh, okay Virginia."

"So you changed your mind about talking to me?"

"I've been thinking about that poor Marine, Stan Turner. After you left, I pulled all of the newspapers articles you wrote about him. He sure doesn't seem like a murderer."

"I don't think he did it."

"So I thought the least I could do was answer your questions."

"I'm so glad you came by Angela. You're doing the right thing."

"I hope so."

"So when did you meet Brett?"

"I've known him all of my life. We are both the same age and have been class mates ever since kindergarten."

"When did you start to date him?"

"In my junior year of high school he asked me out on date for the first time. Before that we were just casual friends. Brett is not a very social person. He always kept pretty much to his self."

"So you were real close to him for three or four years then.

"Yes, that's true."

"I've been told a few things about Brett that I need to verify are true."

"What's that?"

"Well, some people at Quantico say Brett doesn't like Negroes much. Did you find that to be the case?"

"Yes, actually, I think he's afraid of them."

"Afraid? Why is that?"

"I guess it started when he was twelve. Brett's a good baseball player you know. In Little League he was not only an excellent pitcher but also the league leader in home runs two years in a row. One year his team made it to the play-offs for the Little League World

Series and traveled to Houston, Texas for a game. The team won the game due to Brett's three-run homer in the top of the sixth inning. After the game somehow Brett missed the team bus back to the motel. The opposing team had a lot of Negro players. I guess a couple of them caught Brett all alone and beat the shit out of him because they were mad about losing. Ever since that day he has hated Negroes."

"Huh, that's interesting. I assume since you dated Brett for several years you must have found some qualities in him that you liked."

"Yes, he was always good to me. He didn't have any friends so I was the only one he ever talked to. We were very close until-"

"Until what?"

"Until he started hurting me."

"When did this start?"

"About a year ago. I don't know what triggered it but he started having these periods of terrible anger and depression. During these times he would yell at me and sometimes hit me across the face. Sometimes he would give me a bloody nose or a black eye."

"You don't know what brought this on?"

"I don't know. It might have been because of his father."

"What do you mean?"

"His father was always very demanding. Brett had very strict rules he had to follow at all times."

"What kind of rules."

"He had to address his father as "Sir." He was expected to get A's and B's. If he got a "C" he was severely disciplined."

"How was he disciplined?"

"His father would make him cut wood for several hours . . . or maybe make him run four or five miles while his father rode a bike behind him. Sometimes he was confined to his room for weeks at a time and other times he would be whipped."

"Did you ever notice he had a tendency in conversation to ramble on at times about things that really didn't make much sense?"

"That's just the way Brett was. His Mom say's it was because of his head injury."

"What head injury?"

"When he was just a small child, he was riding in his Mom's Hudson. It was pretty much a piece of junk but it was all they could afford I guess when they were young. Anyway the passenger door didn't, you know, latch too well. One day when Brett was riding home with his Mom she took a corner a little too fast and Brett fell out hitting his head on the curb. Since they were so poor they didn't take Brett to the hospital because they knew they didn't have the money to pay for the doctors. Brett recovered from the accident pretty much okay but his Mom's says he's had a tendency to ramble in his conversations ever since. It's not that he's slow, because he's really smart, but he just rambles a lot.

"Now Angela, I know this is going to be difficult for you, but you've heard about the Sunday Night Slasher haven't you."

"Yes."

"Well, would it surprise you to learn that underneath Brett's bed are nineteen newspapers each with a Slasher headline on the front page."

"He liked the Slasher. He was really happy every time he killed one of them Negroes. I told him he should throw those newspapers out but he didn't listen to me."

"Do you think Brett might have been the Sunday Night Slasher?"

"No, he couldn't have done those things. Do you think I would have stayed with him if I knew he was a murderer?"

"But how would you know if he were the Slasher?
Didn't his episodes of anger and depression start about
the same time the Slasher began his killing?"

"I suppose so."

"Then he could have been the Slasher."

"Maybe, but I don't know anything about those
killings."

"I know you didn't help him, but did you ever see
him do anything unusual."

"No, not really."

"Were you ever with him on a Sunday night when
any of the murders took place?"

"Well, we actually never saw each other on
Sunday nights. He said that was when he went to
church. But I knew he didn't go to church. Brett isn't the
church going type. Anyway, I offered to go with him but
he said no, he wanted to pray alone."

"Do you know what he actually did on Sunday
nights?"

"No. I never followed him or nothing."

"Well, Angela you've been a real big help. Now
the FBI might be contacting you in the next few days so
when they do I want you to tell them the same thing you
just told me, okay?"

"I don't want to talk to those FBI agents. They
give me the creeps."

"Well, you really need to so they can do their job."

"What if Brett is the Slasher?"

"Then he needs to get help, he's a very sick
man."

"But I think I still love him."

"If you love him, you'll do what's best for him, and
that is getting him help."

"I don't know."

"The next morning I drove back to Kansas City
and took the first flight out to Washington, D.C.,"

Mrs. Stone said, "When I got to the airport I called you. So what do you think, Stan?"

"I think there's no doubt Brett's the Slasher? But how do we prove it?"

"Maybe the FBI will get their butts down there and solve the case. That's our only hope."

"I can't wait around hoping the FBI will do something. There is only a week to trial and I've got Rebekah coming in tomorrow."

"Well, if you think of anything else I can do, let me know. I've got to get back to Charlotte. I've got a story to write on the Sunday Night Slasher. Hopefully the story will get the FBI moving."

"Thanks a lot, Mrs. Stone. You've really been a life saver."

Chapter Twenty-one
Reunited

I had mixed emotions having Rebekah coming to the trial. I loved her and I desperately wanted to see her, but I needed to spend every moment trying to figure out a way to prove I was innocent. Rebekah was seven months pregnant and I didn't want to leave her alone. I thought of asking Rita to look after her but then thought better of it. Luckily my prayers were answered when I got a call from Steve Reynolds.

"Steve, how are you?"

"A lot better than you I am sure."

"You heard the news I take it?"

"Well, it's been all over the newspapers for the last three weeks. I always knew you'd be famous some day but I didn't expect it to be quite like this."

"Nor did I."

"Hey I called up to see how Rebekah was holding up and she says she coming out to the trial."

"Yeah, I can't wait to see her."

"Listen, I know you're going to be kind of preoccupied with the court martial and won't have as much time to be with her as you'd like. So I was wondering if you'd like me to fly out with her to keep her company and watch out for her?"

"Oh man, that would be fabulous!" I said. "Would you be able to do that?"

"Well, I've got two weeks vacation I can take. I don't feel much like doing the traditional vacation with my best friend on trial for murder."

"That would really take a load of my mind Steve.

I've been worried sick about what I was going to do with her during the trial. I tried to get her to stay home but she insisted on coming."

"Don't you worry? I'll fly up to Portland, pick her up and then we'll fly out to Washington together. I'll leave tomorrow morning and we should be in Washington late tomorrow night."

"Okay, I'll pick you up from Dulles Airport."

"Great."

"Thanks a lot Steve."

Later that day I called the Holiday Inn motel in Woodbridge to make reservations for Steve and Rebekah. The Holiday Inn was the only decent motel in Woodbridge so I was very upset when they told me there was no vacancy.

"What do you mean there's no vacancy? I've never had any trouble getting a room before. I don't recall ever seeing it more than half full."

"There's a big Court Martial starting next Monday. All the networks and news agencies have grabbed up all the rooms."

"Oh crap. You've got to be kidding."

"No, we're booked up for the next three weeks."

"Are there any other motels close by?"

"The nearest good hotels or motels are in Alexandria."

"Damn, that's a long drive from here."

"I'm sorry, Sir."

"Okay, thanks."

I don't know if I was more upset about getting smacked in the face with the reality that my trial was starting next week or the fact that Rebekah would have to drive 40 miles every day to attend the Court Martial. At any rate I called around Alexandria and found a good hotel in which Rebekah and Steve could stay. I got them adjoining rooms so Steve would be close by in case

Rebekah needed him. Unfortunately I would have to sleep every night in the barracks with the Casual Platoon.

The next night I drove to Dulles Airport. It was going to be exciting to see Rebekah since it had been over six months since I had seen her last. The drive to Dulles International Airport was very long and lonely. I began to wonder if I would be taking this same ride again in the near future, hopefully saying goodbye forever to Quantico and the United States Marine Corps. If not, then I'd be rotting in a military prison for the rest of my life, if the military tribunal was lenient. I couldn't bear to think of the other possibility as it was too chilling to even contemplate.

After parking my rent car, I entered the terminal and waited at the gate for Flight 321 from Portland. When the plane arrived, a big tram rolled out to the plane to pick up the passengers and bring them back. I patiently waited as people began to pour out of the exit from the Gate. Then I saw her emerge with Steve close behind.

"Rebekah," I said as I ran over to her and embraced her."

"Hi, sweetheart," she said. "Are you okay?"

"Yes, I'm fine considering everything. You're looking pretty . . . pretty pregnant."

"I know, I am as big as a house."

"Hi, Steve, how was the flight?" I said.

"Smooth as silk," Steve replied.

"How's the little one?" I said.

"You mean Ivan the Terrible? He's been kicking up a storm all day long."

"Oh, really?"

"Yeah, I wish he'd go to sleep."

"Well, let's go get your baggage so we can get you to your hotel. It's getting pretty late and you need your rest."

"I'm not going to bed until you tell me everything that's going on," Rebekah said.

"I will. I'll tell you on the drive to the hotel. You have to stay in Alexandria since all of the closer hotels and motels have been booked up by the press."

"Why is everyone so interested in your trial anyway?"

"You can thank Virginia Stone for that. She's blown this trial up into a big media event. But we shouldn't complain, we're going to get ten percent of whatever she makes from all her stories and books. There might even be a movie."

"Is that right?" Rebekah said.

"Yeah, I signed a contract giving her exclusive rights to the story and she's been doing a pretty good job exploiting it."

"Well you better get acquitted then so we can spend all that money."

"I'm working on it, believe me. I'm doing everything I possibly can and I've got a lot of good people helping me out too."

"Good."

"Listen Stan, if I can do anything don't forget I'm here," Steve said.

"Thanks Steve, you've done a lot already just watching out for Rebekah. But if something comes up where I need your help, believe me, I'll let you know."

When we got to the hotel Steve checked into his room and went to bed. Rebekah and I checked into her room and we got reacquainted. I had to be back in Casual Platoon by midnight so I couldn't stay as long as I wanted. As I was leaving Rebekah said she wanted to meet Lt. Burden, Sgt. Matson and Rita. I wasn't crazy about her meeting Rita but she was adamant about it. She claimed she wanted to personally thank her for her help. Somehow I didn't think gratitude was the reason she insisted on the meeting. Nevertheless, I said I would arrange a get together the next day which was Sunday.

In the morning I called Rita and told her Rebekah was dying to meet her. She said she was likewise anxious to meet Rebekah so we decided to all have lunch together in Woodbridge at noon. After talking to Rita I drove back into to Alexandria to Rebekah's hotel. It was about 9:00 a.m. when I arrived. Steve and Rebekah were both still asleep. I knocked on Rebekah's door and woke her up.

"Good morning," I said as she opened up the door and squinted at the bright sunlight flooding into her room.

"Is it already daylight?"

"Yeah, you must have slept good."

"I guess I was pretty tired last night when you left. When I laid down I fell right to sleep and didn't wake up until I heard you knocking at the door."

"I guess carrying a little baby around kind of tires you out."

"Little, if he were jumping around in your belly you wouldn't think he's so little."

"Maybe not."

"So what are we doing today?" Rebekah asked.

"Well, you have time to grab a free continental breakfast in the lobby and then I thought you'd probably want to go to church at ten."

"Good, we don't want to give God any reason desert us at us at a time like this."

"That's for sure."

"I'll light a candle for you. As a matter of fact I am going to light a candle for you every day until you're home with me in Portland."

"Which will be very soon," I said.

"Do you promise?"

"Yes, of course, I promise. Oh and after Church we're having lunch with Nurse Andrews."

"Oh Good. I can't wait to meet her, she better be ugly."

"She's not exactly ugly but she no match for you."

"Hmm. We'll see about that."

We managed to get Steve out of bed and over to the hotel lobby where we pumped him full of coffee to wake him up. Traveling to Washington, D.C. had wiped him out. We promised him the rest of the week wouldn't be so strenuous. After church we drove to Woodbridge and drove into the parking lot of the Wildbriar Restaurant and Pub. As we were getting out of our car I noticed Rita was just walking into the restaurant. I gave her a hard look which attracted Rebekah's attention.

"Tell me that beautiful brunette with the big boobs was not Nurse Andrews."

"Well, I'm afraid that was her."

"Damn, I knew it."

"Relax, she doesn't look that good up close."

"Yeah, sure."

"I think she's a knockout," Steve said.

"Shut up Steve," I replied.

We walked inside and joined Rita who was talking to the hostess.

"Rita, this is my wife, Rebekah," I said. "And this is my best friend, Steve Reynolds."

"Well, it's so nice to meet you, Rebekah, and you too, Steve. I've heard so much about you, Rebekah. How's the baby?"

"Oh, fine."

The hostess led us back to a booth near the back of the restaurant and a waiter came and took our orders.

"So how was your flight?" Rita said.

"Oh fine, just very long and junior here was kicking all the way."

"I don't know if I am ready for a baby yet," said Rita.

"It's a lot of work, believe me."

"Yeah."

"So, Stan tells me you've been a big help to him since he got sick and then got in trouble."

"Well, he looked so scared and helpless when he walked into the infirmary, I felt sorry for him," Rita said as she looked at me and smiled. "And now that I've got to know him I can say you're a lucky woman to have him."

"Thank you. I hope I get to keep him."

"What?"

"I hope he's not convicted, you know, the court martial."

"Oh yes."

"So how long have you been a nurse?"

"About six years. I graduated from the University of Virginia in 1964."

"Are you married?"

"No, I've been married, but right now I am single."

"Any boy friends?"

"No, after my first marriage cratered, I vowed to be very careful."

"Rebekah, let's not give Rita the third degree," I said.

"Oh, I'm sorry I didn't mean to pry it's just that Stan has told me what a wonderful person you were I was just interested in hearing all about you."

"Oh, its okay I don't mind," Rita replied. "I heard so much about you I feel like we're old friends."

"Maybe we should talk about how we're going to prove that I didn't kill Sgt. Foster," I said. "We only half a week until the trial."

"Does anyone know what the FBI is doing?" Steve said.

"No, Virginia Stone's editor is working on that but no one knows what's happening," I said.

"What about Sgt. Matson?" Rita asked.

"He's talked to all of Sgt. Foster's friends and has come up blank," I replied.

"What about your attorney, Lt. Burden, what's he doing?" Rebekah said.

"He's getting ready for the Court Martial. He's going to have to create a reasonable doubt with the evidence at hand," I said. "At this point he's got to assume the worst, that the FBI won't come through."

"I'm really scared Stan, everyone knows who the real killer is but no one seems to care. They're just going to convict an innocent man and let the killer go," Rebekah said.

"I know. It's very frustrating but something's got to break. I know it will. Don't give up on me yet," I replied.

In an effort to make Rebekah feel better I tried to seem upbeat and confident, but underneath I was scared to death. My life was in the hands of a few FBI Agents who I had never met and who probably didn't give a rat's ass whether I lived or died.

Chapter Twenty-Two
Court Martial - Day One

During the next week I met almost daily with Lt. Burden to discuss various aspects of the trial. He explained to me that I would be tried by a panel of two officers and one enlisted man appointed by the base commander. One of the officers on the panel was a lawyer from the Judge Advocate General's office and that officer would preside at the Court Martial.

One of the decisions Lt. Burden had to make was whether he should let me testify or not. Under the Fifth Amendment to the Constitution of the United States and under the Uniform Code of Military Justice I couldn't be compelled to testify against my will if my testimony might tend to incriminate me. If I did testify I would have to admit that I had made threats against Sgt. Foster. On the other hand if I didn't testify I couldn't explain how my finger prints got on the murder weapon which was critical to my case. I told Lt. Burden that I wanted to testify because I was an innocent man and wanted everyone to hear it from my lips. He said he would make a decision toward the end of the trial depending on how things were going.

On Friday Virginia Stone's news story on the Sunday Night Slasher was published. Within an hour of its publication the press had flooded into Quantico. Dozens of reporters were lined up at the gates of the base seeking permission to interview Lt. Burden, Lt. Hooper, myself and anyone else connected with the Court Martial. The base commander was livid about the article being published on the eve of the trial. Reacting swiftly to it, he refused to allow any interviews to reporters and issued orders restricting me to the base. He even denied me the right to use the telephone so I couldn't be interviewed by reporters. Candidate Brett Billings was placed in protective custody pending an inquiry into the accusations contained in the news article and contact with the FBI. Luckily before I received my orders not to make telephone calls, I had placed a call to Virginia Stone.

"Oh, I am so glad you called. Did you read my article?"

"Yes, it was dynamite. The brass is totally pissed off. Reporters are storming the entrance to the base."

"I know isn't it wonderful. I can see a Pulitzer Prize in my future."

"So what's the FBI doing about the story."

"We don't know. We know they are in Liberal with a team of investigators but we haven't been able to find out what's happening."

"Lt. Burden said to tell you he needs you as a witness."

"A witness?"

"Yes. He want's you testify about what you found in Brett Billings room and he wants you to talk Angela Mayberry into coming to testify."

"I don't think she will. Besides, she doesn't know for sure that Brett Billings is the Slasher."

"Well, try anyway. He thinks her testimony could be important."

As I was on the phone I noticed an officer enter the Casual Platoon Barracks and walk toward me.

"Wait a minute Mrs. Turner, somebody from the JAG office is here to talk to me."

"What does he want?"

"I don't know."

When the JAG officer reached me he took the phone out of my hand, hung it up and said. "Candidate Turner I have been instructed to deliver these orders to you. You are hereby restricted to your quarters and you shall not make telephone calls to anyone without the written permission of the base commander."

"Yes, Sir."

"Who's in charge here Candidate Turner?" he said.

Corporal Lemaster hearing the commotion had entered the main squad room where I was being given my orders.

"I am, Sir," Corporal Lemaster said.

"What's your name?"

"Corporal Lemaster."

"Corporal, here are Candidate Turner's orders. Please see to it that they are obeyed."

"Yes, Sir."

"Thank you, Corporal. That will be all."

The rest of the weekend I was totally isolated from everyone. I couldn't talk to Rebekah, Rita or anyone except Lt. Burden. The hours dragged as I anticipated the beginning of my trial on Monday. I felt totally helpless as my fate was now totally in the hands of others. What was Lt. Burden doing? Did he think I could be acquitted or was he just going through the motions of defending me? Was Virginia going to press on with her investigation or would she quit now that she had her Pulitzer Prize locked up? Was the FBI really expediting their investigation in Liberal or was the investigation bogged down in red tape? All of these questions haunted me.

I was scared and extremely depressed as I lay on my bunk that evening after everyone had gone to the mess hall for dinner. What if I were convicted? Would the judges really sentence me to be executed by a firing squad? How could such a thing happen to an innocent man? I got off my bunk and knelt down on the floor to pray. Praying wasn't something I did a lot of during my young life. I believed in God, but I had never really been close to him. I didn't have a prayer memorized so I just spoke from my heart."

"Dear Lord, please forgive me for all my sins. I am weak and I need your strength to sustain me during these difficult times. You know, Lord, that I am innocent of these charges against me. Please help me open the eyes of my accusers so that they may see the truth.

"Thank you, Lord, for the gift of life, for Rebekah, for Reggi, for our unborn child, for Lt. Burden, for Steve and . . . and for Rita who must surely be your angel sent from heaven. I know I am not worthy, but I promise if you see me through this time of peril, in the years ahead I'll strive with all my heart to be a better Christian and grow in wisdom and understanding. In the name of the Father, the Son and the Holy Spirit. Amen.

On Monday morning at seven hundred hours I was escorted to the mess hall for breakfast and then taken to JAG headquarters to await the beginning of my court martial. Thirty minutes before the proceeding was set to begin, Lt. Burden came in to see me.

"Hi, Stan. How you holding up," he said.

"Okay, I guess."

"Well, all of this will be over pretty soon."

"Yeah, but will I be a free man?"

"We've got enough Slasher evidence to make it difficult for them to convict you. Plus that story that Virginia Stone wrote was a masterpiece."

"Do you really feel that optimistic?"

"I think we can win barring something unexpected."

"Like what?"

"I don't know. If I knew it wouldn't be unexpected."

"Right."

"Now, I need to give you some tips on courtroom demeanor. During the trial I want you to sit up and be very attentive. Don't look bored or fall asleep. I'm going to have Rebekah sit right behind you so the judges can see her pregnant belly and be reminded you're a father with two kids dependant on you."

"Okay. Can I talk to her?"

"Only before or after each session or during breaks."

"Have you heard from the FBI?"

"Nothing yet."

"When are they going to get off their ass and do something?"

"They have a certain procedure they have to follow and it just takes some time to get through it. I think we will be hearing from them before the trial is over."

"I sure hope so."

"Okay, are you ready to go into the courtroom?"

"Ready as I will ever be I guess."

"Then let's go."

We got up and walked across the hall to a large conference room. At the far end was a long judges' table with three empty chairs, the United States Flag at one end and the Marine Corps flag at the other. In front and to the left was a small table at which a court reporter was situated. In front and to the right was a witness stand. Two smaller counsel tables faced the witness stand, the reporter and the judges. Behind the counsel tables were approximately 100 spectator seats all of which were filled with interested persons and the media.

Lt. Burden led me through the spectators and we sat down at one of the counsel tables. Lt. Hooper and his aid were already situated at their table. Rebekah and Steve were directly behind me and I saw Rita sitting with

Sgt. Matson toward the back of the room. Virginia Stone and her photographer were seated near the rear door I suppose so they could leave periodically to make phone calls. I took a deep breath and waited patiently for the court martial to begin. In a few moments a side door opened and two military officers and a sergeant major walked through and took a seat at the judges table. The presiding judge called the proceeding to order.

"I'm Colonel Joseph Abbey and I have been appointed to preside over this general court martial. To my left is Major Calvin Clark and to my right is Sergeant Major Thomas Taft. This general court martial is being convened pursuant to the orders of General Walter Harrison, commander of the United States Marine Corps Base at Quantico, Virginia."

"Lt. Hooper will you please read the charge?"

"Yes, Sir. Candidate Stanley Turner, you are charged with intentional and premeditated murder under Section 555.007 of the Uniform Code of Military Justice. Specifically, on or about Sunday, December 28, 1970 you did intentionally and with malice aforethought sneak up behind and take the life of Sgt. Louis Foster by cutting his throat with a knife," Lt. Hooper said.

"Thank you. You may proceed," the judge said.

"The prosecution calls Lt. Warren Stevens, United States Navy."

"Lt. Stevens, do you swear to tell the whole truth and nothing but the truth so help you God?" the judge said.

"I do."

"Lt. Stevens, what is your current assignment."

"I am presently assigned as chief coroner at Quantico Naval Hospital."

"And were you called to investigate a crime scene on December 28, 1970."

"Yes."

"What did you find?"

"When I arrived at the Staff Parking Lot near OCS "C" Company, I found Sgt. Louis Foster lying on the pavement next to his car."

"What was his condition?"

"He was dead. His throat had been lacerated by a sharp object."

"Did you find any weapons or instruments in your investigation that could have caused these lacerations?"

"Yes."

"What did you find?"

"A linoleum knife."

"Where did you find it?"

"In a vacant lot about a half mile from the scene of the crime."

"Did you conduct any tests to determine if this linoleum knife was the murder weapon?"

"Yes, we analyzed the blood that was on the knife and it matched the blood of the victim."

"Did you do any studies to determine the time of death?"

"Yes."

"What, in your opinion, was the time of death?"

"Approximately 2330 hours."

Lt. Hooper continued to question Lt. Stevens for some time. Finally he passed the witness.

"Lt. Burden," the judge said. "Your witness."

"Lt. Stevens. Was Sgt. Foster wearing his shirt at the time you found him?"

"No, he was naked from the waist up."

"Were there any other lacerations other than those on the victims throat?"

"Yes, there were some lacerations on the victim's chest."

"Could you describe them?"

"There was one approximately four inches long

and one-quarter inch deep starting two inches down from his throat. A second laceration crossed through the first laceration approximately one-third down from its beginning."

"Did these lacerations appear to have any meaning?"

"They appeared to represent a small "t" or a cross."

"Did these lacerations contribute to Sgt. Foster's death?"

"No."

"Do you have any explanation as to why the killer made these marks?"

"Objection, calls for speculation," Lt. Hooper said.

"Sustained," the Judge replied.

"No further questions," Lt. Burden said.

"You may step down," The Judge said. "You may call your next witness."

"The prosecution calls Corporal Marvin Meeks," Lt. Hooper said.

The witness was sworn in and Lt. Hooper commenced direct examination. "Corporal Meeks. What is your current assignment?"

"I am an investigator for the Judge Advocate General's office here at Quantico Marine Base."

"Were you called to the scene of a crime on December 28, 1970?"

"Yes. I was called to the crime scene where Sgt. Louis Foster has been murdered."

"And what was your function in the investigation?"

"I'm a finger print expert."

"And did you find any finger prints at the scene of the crime?"

"Well, not at the scene of the crime, but on a linoleum knife that was found about a half mile away and later was determined to be the murder weapon."

"How many finger prints did you find?"

"Just one thumb and an index finger."

"Did you ascertain whose prints were on the knife?"

"Yes, Candidate Stanley Turner."

The crowd stirred and the Judge banged his gavel for order. Lt. Hooper continued questioning the witness for awhile and then said,"No further questions Your Honor."

"Lt. Burden," the Judge said.

"Corporal Meeks. You said there were only two prints on the alleged murder weapon."

"Yes."

"Is there any way you can determine when those prints got on the linoleum knife?"

"Not exactly."

"So, Candidate Turner might have picked up the linoleum knife a day or two before the murder and left his prints on the knife."

"Well-"

"That's possible, isn't it?"

"Yes."

"Is it possible that Candidate Turner picked up the knife and then a second party wearing gloves perhaps picked up the linoleum knife and killed Sgt. Foster."

"That's possible but-"

"No further questions," Lt. Burden said.

"Lt. Hooper, any rebuttal?" The Judge asked.

"No, Your Honor."

"Then call your next witness."

"The prosecution calls Candidate Howard Benton."

The Judge swore in Candidate Benton and Lt. Hooper began interrogation. "Where are you assigned now, Candidate Benton?"

"C-Company, Officer Candidate School, Sir."

"And do recall the night of December 28, 1970?"

"Yes, sir."

"What happened that night, soldier?"

"Candidate Stanley Turner and Candidate Brett Billings had just returned from being severely disciplined by Sergeant Foster. They kind of staggered into the squad room and were really mad and upset."

"Do recall what Candidate Turner said."

"He said, referring to Sgt. Foster: He's a bastard. I hope he rots in hell."

A commotion broke out in the courtroom and the Judge quickly picked up his gavel and banged it. "Order . . . Order in the courtroom."

"Did he say anything else?"

"Yeah he also said he would like to stick the Sergeant's plastic stick up his ass."

"That's all thank you," Lt. Hooper said.

"Lt. Burden," the Judge said.

"Do you recall what Candidate Billings said after this period of discipline?"

"Yes, I believe he said that no human being can take that kind of punishment and that Sgt. Foster was a fucking lunatic."

The courtroom again erupted in conversation. The Judge raised his gavel and glared at the spectators.

"Anything else?"

"Yes. He said he'd like to meet Sgt. Foster on a dark street."

"What was Candidates Billings and Turner's condition after being disciplined?"

"They were totally exhausted, they could hardly walk and we had to help them into their bunks because they didn't have the strength to climb up into them."

"Thank you, Corporal . . . that will be all."

"Any redirect, Lt. Hooper?" the Judge said.

"No, Your Honor."

"Then call your next witness."

Lt. Hooper called Lt. Littleton next. His testimony wasn't particularly helpful. After he was excused the presiding judge ordered a recess for lunch. I ate with Rebekah since I hadn't seen her all weekend. It was obvious she was very distressed by what had transpired during the morning. The baby apparently was also feeling her anxiety and was very active. I tried to cheer her up but with little success. I suggested she might want to go back to the hotel for the afternoon but she refused. After lunch the trial resumed with Sgt. Matson as the first witness.

"Sgt. Matson, do you know the defendant?" Lt. Hooper asked.

"Yes, sir."

"How did you meet him?"

"We were in the hospital together. We bunked next to each other."

"Now on December 28, 1970 were you and Candidate Turner still bunking next to each other at the hospital?"

"Yes."

"Did anything unusual happen that day?"

"Well Nurse Andrews came to see Stan and told him about Sgt. Foster's murder."

"How did he respond to the news?"

"He seemed surprised to hear it."

"Surprised?"

"Yes, he said he just couldn't believe it. Then Nurse Andrews suggested he might be a suspect and he got very upset. She had to hold him to settle him down."

"Hold him?"

"Yes she put her arms around him and pulled his head onto her bosom. Then she began stroking his hair to console him."

"Were Candidate Turner and Nurse Andrews

romantically involved?"

"I don't know for sure but they definitely had more than a nurse-patient relationship."

"What did they do to make you think that?"

"Well Nurse Andrews spent a lot more time with Stan than anyone else on the floor. They would walk around the hospital together when Nurse Andrews was on break flirting and carrying on. It was obvious they liked each other a lot."

"Did Candidate Turner ever admit to or brag about having a sexual relationship with Nurse Andrews?"

"No, he denied any sexual interest in her. He has a pregnant wife and a kid, you know."

"Now on the night of the murder did the Defendant leave his hospital bed?"

"I don't know for sure but I woke up once around eleven and he wasn't in his bed. He might have gone to the bathroom or something I just didn't see him when I woke up."

"Did you see him return to his bed?"

"No. I fell back to sleep and didn't wake up until morning. He was there in the morning."

"No further questions, pass the witness," Lt. Hooper said.

"Lt. Burden, your witness," the Judge said.

"Thank you, Your Honor," Lt. Burden replied.

"So, Sgt. Matson, you didn't see the Defendant leave the hospital, did you?"

"No, Sir."

"And you didn't see him return to the hospital if indeed he ever left?"

"True."

"You were asleep the entire time right?"

"Yes, except for a minute or two when I woke up."

"No further questions Your Honor."

"All right Lt. Hooper call your next witness," the Judge said.

The court took a short break after Sgt. Matson's testimony. During the break Sgt. Matson hailed me in the hallway.

"Stan."

"Oh, hi, Sgt. Matson."

"I'm sorry I couldn't provide you with an alibi."

"Well you've got to tell the truth, but I don't understand why you brought up all that crap about Nurse Andrews and I being romantically involved. I've told you before there's nothing going on between us."

"Well maybe you don't see it but Nurse Andrews is in love with you. Anyway, it doesn't make any difference. She can't even testify that you were at the hospital all night."

"You're right, it probably doesn't affect the trial but it sure doesn't help my marriage."

"I'm sorry if I caused you any problems with Rebekah. Maybe I should go talk to her?"

"No, no . . . please don't. It won't be necessary, we'll work it out."

"Okay, Is there anything else I can do for you?"

"Not unless you've got a pipeline into the FBI. I'd sure like to know if they are ever going to come and rescue me from this mess."

"Well Agent Sierra left me his card and said to call him if anything came up. I guess I could call him and ask him what they're going to do."

"What? You've talked to Agent Sierra?"

"Well sure, when he was here late last year looking for Brett Billings in connection with that Sunday Night Slasher investigation."

"Why didn't you mention that earlier?"

"It never came up. I thought Lt. Burden would have known about it."

"How was it the FBI came to you?"

"I'm in the personnel office. They came to me to find out where they could find him."

"Well, give Agent Sierra a call and tell him to get his butt down her and arrest Brett Billings before this fucking trial is over."

"Okay, I'll call him right away."

After the break Lt. Hooper called several minor witnesses whose testimony took less than thirty minutes each and then he called Rita Andrews.

"Nurse Andrews, where are you employed?" Lt. Hooper asked.

"I'm employed at Quantico Naval Hospital."

"Are you a member of the Armed Services?"

"Yes, I'm a Navy staff nurse."

"On the night of December 27, 1970 were you on duty?"

"Yes, I was on duty at the OCS Infirmary. I have to staff the infirmary one night per week."

"Did you have an occasion to treat the defendant on that night?"

"Yes he came in complaining of hematuria. He was examined and some tests were administered. Several of the tests were positive so he was sent to the hospital for further testing and observation."

"For the benefit of us without a medical education would explain the term "hematuria."

"Hematuria is basically having blood in your urine."

"I see, and the defendant had blood in his urine?"

"Yes, a microscope analysis showed blood cells in his urine."

"Did the defendant give an explanation as to why he might have hematuria?"

"He indicated that Sgt. Foster had forced him to do excessive physical exercise and had hit him on his back repeatedly with a plastic stick."

"How would you characterize his physical state other than the hematuria?"

"He was suffering from complete exhaustion, muscle ache, swelling of his wrists and he had numerous bruises on his back."

"How would you characterize his mental condition?"

"He was angry, confused and generally upset."

"What did he say to you to indicate he was angry?"

"Oh I don't really remember . . . I guess it was just his excited state."

"He must have said something?"

"Well, Lt. Chamberlain told him he could file a complaint against Sgt. Foster with the JAG office but Candidate Turner didn't think that would do much good. He didn't think anybody would believe a new recruit over a seasoned drill sergeant."

"Objection Your Honor, the witness is being non-responsive and evasive. Would you instruct the witness to answer the question?"

"Nurse Andrews you must answer the question," the Judge warned.

"What was the question?"

"What did the defendant say to make you think he was angry?"

Rita looked at me and then covered her face with her hand. Finally she dropped her hand and said, "He said Sgt. Foster would get his just reward. But he didn't say it in anger. He said it quite calmly without any sign of emotion."

"Now Nurse Andrews did you have occasion to see the defendant in the hospital after December 27th?"

"Yes, he was one of my regular patients at the hospital."

"And were you on duty on the night of December 28, 1970?"

"Yes, I was on the three to eleven shift."

"During your shift did you see the defendant?"

"Yes, I talked to him several times and I administered his medication."

"Isn't it true you took a walk with him during the evening?"

"Yes, during my break I did. He was depressed and I was trying to cheer him up."

"Did Candidate Turner leave the hospital at any time during your shift?"

"I don't think so. I never saw him leave."

"You didn't see him leave . . . but did you ever observe him missing?"

"No."

"I must remind you Nurse Andrews you're under oath."

"Is that a question?"

"Don't be smart with me Nurse Andrews. This is a military tribunal."

"I am not trying to be smart. I am trying to understand if you're asking a question or what."

"The question is: Was Candidate Turner in the hospital during your entire shift? Was he ever missing?"

"No . . . not to my knowledge."

"Isn't it true that you and Candidate Turner have been having a romantic affair?"

"Objection Your Honor, counsel is leading the witness?" Lt. Burden said.

"Your Honor, we've already had testimony on Nurse Andrews' romantic interest in Candidate Turner, please allow me to treat her as a hostile witness."

"Permission granted," the Judge said.

"Okay Nurse Andrews, Isn't it true that you and Candidate Turner have been having a romantic affair?"

"No."

"Isn't it true you spent an inordinate amount of your time on duty tending to every need of Candidate Turner?"

"I took good care of him."

"You liked him didn't you?"

"Well sure . . . he's a nice guy."

"Isn't it true when you found out he had to go to Bethesda, Maryland for tests you insisted on personally taking him there?"

"Well, I didn't want him to go all that way in a jeep with a total stranger."

"Isn't it true you left with him at nine hundred hours when your appointment at Bethesda wasn't until fourteen hundred hours?"

"I don't know, that was a long time ago."

"How long a trip is it to Bethesda?"

"About two hours."

"What did you do during the other three hours?"

"We went to an art studio."

"Was this part of his treatment?"

"No."

"Was taking him to your apartment part of the treatment?"

"Objection! Assumes facts not in evidence and argumentative," Lt. Burden said.

"Withdrawn, I'll rephrase. Did you take Candidate Turner to your apartment?"

Rita squirmed in her seat, gave me a hard stare and then looked over at Rebekah.

"Yes, I forgot something so we stopped by to get it."

The spectators began to chatter, the Judge smacked his gavel on the table and demanded order. Rebekah stared coldly at Rita.

"You forgot something?"

"Yes."

Lt. Hooper shook his head. "Isn't it true you took him to your apartment to have sex with him?

Rita sat up straight in her chair and glared menacingly at Lt. Hooper without responding.

"Nurse Andrews, did you take him to your apartment to have sex with him?"

She looked over at me and then the judges before finally saying,"Yes."

Again the crowd broke into excited conversation, the Judge banged his gavel and threatened to clear the courtroom if he didn't get order. Rebekah got up and started to leave the room.

"Do you love Stan Turner Nurse Andrews?" Lt. Burden asked.

The room grew silent and Rebekah interrupted her exit to look at Rita as she gave her response.

"Yes. . . . Yes. . . . I love him," She said as she began to weep.

Rebekah let out a cry and left the room.

"Then you would lie for him to save his neck wouldn't you?"

"Yes. . . . I mean, no. . . . I wouldn't have to lie, he didn't do anything."

"That's all Nurse Andrews," Lt. Hooper concluded.

"Your witness Lt. Burden."

"Thank you, Your Honor. Nurse Andrews, now you said you took Candidate Turner to your apartment to have sex with him."

"Yes."

"But did you have sex with him?"

"No."

"Why was that?"

"He refused to have sex with me. He said he was a married man and he believed in commitment."

"So what did you do in your apartment?"

"We just talked. . . . I showed him my paintings and then we left."

"Now you have professed your love for Candidate Turner before this court but I ask you has Candidate Turner ever asked you to lie for him?"

"No. In fact, he told me he didn't want me to commit perjury. He said just tell the truth. Since he was innocent he said he didn't need anyone to lie for him."

"And have you lied to this Court today."

"No, Sir."

"Thank you, Nurse Andrews. No further questions at this time," Lt. Burden concluded.

"Any redirect Lt. Hooper?" the Judge said.

"Yes, just one question, Your Honor."

"Proceed."

"Nurse Andrews, haven't you forgot to tell us one additional thing Candidate Turner said to you at the infirmary on the night of Sgt. Foster's murder?"

"I don't think so."

"Are you sure? I could call Lt. Chamberlin in to refresh your memory."

Rita shifted in her chair and took a deep breath. "No, that's not necessary."

"What did he tell you he would like to do to Sgt. Foster, Nurse Andrews."

She took a deep breath. "He said . . . he said he'd like to kill him."

The crowd broke into hysteria, the judge banged his gavel and demanded order but the crowd refused to be calmed. Finally the judge looked at his watch, conferred briefly with the other judges and then recessed the court martial until the following day at nine hundred hours.

Chapter Twenty-Three
Court Martial - Day Two

Rebekah had not taken the first day of trial well. She was not the type that yelled, screamed and threw pots and pans when she was mad. She would just withdraw and wouldn't talk to me for hours or even days at a time. After that first dismal day of trial I went to her but she refused to talk to me. I tried to explain to her that Rita's feelings were not mutual and that nothing had happened between us. She obviously didn't believe me. I told Steve to keep an eye on her for me and then they left to go to their hotel. I wondered if Rebekah would even come to the second day of the court martial.

That night Lt. Burden and I spent hours preparing for my testimony. He had decided that I must testify if there was to be any chance of an acquittal. In addition to my testimony it was expected that Candidate Billings would be called as a witness. I could tell Lt. Burden was excited about the prospect of cross-examining the now infamous Sunday Night Slasher. He was about to get some unexpected national media exposure which could do wonders for his employment prospects after his tour of duty with the Navy.

The next morning I waited anxiously to see if Rebekah would show up with Steve. By the time the court martial was set to begin they had not arrived. I began to have doubts that my marriage would survive this ordeal. While I was waiting anxiously for Rebekah to arrive, Sgt. Matson showed up.

"Stan."

"Hi, Sergeant."

"They're here."

"Who's here?"

"The FBI."

"You're kidding?"

"No. I called them like you asked and Agent Sierra said they planned to be there for Brett Billings direct examination. He said they had completed their investigation in Liberal and were going to follow up here at Quantico."

"Have you seen them?"

"Yes, they're already in the gallery?"

"Where are they?"

"They're inside talking to Virginia Stone trying to find out if she has any evidence they don't have."

"Wow, this is great news. Thanks, Sergeant. I've got to get inside. I'll talk to you later."

I went back into the courtroom and at precisely 900 hours, the three judge panel walked in and sat down and the presiding judge called the court martial to order. Lt. Hooper immediately called Candidate Brett Billings. A side door opened and he appeared in full dress uniform. His cast had apparently been removed but he still walked with a distinct limp."

"Do you swear to tell the whole truth and nothing but the truth so help you God?" the Judge said.

"I do."

"Candidate Billings, could you tell us where you are currently assigned?"

"I'm in OCS Casual Platoon pending recovery from a broken ankle."

"Were you previously a member of OCS C-Company."

"Yes, Sir."

"Do you recall the evening of December 28, 1970?"

"Yes, Sir."

"Could you briefly describe what happened that evening?"

"After dinner Candidate Turner and myself had been ordered to report to Sgt. Foster's office. We had been caught talking in line and were to be punished for disobeying the Sergeant's orders not to talk. After we arrived, the Sergeant ordered us to do hundreds of pushups, sit-ups, jumping jacks, squat thrusts and then told us to run in place. If he didn't like the way we were doing the exercise he would hit us with a hard plastic stick."

"So how long did this punishment last?"

"About two hours."

"Now had you already had significant exercise that day?"

"We had run 6 miles and marched another 4 miles earlier in the day."

"How did Candidate Turner take this punishment?"

"He was very upset and in a lot of pain. He denied he had talked in line and thought he was being treated unjustly."

"How about you? How did you feel about the punishment?"

"I deserved the punishment because I had talked in line so I accepted it. It was, however, excessive punishment considering the crime."

"After you returned to the squad room what was said, if anything, about Sgt. Foster and the punishment he had given you?"

"He said St. Foster was a maniac and he wanted to kick his ass."

"Now later on that night did Candidate Turner leave the barracks?"

"Yes, he got up and went to the bathroom and when he came back he said he was bleeding and had to go to the infirmary."

"So, he left."

"Yes."

"Now the following night, December 28, 1970, did you leave your barracks at any time?"

"No, I was in my barracks the entire evening."

"What time did you get to the barracks that night?"

"At approximately eighteen hundred hours, right after dinner."

"Did you leave your barracks for any reason that night?"

"No, Sir."

"Now there has been some accusations made that you are the so called Sunday Night Slasher. Have you heard that?"

"Yes, I was questioned by the FBI about it about six months ago."

"Did they bring any charges against you?"

"No, it's a ridiculous accusation."

"Do you come from a long time Marine Corps family."

"Yes, my father and brother are Marines, my grandfather and great grandfather were Marines."

"So you are just following in their footsteps."

"Yes, Sir. I am proud to be a Marine."

Lt. Hooper continued to examine Billings for sometime. He asked him about his family, his life in Liberal, Kansas and his plans for the future as a Marine Corps officer. Billings put on an appearance of a clean-cut, American boy proudly serving his country. I wondered, as I heard him testify so rationally, how he could have killed 19 innocent men. Finally the lies ended.

"Pass the witness, Your Honor."

"Lt. Burden," the Judge said.

"Thank you, Your Honor."

"Candidate Billings. You've testified you're from Liberal, Kansas, is that right?"

"Yes, Sir."

"You've testified you're familiar with the Sunday Night Slasher, right?"

"Yes. I've heard about him. It was a big story in Liberal."

"How many persons did he kill?"

"I believe nineteen."

"Were they all Negroes?"

"Yes, as I recall, they were."

"For the record was Sgt. Foster a Negro."

Billings frowned. "Yes, but I'm not the Sunday Night Slasher, so I don't see what that has to do with anything."

"Humor me, Candidate Billings. Since Lt. Hooper so graciously brought up the subject of the Sunday Night Slasher I have a right to ask you about it too."

"Maybe so, but-"

"I know you testified you were sound asleep in bed when Sgt. Foster was killed."

"That's right," Billings said.

"What day of the week was that?"

"You know it was Sunday."

"You're right, but I just wanted to hear you say it. . . . Now, on what night did the Sunday Night Slasher kill?"

"Obviously it was on Sunday night, but that could easily be a coincidence."

"True. An there were other coincidences, weren't there? The Slasher slit his victims throat, the same way Sgt. Foster died, isn't that right?"

"I suppose," Billings said.

"The Slasher was right handed, wasn't he?"

"How should I know?"

"You're right handed, aren't you, Candidate Billings?"

Billings shook his head. "So what, most of the planet is right handed."

"Of course, another coincidence. . . . Now, Did the Sunday Night Slasher leave a signature on his victims?"

"I don't know."

"You don't know? That's surprising since you had 19 opportunities to learn about it back in Liberal. Don't you watch TV?"

"Okay, I heard something about it? It was a cross or something carved on the victim's chest."

"Was such a cross carved on Sgt. Fosters chest the night he was murdered?"

"Yeah, so what. Maybe the killer wanted to make it look like the Sunday Night Slasher had done it just to throw everybody off his trail."

"You think someone is trying to frame you, Candidate Billings?"

"Objection," Lt. Hooper said. "Counsel is relentlessly badgering this witness. Candidate Billings has testified he is not the Sunday Night Slasher over and over again, yet Lt. Burden insist on twisting his testimony at every opportunity."

"Sustained," the Judge said. "Let the witness do the testifying, Lt. Burden."

"I apologize, Your Honor. . . . Candidate Billings, are you a fan of the Slasher?"

"What do you mean?"

"Do you admire him?"

"No, of course not."

"Why is it then that you have a collection of newspapers under you bed back in Liberal, each with a Slasher story on the front page?"

The gallery erupted in excited chatter, the judge banged his gavel and demanded order.

"Objection! Assumes facts not in evidence," Lt. Hooper screamed.

"What! . . . You've been under my bed?" Billings said obviously shaken.

"Do you deny it?" Lt. Burden said not waiting for the judges ruling.

Billings took a deep breath as he contemplated the question. He glared at Lt. Burden not knowing what to say. Lt. Hooper was on his feet looking at the judge, waiting for him to say something. The courtroom was still in anticipation of Candidate Billing's response.

"Overruled, I want to hear this," the Judge said.

Billings suddenly smiled and sat back in his chair. "No. I don't deny it. The slasher interests me, so what?"

"He interests you?"

"Yes."

"Kind of a hero worship?"

Billings didn't answer.

"Your honor, would you instruct the witness to answer the question?" Lt. Burden asked.

"Candidate Billings, you must answer the question."

"Yes, . . . yes, he is a hero."

"You condone the killing of innocent Negro leaders?"

He laughed. "Innocent? They're not innocent. They're nothing but a fraud. They preach the liberation of their people, but their people have been free for a hundred years. Their true goal is not liberation but enslavement of the white race. They don't want liberation, they want revenge!"

The crowd reeled in shock. Reporters wrote furiously to get down every word out of Billings mouth. Lt. Burden smiled. The panel of judges shook their heads.

"Are you a member of the KKK?" Lt. Burden

continued.

"Are you kidding? The Clan is dead. Kennedy and the Northern Liberals killed it. Now it's up to men like the Slasher to stop the conspiracy."

"When was the last Slasher killing?"

"December 11, 1969?"

"When did you leave for OCS training?"

"December 16, 1969."

"Why did you join the Marines anyway?"

"My Dad wanted me to be a Marine. He expected me to be a Marine. Marines are the finest fighting men in the world. They protect our nation from its enemies. Marines are trained killers . . . nobody messes with a Marine."

"So you don't want anyone to mess with you, is that it? You figure once you've been trained by the Marines you'll be invincible."

He laughed. "I don't need the Marines for that. My Dad already taught me everything he's learned in twenty-two years as a Marine. I'm already an expert with a rifle."

"How about a knife?"

Billings didn't answer, he just gave Lt. Burden a demonic grin. A chill ran down my spine. I squirmed in my seat.

"When you first met Candidate Turner did you tell him that you joined the Marines so you could go to Vietnam and kill Cong."

"Yes, isn't that what this war is all about?"

Lt. Burden responded, "Apparently it is, Candidate Billings, at least for you. . . . Now, you testified as to some things that Candidate Turner said the night you two were disciplined. What about you, did you have anything to say about what happened?"

"I'm sure I did."

"Do you recall saying, 'That's what you get for

giving Niggers a little power?'"

"Yes, that's sounds like something I would say."

"How about, 'He'll wish he hadn't fucked with me.'"

"And I meant it to. Unfortunately I was all tied up in training so Turner got to him before I had the opportunity," he said with a grin. "I congratulate him. Good work, Stan."

Everyone turned and looked at me. I became nauseous, my shoulders tightened and my head began to pound. Turning away to avoid eye contact with my accusers I thanked God Rebekah wasn't here to see this torture.

"Didn't you have just as much reason to kill Sgt. Foster as did Candidate Turner."

"I suppose so."

"I think you had more reason, . . . you've already told us you don't like Negroes, particularly Negroes who have power. You didn't like taking orders from Sgt. Foster, did you?"

"Not much."

"Now do recall the first night at Quantico?"

"I don't know, I guess."

"Do recall bumping into Candidate Turner on your way to the can?"

"I'm not sure?"

"Do you recall the tool box getting knocked over?"

"The tool box?"

"Yeah, and all the tools getting scattered around?"

"No."

"Isn't true that Candidate Turner knocked over the tool box and when he was returning the tools to the box he cut his finger on the linoleum knife?"

"I wouldn't know."

"And isn't it true you seized that opportunity to

take the linoleum knife with Candidate Turner's finger prints on them to kill Sgt. Foster. Of course, you used plastic gloves so your fingerprints wouldn't be on the knife."

"Objection, Your Honor, Lt. Burden is testifying."

"Sustained, Lt. Burden, please no more speeches," the Judge said.

"That's okay, Your Honor, we've heard enough lies. I'm through with this sorry excuse for a human being."

"Objection Your Honor, argumentative."

"Sustained, I'm warning you Lt. Burden you better conduct yourself like an officer or I'll find you in contempt of this Court."

"I withdraw the comment, Your Honor," I apologize.

"Lt. Hooper. . . . Redirect?" the Judge asked.

"Thank you. . . . Just two questions to clarify your testimony, Candidate Billings, if you don't mind."

"Yes, Sir."

"It doesn't matter whether you liked Sgt. Foster or not, whether you're prejudiced or even if you are a racist. None of those things constitute a crime. The relevant question here is did you have anything to do with the killing of Sgt. Foster?"

"No, I did not."

"And whether you admire the Sunday Night Slasher or not is not an issue in this trial. The only relevant question at hand is whether you are, in fact, the Sunday Night Slasher?"

"No, Sir, I am not."

"Thank you, no further questions," Lt. Hooper said."

"Any re-cross, Lt. Burden."

"No further questions, Your Honor."

"The witness may stand down. We'll take a ten

minute recess before the next witness," the Judge said.

Billings stood up, picked up his hat and walked to the door in which he had entered. As he got to the door Agent Sierra and two MP's were waiting for him. The two MP's grabbed Brett's arms, swung them behind his back and cuffed him.

"Brett Billings," Agent Sierra said. "We have a warrant for your arrest in conjunction with an extradition request from the state of Kansas to answer a seven-count indictment for murder. Please come with me, we have a car waiting outside."

Several members of the media had observed the arrest and had their cameras rolling. Billings not only did not put up a fight but he almost looked relieved. The members of the press by now had crowded around the FBI and their prisoner. Cameras were flashing and the reporters were frantically asking questions of Agent Sierra and Billings. The MP's gradually moved Billings to the front door and he was finally escorted out to a waiting car and taken away. Suddenly the reporters turned around and began a stampede toward me.

"Mr. Turner, do think Brett Billings arrest will have an impact on your trial?" the first reporter asked.

"I certainly hope so. He clearly is Sgt. Foster's killer."

"Do you expect the charges against you to be dropped," a second reporter asked.

"I don't know, but I would think so."

"How did you make the connection between the killing of Sgt. Foster and the Sunday Night Slasher," a third reporter asked.

"Actually a friend of mine made the connection when I told him Brett was from Liberal, Kansas."

As I was fielding questions Lt. Burden came out of the court room and motioned for me to come inside.

"I'm sorry ladies and gentlemen but the court

martial is about to reconvene."

I walked inside and sat down at the counsel table next to Lt. Burden. The side door opened and the three judges came through the door and sat down. Lt. Burden immediately got up to address the Court.

"Your Honors, in light of the arrest of Brett Billings pursuant to a Kansas extradition request and the similarities between the killing of Sgt. Foster and the victims of the Sunday Night Slasher I request a dismissal of all charges against Stan Turner."

The three judges conferred with other briefly and then the presiding judge said. "Request denied, Candidate Billings has testified and we will certainly take his testimony into consideration but we cannot make any assumptions based on his arrest. We must decide this case upon the evidence presented during this Court Martial. To do anything else would be improper."

"But Your Honors, clearly there is as strong likelihood that Brett Billings is the killer."

"You've heard our ruling, now let's proceed," the presiding judge said.

"Your Honors, then I request a thirty day recess of this case in order to more fully explore the impact of Brett Billings' arrest on the defendant's guilt or innocence," Lt. Burden said.

"Your Honors, if the Court will permit us to present our last witness, it will become apparent that a recess is not necessary," Lt. Hooper said.

"All right, call your next witness."

"The prosecution calls 2nd Lt. Peter Greer."

"Objection, Your Honor, this name was not on the witness list."

"Your Honor, when Virginia Stone's newspaper stories came out and it became apparent the defense was going to try to pin Sgt. Foster's killing on Brett Billings we felt we had to immediately search out rebuttal witnesses to refute their contention. For the past few days our investigators have been interviewing every candidate in C-Company to see if anyone had any relevant evidence to give this tribunal. We just this morning found Lt. Greer. After our direct examination of Lt. Greer we would not oppose a recess until tomorrow in order for Lt. Burden to prepare his cross examination," Lt. Hooper argued.

"That seems fair under the circumstances. You may proceed."

The side door opened and a very young officer walked in and sat at the witness table. He looked familiar but I didn't know why. The judge administered the oath.

"Lt. Greer, were you a member of C-Company with Candidates Turner and Billings."

"Yes."

"C-Company has now graduated from OCS is that correct?"

"Yes, we just completed our training and received our commissions."

"Do you recall the first few nights at OCS?"

"Yes, quite vividly."

"Do recall the night of December 28, 1970, the night Sgt. Foster was killed?"

"Yes."

"Where were you that night?"

"I was in my bunk in the squad room at C-Company."

"Between 11:00 p.m. and midnight, were you asleep?"

"No. I couldn't sleep I had a mild case of diarrhea apparently from something I ate at dinner."

"Could you describe what you were doing during this one hour period?"

"I was running back and forth between my bed and the toilet."

"How many times did you go back and forth?"

"At least four or five times."

"What was the longest period of time you were away from your bunk?"

"Ten minutes."

"Do you sleep on the top or bottom bunk?"

"The bottom."

"Who slept above you on the night of December 28, 1970?"

"Candidate Brett Billings."

"Was Brett Billings in his bunk in the squad room of C-Company on the night of December 28, 1970?"

"Yes."

"The entire one hour period between 2300 hours and midnight."

"Yes."

Pandemonium broke out in the Court room. My heart sank. I was so shocked by Lt. Greer's testimony I couldn't breathe. Reporters swarmed around me shoving their microphones in my face. I leaned forward and buried my face in my hands to avoid the reporters. I could hear the judge banging his gavel and demanding order. Then I heard whistles blowing as MP's swarmed into the court room to restore order. Two MP's pushed and shoved reporters away from me and pulled me out of the courtroom to safety.

After I was taken to the JAG office, I was met by Lt. Burden.

"Are you all right?" Lt. Burden asked.

"No, not after that last witness."

"I don't know where they found that guy but he just destroyed our defense."

"I just can't believe it. The fucking FBI finally comes in and arrests Brett Billings and finally I think I'm about to get out of this mess. Then Lt. Greer shows up and hands me a live hand grenade."

"He appears to be a pretty credible witness too. I doubt if I am going to be able to impeach him."

"Fuck!"

"Okay Stan, let's not panic. If Brett Billings did not do it somebody else must have done it."

"But who would that be?"

"Obviously I don't know but at least the Judge has recessed the court martial until tomorrow. Between now and then I suggest you consider every other possible suspect. If we don't come up with something really soon I afraid you're going to get convicted."

"Maybe I should just give up."

"No, you can't do that. . . . You have a wife and children to consider."

"Rebekah's not even talking to me. My marriage is probably over. No one's going to care if I go to prison or get taken out by a firing squad."

"Oh come on. Rebekah still loves you. She's just a little confused over your relationship with Rita. Hell, I'm confused about your relationship with Rita. But don't worry, if you're telling the truth and Rita is just a friend, then Rebekah will eventually realize that and you two can get back together."

"I wish I could believe that. I'll probably never see Reggi again and the baby will grow up never knowing his father."

"Don't talk like that. We'll figure a way out of this somehow. Just don't give up the fight. You've got to testify tomorrow. If you've given up the Judges will sense it and assume you're guilty. Will you hang in there?"

I wiped the tears from my eyes and said, "I'll try."

"A few prayers wouldn't hurt either."

That night after dinner I lay on my bunk trying to make sense of everything that had happened. Who else could possibly want Sgt. Foster dead. We had gone through all of the candidate files for C-Company and nobody really stuck out. Maybe it was someone from a previous OCS class. Probably someone who was washed out and was waiting for an opportunity to get revenge on Sgt. Foster. But whoever it was knew about the Sunday Night Slasher because they made it look like he did it hoping Brett Billings would take the rap for it. As I was pondering these possibilities Corporal Lemaster came into the squad room and informed me I had a visitor outside. He said I had fifteen minutes to talk to her. I rushed outside hoping to see Rebekah but instead Rita was standing there with her caring eyes and sweet smile.

"Stan, are you okay?"

"More or less."

"I was so worried about you after Lt. Green dropped that bombshell and the reporters mobbed you."

"I'm okay. Thanks for coming to see me. It's pretty lonely around here."

"Listen I knew you would probably have trouble sleeping tonight so I slipped out some sleeping pills for you."

"That was nice of you. Couldn't you get into a lot of trouble doing that?"

"No. The nurses do it all the time. None of them ever pay for medicine."

"Hmm. One of the perks of your trade I guess."

"Yeah, one of the few."

"Well, I've been sitting here thinking of who might have a motive to kill Sgt. Foster. It's got to be a former Candidate who was washed out on account of something Sgt. Foster did."

"That makes sense."

"But there is no way we are going to be able to get every previous Candidates file in time to do us any good," I said.

"Didn't Sgt. Matson tell you there was some kind

of Court of Inquiry for something Sgt. Foster had done in the past," Rita replied.

"Yeah, I think you're right. Could you check with him and find out more about it?"

"Sure, I'll check on it tonight and get with you before the trial in the morning."

"Great, thanks so much for coming."

"Your welcome, but before I go let me give you one more thing."

"What's that?"

Rita stepped up directly in front of me, put her arms around my neck and kissed me passionately. Her lips were soft and sweet and they greatly aroused me. Without conscious thought I began to respond to Rita's affection wrapping my arms around her pulling her body next to mine. As we embraced, I heard the sound of a vehicle driving up. I pulled my lips away momentarily to see who was arriving and was horrified to see that it was Rebekah. The vehicle stopped a second and Rebekah gave me a chilling stare and then motioned for the driver to go on.

"Rebekah, come back! Please come back," I yelled to the car hustling away in the darkness. I looked at Rita in despair.

"I'm sorry," she said. "I didn't intend to destroy your marriage. Will you ever forgive me?"

"It's not your fault. You've just tried to be good to me. I don't know what I would have done without you. You know when you testified in the court martial that you loved me it made me do some soul searching about how I felt about you. I think I do love you. If I wasn't already married, I would certainly want you to be my bride. But my life is just so confusing right now. I can't give you anything at this moment but grief and agony. You would be better off to forget you ever met me."

"Well, I can't do that. I'm going to stand beside

during this ordeal and I hope when it's all over we can be together."

"I can't promise that."

"I know."

"Turner! Your time is up," Corporal Lemaster yelled.

"Okay, Corporal. . . . I'll be right there. I'll see you tomorrow Rita, okay?"

"Yes, I'll come by first thing."

If I was depressed earlier in the evening it was nothing compared to what engulfed me after Rita left. What thin strands of hope I had for the salvage of my marriage had been severed. The chances of finding Sgt. Foster's killer were minuscule at best. I laid back on my bunk and suddenly realized I had a bottle in my hand. I lifted it up in front of my eyes so I could read the label. "Seconal - twenty-four tablets - take two tablets every four hours as needed."

After opening the bottle I took out three tablets and went to the can to get some water to wash them down. I figured in my condition I needed an extra strong dose. When I got back, I lay on my bunk. I began to feel light headed almost immediately and my vision became blurry. A peaceful feeling gradually overcame me and I fell asleep.

When I awoke, I suddenly realized that this might be my last night in Casual Platoon. If my testimony was not convincing I would be convicted and immediately sent to prison. I couldn't live in prison. The thought of it made me nauseous. I'd rather be dead. After I got up, I showered and got dressed. Before I put on my boots I carefully wrapped the twenty-one remaining tablets in a Kleenex and concealed them in my boot. If I were going to die, I'd rather just fade off into dreamland and never wake up.

I was scheduled to meet with Lt. Burden at eight

hundred hours to get ready for my testimony. Rita was supposed to come by before I left to tell me what she had found out from Sgt. Matson. I waited until 0755 hours but she didn't show up so I left to go to the JAG office. Lt. Burden hadn't arrived yet so I sat in the waiting room to wait for him. Suddenly the door flew open and there was Rita.

"Hi, I'm sorry I missed you at the barracks but I wasn't able to see Sgt. Matson until early this morning."

"So what did you find out?"

"Not much more than what you told me. He couldn't remember the name of the Candidate who was killed but he did say that Lt. Hooper was the officer in charge of the Court of Inquiry."

"Well, I'm sure Lt. Burden can get a copy of the file or a transcript of the proceeding so we can review it for possible suspects."

"If he can get the file I'll go through it while you're testifying."

"Okay."

The door flew opened again and Lt. Burden entered the waiting room.

"Hi, Stan. . . . Rita. How are you holding up, Stan?"

"I've had better days," I replied.

"I'm still reeling from Lt. Greer's testimony." Lt. Burden said. "I thought we had this case licked. Now we're backed up on the 10-yard line, the clock's running out and we have no time outs."

"We have one possibility left," I said.

"What's that?"

"Sgt. Matson said a couple of years ago a Candidate was killed in Sgt. Foster's OCS Company. There was a Court of Inquiry but no Court Martial. Apparently Sgt. Foster convinced the Court that it was an accident. Sgt. Matson says it was a whitewash."

"Hum. . . . That's an interesting idea. That must of happened before my time. I don't remember it at all."

"Can you find the file so we can see who might have had a motive to kill Sgt. Foster?"

"All court files after one year are sent to a central storage facility in Trenton, New Jersey. It would take two or three weeks to retrieve that file."

"Apparently Lt. Hooper was the officer in charge of that investigation. Do you think he might discuss the case with you?"

"In the middle of a murder trial, I seriously doubt if he's going to reminisce with me about a Court of Inquiry held two years ago. He has a duty to advise me and the Court of any exculpatory evidence that he discovers or is brought to his attention. He doesn't have to go looking for it or even help me look for it, . . . unless-"

"Unless what?"

"Unless I called him as a witness."

"You can do that?"

"It's highly irregular, but if he has knowledge relevant to the crime then I could call him. I'd have to be sure though. If it turned out he didn't know anything I'd be in serious trouble."

"So all we have to do is get him to tell us everything he can remember about the Court of Inquiry, right?"

"That would be a start."

"There may be another way to do that. . . . Is Lt. Hooper single?"

"I believe so."

"Where does he hang out?"

"During the week he usually goes to the Officers' Club after work."

"Does he have a girlfriend?"

"I don't know. I haven't seen him with any one girl

on a regular basis. Why all these questions?"

"There is a girl I met in DC who might help us out."

"Don't tell me what you're planning to do. I can't participate in anything unethical."

"Don't worry, you don't know anything about it."

"About what?"

"I don't know."

At nine hundred hours the court martial resumed. The presiding judge warned the spectators that if there was one single outburst like the preceding day he was going to clear the courtroom for the rest of the trial. Lt. Hooper smelling victory rested. The judge asked Lt. Burden to present his case.

"The defense calls Lt. Peter Wallace," Lt. Burden said.

Lt. Wallace took the stand and was administered the oath.

"Lt. Wallace, where were you stationed on December 28, 1970?"

"I was a candidate in C-Company OCS."

"And what were you doing on the night of December 28, 1970."

"I was on guard duty in the Candidate Parking Lot."

"During what hours?"

"From 2200 hours on Sunday night to 0600 hours on Monday."

"Where is the Candidate Parking lot in relation to the Staff parking lot?"

"If you were coming from the C-Company barracks to the staff parking lot you would have to go by the OCS Parking Lot."

"Did anything unusual happen on the night of December 28, 1970?"

"Yes, about 2205 hours a Marine walked by the

OCS Parking Lot heading toward the staff parking lot. I didn't pay much attention to him until a few minutes later he came back and he was in a hurry. He stopped not too far from me, threw something toward a dumpster across from the parking lot and then kept on moving. I yelled at him to stop but he ignored me."

"What did he throw in the dumpster?"

"I didn't look right then, but later on I found two rubber glove near the base of it."

Lt. Burden questioned Wallace for another half hour about the Marine, his description, what he was wearing, and every other detail he could come up with but it added nothing to what had already been said. Finally he passed the witness.

"Your witness," the Judge said.

"Lt. Wallace, can you identify who the person was who walked by you that night."

"No, Sir, like I said, it was very dark."

"Do you think the man you saw was Sgt. Foster's killer?"

"Yes, Sir."

"Why is that?"

"When he came back he acted panicky. He was obviously running from something. I didn't know exactly what it was at the time but I knew something was wrong."

"When you told him to halt and he ignored you, why didn't you do something."

"I didn't know what to do. I couldn't leave my post. About the only thing I could have done was shoot him and I just didn't think that was an appropriate response."

"I see. Now, I want you to take a look at the Defendant, Stanley Turner. Could he have been the man who you saw on December 28?"

"It's possible but like I say I really couldn't see him very well."

"But it could have been Candidate Turner?"

"Yes."

"No further questions Your Honor."

"You may step down. Let's take a short recess. The Court will reconvene at 1030 hours," the Judge said.

While the Court was in recess I rummaged through my wallet for the note Nicole had given me with her phone number. I knew I wasn't supposed to make any phone calls but I needed her help. I found the note and then slipped into an empty office to make the call.

"Hello. . . . Warren Chiropractic," a voice said.

"Is Nicole there?"

"Yes, I'll get her."

"Hello."

"Nicole?"

"Yes."

"This is Stan Turner."

"Stan Turner?"

"Yes, the man you picked up at the Senate Gallery Club."

"I know who you are. I've been following your trial. I am just surprised you're calling me?"

"Well, you remember that little note you gave me when you left?"

"Oh yes, my little desperate note. Well, do you need a massage or do you want to talk?"

"Both."

"Well, I hope they find you innocent because somehow I don't think they will let me in to give you a massage in your jail cell."

"Actually I wonder if you would give the massage to someone else?"

"Now wait a minute. I'm not some two bit hooker."

"No, no. I really need your help. As you probably have read the court martial is not going too well for me right now. We had built our defense on our assumption that Brett Billings killed Sgt. Foster. Now we know he didn't do it. If we don't find out who did it in the next twenty-four hours I'm going to be convicted."

"So how can I help?"

"Well you are one sexy lady with a set of magical fingers. There is some information we need to get out of someone and I'm sure you wouldn't have any trouble getting it."

"Who has this information?"

"Lt. Hooper."

"The prosecutor?!"

"Yes, he was the officer in charge of a Court of Inquiry that took place a couple of years ago when a candidate in Sgt. Foster's company died. We believe someone who was close to that Marine has to be the murderer."

"That's a really long shot isn't it?"

"It is, but it's all we got. If we don't find something here, I'm afraid it's all over for me."

"So what do you want me to do?"

"Lt. Burden goes to the Officer's Club every evening for an hour or so. If a pretty young lady were to take an interest in him I'm sure he would tell her all about himself, particularly all about the Court of Inquiry."

"I'm not sleeping with him."

"Oh no, just use those magical fingers to put him to sleep when you're through with him."

"How do I get into the base?"

"I'll have a friend of mine, Rita Andrews, call you. She'll get you on the base and take you to the Officer's Club. When you're done you can give her any information you've found out."

"Okay, but this is really bizarre."

"I know, but my life is at stake and I don't know where else to turn. If you do this for me I don't know how

I will ever repay you but I hope someday I'll be able to."

"Good luck today in trial."

"Thanks."

I put down the phone and breathed a sigh of relief. Maybe there was hope yet. I slipped out of the office and headed back to the court room. The judges were on the bench and all eyes were on me when I entered the court room."

"Well, good of you to come back to your court martial Candidate Turner. We thought maybe you had decided to flee the country," one of the Judges said.

The spectators broke out in laughter. I sat down, smiled and said, "No, Sir, just lost track of time."

"Lt. Burden, please call your next witness," the Judge said.

"Thank you, Your Honor.   The defense calls Candidate Stanley Turner."

"Candidate Turner, Do you swear to tell the truth, the whole truth and nothing but the truth so help you God?"

"I do."

Lt. Burden questioned me the rest of the morning and all afternoon. He started with my background, education, family life and then went through each hour of my Marine Corps experience from the moment I stepped off the airplane at Dulles International Airport to the day of the murder. I told the Judges my side of the story as convincingly as I could. I looked into their eyes and told them honestly and sincerely that I was innocent. Did they believe me? Who knows? But they did seem to be listening. Then Lt. Burden asked me the ultimate question.

"Did you murder Sgt. Foster?"

"No, absolutely not."

"Do you know who did?"

"I thought Brett Billings had done it, but now I

don't know. All I know is I didn't do it."

"No further questions Your Honor."

"All right, Lt. Hooper, your witness," the Judge said.

"Candidate Turner, you heard Nurse Andrews testify that you told her you'd like to kill Sgt. Foster? Was Nurse Andrews telling the truth?"

"Yes, but I didn't mean it literally. I just meant I was mad at him for mistreating me."

"You were really mad, weren't you? Didn't you also say you'd like to kick his ass?"

"Yes."

"And didn't you say some day he would get his?"

"Yes, but I meant God would take care of him."

"Well, did you decide to help God out perhaps?"

"No."

"Isn't it true that on Sunday night, December 28 you left the hospital unnoticed and made your way to the Staff Parking Lot near C-Company barracks?"

"No."

"And then waited for Sgt. Foster to come back from his poker game so you could kill him?"

"No, I never left the hospital."

"Isn't it true that you were Brett Billings only friend?"

"I hardly would call him a friend since I had only known him two days."

"But you were the only one he talked to, isn't that right?"

"I suppose so."

"He told you or you discovered somehow in talking to him that he was the Sunday Night Slasher, isn't that right?"

"No way, how would I figure that out?"

"Well, somehow you figured out he was the Slasher because you managed to get the FBI to come here and arrest him."

"But that was later."

"How do we know that? You could have found out he was the Slasher and decided it was a perfect opportunity to kill Sgt. Foster and pin the murder on him. That's why you carved the cross on Sgt. Foster's chest and murdered him on a Sunday night."

"That's ridiculous."

"Is it? Well it almost worked. If you'd of done a better job of disposing of the murder weapon you probably would have gotten away with it," Lt. Hooper said. . . . "No further questions."

"All right, we'll recess until tomorrow morning at 1000 hours."

That night Nicole was set to have her rendezvous with Lt. Hooper. I had arranged for Rita to pick her up and get her to the officer's club. I couldn't believe that my life was in the hands of a woman who I had known less than twelve hours. It was amazing that she had agreed to play our little game of deception. I began to doubt my sanity in setting up such a ridiculous stunt.

The evening dragged on ever so slowly. For a while I tried to read a book to make the time pass more quickly. Unfortunately, I couldn't concentrate and would end up starring at a single page for several minutes. I tried to take a nap but my eyes wouldn't stay closed. I looked at my watch and it was twenty-one hundred hours. How was Nicole doing, I wondered? Had the caper worked or was it bust? I walked outside and looked up and down the street hoping to see Rita's car rolling up to give some news but the streets were empty.

After a while I went back inside again and looked at my watch. It was 2230 hours. There were only thirty more minutes until lights were out and I would be forced to wait until morning to find how Nicole had done. Finally at 2235 I heard a car drive up outside and I ran to the door to see who it was. Seeing Rita getting out of her car, I went outside to meet her.

"Finally you got here."

"Well getting a drunken Marine to talk is not easy."

"So what happened?"

"Well, I had to stay clear of the officer's club because if Lt. Hooper had seen me he would have known something was up. So this is Nicole's account of the evening."

"Okay, let's hear it."

Well Nicole obviously took her assignment seriously. She went to the beauty shop and got a gorgeous hairdo and had her nails done quite exquisitely. She arrived at the club in a short black cocktail dress that exposed a considerable portion of her female anatomy. As she entered the club, she immediately became the object of may lustful stares. Lt. Hooper was playing pool at the time and, immediately upon seeing her, lost all concentration on his game.

Nicole went to the bar and ordered a drink. Several Marine Officers attempted to pick her up but she artfully repelled them. Finally, Lt. Hooper made his move. He casually walked up to the bar and sat down beside her.

"Hi, there, Miss."

Nicole glanced over at Lt. Hooper and gave him a cursory inspection and then said. "Hi, aren't you Lt. Hooper."

"Yeah, how did you know?"

"Hell, you've been on TV all week."

"Oh, I guess you're right. I never watch TV. I'm too busy working or unwinding from work."

"I can understand that. You're under a lot of pressure being a prosecutor."

"Boy, you got that right."

"What's it like trying to put someone in prison for the rest of their life?"

"Well, if they deserve it, then it feels good. It feels like justice has been done."

"But don't you ever worry that maybe the guy you're trying to put away is innocent?"

"Sure, I worry about that. But it's not my job to defend the prisoner. There's another lawyer that handles that and if everybody does their job then justice should be done."

"That's fascinating," she said and then turned away.

She finished her drink and started to leave.

"Wait a minute, let me buy you another drink," he said.

"You sure?"

"Of course, our conversation was just getting interesting."

"I'll take another Margarita," Nicole said.

"Bartender. Another Margarita for the lady."

"Coming up," the bartender replied.

"So what do you do?" Lt. Hooper said.

"I'm a massage therapist."

"Really?"

"What does a massage therapist do exactly?"

"Well, if people injure their back in a car wreck, slip and fall or other accident I help them rehabilitate themselves with certain types of massages."

"Huh. . . . Is that kind of treatment effective?"

"Yes, in a lot of cases it is. I also give a lot of massages to executives and professionals that are under a lot of stress. Maybe sometime I could give you one."

"I could really use one right now. I'm just about to wrap up this case against Stanley Turner and I'm scared to death they have some trick up their sleeve."

"Why is that?"

"Well, any defense counselor that can dig up a serial killer from Kansas to take the rap for his client is someone to be reckoned with. I've got a bad feeling about this case."

"Oh now, from what I've seen on TV you got the case all but won."

Lt. Hooper smiled and said, "I don't know about that, but what I do know, is I could really use that massage. You know we could go to my place."

"Lieutenant, I don't make house calls."

"I'll be a gentlemen. . . . Don't worry."

"Can I trust you?"

"Yes, you have my word as an officer."

"Okay, you better be a man of your word or I'll complain to your commanding officer."

"Don't worry. My car is just outside."

Nicole and Sergeant Hooper left the club and went outside to Lt. Hooper's car. Lt. Hooper opened the passenger door for Nicole and she got in. "Thank you," said Nicole. Lt. Hooper went around to the drivers side and got in.

"I live just about twenty minutes from here."

"In Woodbridge."

"Right."

"Do you try a lot of murder trials?"

"No, this is actually my first one. Not too many people get murdered on a military base."

"I thought I read about you trying one a couple of years ago."

"No. . . . Oh, you must have read about the Court of Inquiry into the death of Candidate Samuel Matson."

"Maybe so. What's a Court of Inquiry?"

"It's an investigation to determine if there are enough facts indicating a crime was committed such that a Court Martial should be convened."

"So why did they have a Court of Inquiry in this case?"

"Because there were some charges that Sgt. Foster had abused Candidate Matson."

"Is that the same Sgt. Foster that Candidate Turner has been charged with killing."

"Yes, as a matter of fact it is."

"So your Court of Inquiry found Sgt. Foster innocent?"

"Well, not innocent exactly, but we determined there wasn't enough evidence to bring charges."

"Do you think he was guilty?"

"Guilty as sin but we just couldn't prove it. Everybody who knew anything clammed up."

"Well, I guess he got what was coming to him."

"Wait a minute, you're starting to talk like you're on the defense side."

"Don't be silly. I want to see justice done."

Lt. Hooper pulled his car up into his driveway and shut off the engine. "Okay, this is it." Nicole and Lt. Hooper got out and went inside the apartment.

"Nice place."

"Excuse the mess, I don't bring too many pretty ladies to my apartment."

"Now Lt. Hooper, if I asked you that question under oath would your answer be the same."

"No, I'd have to take the fifth and when you're in my house you can call me Martin."

"That's what I thought, Martin."

"How about a drink."

"Yes, please."

Lt. Hooper walked over to his stereo and put on some soft music. Then he went and fixed Nicole and himself a drink. They talked for a while and had a few more drinks until finally he put his arm around Nicole and tried to kiss her.

"Martin, . . . how about that massage now."

"Now?"

"Yeah, you're looking pretty stressed out."

"I'm as loose as a moose," he protested.

Nicole moved around behind Martin and began playing with his shoulders.

"No, you're very tight. Lay down."

Lt. Hooper obeyed and Nicole began massaging his back. He sighed with delight over Nicole's soothing touch. Before long he fell sound asleep and Nicole left the apartment and found me waiting for her outside.

"So that's it," Rita said.

"Samuel Matson. He must be related to Sgt. Matson. You don't suppose Sgt. Matson is the killer?" I said.

"If Samuel was his son, he sure would have a good motive," Rita replied.

"Damn. We've got to call Lt. Burden and tell him what we found out."

"I'll call him since you've got exactly two minutes until lights out."

"Thanks Rita, you're a lifesaver. Did you thank Nicole for me?"

"Yes, but I think she's going to want a personal thanks."

"I hope I'll be able to give it to her."

"You can send her a thank you note."

I laughed. "A thank you note? Do I detect a tinge of jealousy?"

"Perhaps. She likes you just a little to much for my taste. I think she'd like to sink her hooks in you."

"Well that's not really your problem, is it?"

"Maybe it is, maybe it isn't," she replied.

I looked at her and shook my head. "Listen, if I resisted you I can resist anyone."

"Is that supposed to make me feel better?"

I smiled. "Okay, lets stop playing these little mind games. Just go talk to Lt. Burden."

"Don't I get a kiss for all of my hard work?"

I laughed. "I don't know, kissing you can be dangerous."

"That's what makes it so sweet."

Rita put her arms around me and gave me a passionate kiss. I looked up and down the street for signs of Rebekah, but the streets were empty. I wanted to let myself go but I couldn't do it. I longed for my Rebekah. When I got inside, I went to see Corporal Lemaster. I begged him to let me use the phone to call Rebekah. He refused saying he couldn't disobey orders but he did say he would call her and convey to her any message I might have. He dialed the hotel.

"Hello, can I have Rebekah Turner's room," Corporal Lemaster said.

"I'm sorry, Sir but Rebekah Turner has checked out of the hotel."

My heart sank when Corporal Lemaster relayed the desk clerk's words. I knew she was mad at me but I thought for sure after a while she would get over it and forgive me. But the fact she went home in the middle of my murder trial meant she had given up on me. She didn't care about me anymore. Our relationship was over. I couldn't believe she had deserted me. I had been faithful to her despite overwhelming temptations. It wasn't fair. It just wasn't fair. Not only had the Marine Corps managed to destroy my dream of becoming an attorney, now it had fucked-up my marriage as well. My life had been reduced to nothing more than a pile of rubble and I didn't care if I lived another day.

Chapter Twenty-Four
Court Martial - Day Three

Rita contacted Lt. Burden and advised him of the fruits of Nicole's espionage. He worked all night to prepare his new defense. It wouldn't be easy because once Sgt. Matson figured out that we were on to him he would clam up. If it became necessary to call Lt. Hooper as a witness he would certainly protest and the Court might sustain his objection. Again we were caught in the dilemma of knowing who the killer was, but not being able to prove it. The Court Martial resumed at precisely 1000 hours.

"All right, Lt. Burden, do you have any more witnesses?"

"Yes, Your Honor, the defense recalls Sgt. Harry Matson."

Sgt. Matson got up slowly and walked to the witness box.

"Sgt. Matson, I'm sorry we had to bring you up here again but we just have a few more questions," Lt. Burden said. "You realize you're still under oath."

"Yes, but I've already told you everything I know."

"Well, I'm not sure about that. Are you a married man sergeant?"

"Divorced."

"Do you have any children?"

"No."

"Did you ever have any children?"

"Why is that relevant?"

"It is, please answer the question."

"Objection Your Honor, this can't possibly have

any relevance to this case," Lt. Hooper said.

"Your Honor, if you will bear with me it will become clear that it is quite relevant."

"Objection overruled, proceed."

"Now, have you ever had any children?"

"Yes, I had a son."

"What was his name?"

"Samuel Matson."

"Now I presume your son is dead."

"Yes."

"How did he die?"

"He died in an accident."

"Was he a candidate at OCS here in Quantico?"

Sgt. Matson squirmed in his chair. "Yes."

"Who was his Drill Sergeant?"

"I don't understand what this has to do with anything?"

"Just answer the question please," Lt. Burden said.

Sgt. Matson took a deep breath and then looked at the judge as if he were going to rule on his objection.

"Your Honor, will you please instruct the witness to answer the question," Lt. Burden asked.

"Sgt. Matson, you must answer the question."

"Sgt. Foster," he mumbled.

"The same Sgt. Foster who was killed on December 28, 1970?"

"Yes."

The crowd again became boisterous and the Judge smacked his gavel.

"Was there a Court of Inquiry into the death of your son?"

"Yes."

"And who presided over that Court of Inquiry?"

"Lt. Hooper."

The judges looked at Lt. Hooper and then at each

other.

"What was the result of that Court of Inquiry?"

"Nothing. No action was taken against Sgt. Foster for what he did."

"How did you feel about that?"

Sgt. Matson glared at Lt. Burden and then pulled a small index card out of his pocket. He began to read, "As is my right under the Constitution of the United States of America and the Uniform Code of Military Justice I respectfully decline to answer that question on the grounds it might incriminate me."

Lt. Hooper looked over at us obviously stunned at what was transpiring. I could feel his mind working frantically to come up with a strategy to thwart Lt. Burden's new line of questioning. Finally he shook his head and fell back into his chair without uttering a word.

"Isn't it true you work in the base personnel department?" Lt. Burden continued.

"Yes."

"Isn't it true the FBI contacted you and told you Brett Billings was under suspicion of being the Sunday Night Slasher?"

"As is my right under the Constitution of the United States of America and the Uniform Code of Military Justice I respectfully decline to answer that question on the grounds it might incriminate me."

"Isn't it true that when you found out there was a serial killer on base you thought you had found the perfect opportunity to kill Sgt. Foster and then blame it on him."

"As is my right under the Constitution of the United States of America and the Uniform Code of Military Justice I respectfully decline to answer that question on the grounds it might incriminate me."

"So you immediately kept a close eye on C-Company for the right opportunity to make your move.

When you heard about Brett Billings getting in trouble with Sgt. Foster you knew the time was right. So you paid a visit to C-company on December 27 and planned the murder. You saw the work being done on the showers and discovered a linoleum knife amongst the tools. You thought if you killed Sergeant Foster with the linoleum knife that everyone would assume Brett Billings had done it. Isn't that right?"

"Objection!" Lt. Hooper exclaimed. "Compound question. Your Honor, Lt. Burden is testifying."

"As is my right under the Constitution of the United States of America and the Uniform Code of Military Justice I respectfully decline to answer that question on the grounds it might incriminate me."

The judge said,"Sustained. Lt. Burden, please, one question at a time."

"Yes, Your Honor. . . . So sometime on Sunday night you left the hospital and took the linoleum knife from the tool box and laid in wait for Sgt. Foster to return from his poker game, right?"

Sgt. Matson rubbed his forehead, looked around the room nervously and then read again from his card.

"When Sgt. Foster drove up you approached him from behind and sliced his throat before he knew what hit him. Then you ripped off his shirt and put the Sunday Night Slasher's signature on the victim so that everyone would think Brett Billings had done it. Isn't that right?"

Sgt. Matson took a deep breath and looked down at the floor in front of him. Then he looked at his card and took the 5th Amendment one more time.

"You are left handed, aren't you Sgt. Matson? I know. Don't bother to answer, . . . go ahead and take the 5th amendment."

"What you didn't count on was that Stan Turner accidentally got his fingerprints and blood on the linoleum knife. Now I can almost understand your lack of concern for a serial killer taking the rap for one more murder. What difference would it make anyway? But Sgt. Matson were you going to sit by and let Stan Turner go to prison or be executed when you knew he was innocent?"

"No! No, I wasn't going to let that happen. I've grown very fond of Stan and I certainly didn't want him to get hurt. Sgt. Foster was a disgrace, a blemish on the image of the United States Marine Corps. I planned the murder so carefully I was sure the killing would be blamed on the Slasher. Like you said, what's one more murder when you've already committed nineteen? It was so perfect.

Sgt. Matson continued. "I was totally shocked and appalled by Lt. Greer's testimony providing an alibi for the Slasher. I had no idea what to do. But I wouldn't have let an innocent man die for my crime. I would have confessed had Stan Turner been convicted. Yes, I killed Sgt. Foster and I would kill that sorry bastard again if I had the chance."

Total chaos overtook the courtroom, cameras flashed, reporters ran to the telephones to relay this startling confession to their news departments and Judge pounded his gavel trying desperately to restore order. Finally the MP's again stormed in and restored order.

"Your Honor, in light of Sgt. Matson's confession I move that all charges against Stan Turner be dismissed," Lt. Burden asked.

"Lt. Hooper, do you have a response?" the Judge said.

"The prosecution has no objection," Lt. Hooper replied."

"All charges against Candidate Stanley Turner are hereby dismissed. Sgt. Harry Matson you shall be bound into custody until you are formally charged with the Murder of Sgt. Louis Foster. This proceeding is concluded."

When Harry made his confession, it was like waking up from a bad dream. The excruciating fear and anxiety in which I had been engulfed since I had become a Marine suddenly vanished. I was thrilled by our victory and joy and happiness invaded every inch of my body and soul. Rita rushed over to me and embraced me wildly. Lt. Burden and all my friends came over to congratulate me. The reporters fought desperately for an interview but were kept at bay by the Military Police as I had promised Virginia Stone my exclusive story.

In fact, as Virginia and I embraced she told me she had already arranged a TV interview that was going to take the rest of day. I acquiesced willingly, but before I left, Rita informed me that she and Nicole were throwing a victory party that night at the Senate Gallery Club in DC starting at 2100 hours and I was not to be late. I assured her there was no way I'd miss my victory party.

The thought of the TV interview was exciting. Never had I imagined that I would be such a celebrity. But in the midst of all the celebration I felt Sgt. Matson torment. I could feel his pain and loneliness as he contemplated his fate. I had been moved by his profession of fondness for me as I too had felt a bond had developed between us. Our eyes met and I was drawn toward him. I knelt down as if to tie my boots and then slowly slipped my hand inside and pulled out the twenty-one seconal tablets wrapped in Kleenex. I pressed forward toward Sgt. Matson. The MP warned me to stay away but I forced my way through to embrace him. As we clutched each other we wept and he told me he was sorry for what he had done to me. As I handed him the Kleenex to wipe his tears I told him that I forgave him. After he had wiped his brow, he squeezed the Kleenex and felt the hidden contraband. He looked confused momentarily and then he looked up at me and smiled. I never saw Sgt. Matson again.

As I was escorted to a temporary studio set up near the courtroom I searched the crowd hoping, wishing that I would see Rebekah. I wanted her beside me to share my victory. Without her at my side my triumph was empty for she was the reason that I lived. Yes, I was a free man and certainly I would cherish my liberty so much more in the future, but was the price of liberty the loss of love and happiness?

I could understand how Rebekah could have misunderstood what she had seen. I didn't blame her for being mad, but I couldn't understand how she could just up and leave me. Was she blind to the fact that I loved her more than any person or thing on earth? Was her trust and faith in me so shallow that it would be destroyed by one simple kiss of gratitude to a friend? Could she not give me the benefit of the doubt and allow me to explain? After all we had created two children together and were responsible for their lives. I thought I knew Rebekah. I thought she knew me, but I guess we were both wrong. Now how could I resist her adversary.

Steve picked me up to go to the party at 1930 hours. On the way I made him stop so that I could call Rebekah. Her mom answered the phone and told me she was glad that I had been acquitted and hoped to see me soon but that Rebekah didn't want to talk to me. I explained to her what had happened and asked her to explain to Rebekah. I told her about the party and told her to tell Rebekah I would call her after it was over and that I loved her and really needed to talk to her.

As we drove down the freeway to DC I looked at my watch and saw it was 2000 hours and time for the news. I turned on the radio so I could hear what the press was saying about my trial.

"This is Paul Flemming with the DC Metro News. Today in Washington the Senate repealed the Gulf of Tonkin Resolution. The Resolution was first passed on August 7, 1964 at the request of the President, Lyndon Johnson, and has since been the legal authority for U.S. troop involvement in South Vietnam. In recent months antiwar sentiment has been growing steadily culminating in today's Senate action."

In Quantico, Virginia the case against United States Marine Corps Officer Candidate, Stanley Turner, for the alleged murder of his drill instructor, Sgt. Louis Foster, was dismissed when his defense counsel elicited a confession from the actual murderer, Sgt. Harry Matson. Matson's motive for the murder was the unexplained death of his son, Samuel Matson, at the hands of the murder victim, Sgt. Louis Foster. In a late breaking story we take you to Howard Hunter at Quantico Naval Hospital where we are told Sgt. Matson has just died of an overdose of sleeping pills."

"Yes Paul, just minutes ago Sgt. Harry Matson was found dead in his cell in the brig at the Quantico Marine Base from an apparent overdose of Seconal. Military police are unsure how Sgt. Matson got the pills past jail security but conjecture that he planned the suicide before he took the stand today and made his dramatic confession. That's all we have for now, back to Paul in DC"

"In related news, Brett Billings, the alleged Sunday Night Slasher, was indicted today in Kansas State District Court on nineteen counts of murder. His arraignment is scheduled for next Tuesday when he is expected to plead not guilty on grounds of insanity."

"And in Paris Island, S.C. a Court of Inquiry was convened in connection with the hospitalization of forty-four new Marine Recruits last December as a result of a controversial back country military exercise conducted by the company's drill instructor."

I shut off the radio and thought about poor Harry. Hopefully he was finally at peace. I didn't feel guilty about what I had done. Harry had made the choice. I just gave him the option. I didn't feel much like a party when we finally arrived at the Senate Gallery Club, but my guest gave me no choice. Everyone was there, Rita, Steve, Lt. Burden, Randy Price and a couple guys from D-Company, Nicole and her friends and Virginia Stone and her editor. It was a great night and before everyone got too stoned to listen to me speak I asked for their attention."

"I want to thank all of you for everything you did for me. Most of you barely knew me when I got in trouble and needed your help. I don't know why you went so far out of your way to help me but I am truly grateful that you did. Every one of you will have a special place in my heart and I want all of you to keep in touch because some day I hope to find a way to repay you."

Chapter Twenty-Five
Moment of Truth

After the party I said goodbye to Steve. He was taking a late flight back to California. It was the first time that I had been able to talk to him since Rebekah had left.

"Do you know why Rebekah left me?"

"After she heard Rita confess her love for you she was livid. She was sure you had betrayed her. That night she decided to go see you to confront you with her suspicions. When she drove up and saw you kissing Rita there was no need in her mind to even talk to you."

"But Rita was just giving me a kiss good night. She had just saved my life for godsakes. What was I supposed to do push her away? I couldn't deny her one small kiss."

"I know, but Rebekah is a proud woman and she didn't understand what was going on."

"But now she knows what happened yet she won't even talk to me."

"I don't know what to tell you. I tried to get her to stay around for the rest of the trial and talk to you but she insisted on leaving. She said she was getting a divorce."

"What?"

"I told her she was being a little rash but she said she wasn't going to stay married to a man who she couldn't trust."

"Damn it. Well I'm going to call her one more time and if she rebukes me again then I guess it's over."

"I'm sorry Stan."

"Me too."

Rita and I took Steve to the airport and then drove back to Woodbridge. Lt. Burden had arranged a three-day pass for me so for the first time in many months I was truly a free man. Rita snuggled up close to me in the car on the way home and I knew the moment of truth was at hand.

"I've got to make a phone call before we go to your place."

"I knew you were going to say that."

"It's something I've got to do."

"Why do you still love that bitch? She ran out on you."

"She not a bitch. Rebekah just doesn't tolerate betrayal. I knew that when I married her. I haven't betrayed her but she's too proud and stubborn to realize that."

"Well you're going to have to make a decision tonight because I am sick and tired of being second fiddle to that woman."

"Just let me make this last call and then it will over one way or another."

"I'm going to the ladies room. Make your damn phone call."

We stopped at a gas station. Rita went to the bathroom and I walked over to the pay phone. I dialed the number and waited.

"Hello."

"Mom, is Rebekah going to talk to me?"

"I'm sorry Stan, but I can't convince her to come to the phone. I've tried but she won't listen to me. I've told her you've been through a lot and she should give you a chance to explain but you know how stubborn she is."

"I don't understand why she won't talk to me. This

is so childish. Go ask her to come to the phone one more time would you please."

"Okay, hang on."

A few seconds later she returned to the phone, "I'm sorry Stan, she won't talk to you."

"Okay, I'm sorry it turned out this way. Goodbye Mom."

"Goodbye."

My eyes began to swell and I struggled to keep from crying. I had never dreamed this day would come but I figured I'd just have to accept my fate and move on. Had I been so bad to deserve this? Well, at least I had another woman who loved me. Rita was a beautiful and wonderful girl. I would be happy with her. She certainly had saved my life these past few months. When I got in the car, Rita was starring out the window and biting her finger nail. She didn't look at me. I started the car and we drove off.

"Rebekah wouldn't talk to me."

"That's too bad. She's making a big mistake. There aren't many men like you out there in this world."

"I don't know, maybe she's right. I let you get a little to close perhaps, but I am a man, you're beautiful and I am weak."

"Weak my ass, nine out of ten men would have given in long ago and most of them wouldn't of had any remorse."

"Oh come on, most men are faithful to their wives."

"What world do you come from?"

"Well anyway from now on it's just you and me, that is if you still want me."

"No, I've just been busting my ass to keep you out of prison for my health."

Rita laid her head on my shoulder as we made our way down the dark highway to Woodbridge. When we arrived at Rita's apartment, I was scared. I knew in just a few moments a great change would take place in my life. Would I be happy with Rita? Did I really love her? Could I forget Rebekah? What would become of my children?

We were both silent as we walked into Rita's apartment. Rita told me to make us a couple of drinks while she went to change clothes. I poured her a glass of wine and made me a highball. I turned on the stereo and relaxed on the sofa and contemplated the pleasures that were about to ensue. After about five minutes Rita emerged from her bedroom in a long black nightgown. She had let down her long brown hair and was as radiant as cluster of diamonds. My body was greatly aroused but my mind was numb. I wanted her, yes I wanted to ravish her body but my heart wouldn't allow it. She saw the pain in my eyes and let out a sigh of disgust.

"Damn you, Stanley Turner! You still love that bitch. Get the hell out of my apartment, get out of my life. I don't know why you can't love me the way you love Rebekah. I love you so much. I've done everything I could to make you love me, but it's obviously impossible."

"Don't hate me, Rita. If I wasn't already in love with Rebekah I surely would have fallen in love with you. Please forgive me."

"Just get out of here and go talk some sense into that bitch."

"Okay, but I need one more favor."

"What?"

"A ride to the bus depot."

"Come on, let's go."

Rita took me to the bus depot and I got the next bus to DC and then took a cab to the Dulles Airport. After I boarded the plane I began to wonder what I was going to do and say to Rebekah when I got to Portland. What if she still refused to see me? Then I'd camp at her doorstep until she talked to me or maybe even break in and confront her. She had to talk to me and understand that I loved her. But if she didn't talk to me and wouldn't take me back now I had lost Rita too. It was a long night, perhaps longer even than those lonely nights in the Quantico brig. I was confused and depressed, but mostly scared.

When my plane arrived, I walked quickly through the terminal to get a cab. As I walked out onto the sidewalk I was shocked to see Rebekah struggling to get out of a cab. I rushed over to help her out.

"What are you doing here?"

"To pick you up."

"How did you know I was coming?"

"Your friend Rita called me. She's a real bitch you know it? She chewed me out for not talking to you. She said she's been after you for six months but you wouldn't touch her. She said she planted that kiss on you in front of the barracks and you tried to push her away but she had death grip on you. She even said some girl named Nicole tried to seduce you and few times but wouldn't touch her either."

"I can't believe she called you."

"She said I was the luckiest girl in the world and I ought to put hand cuffs on you so you'd never get away."

"She's really funny, isn't she?"

"I'm sorry Stan, but I just couldn't handle someone else in love with you. You belong to me. I won't share you with anyone."

With that I put my arms around Rebekah and held

her tightly. It was such a relief to have her back in my life I was overwhelmed with tearful joy.

"Don't squeeze me too hard the baby will kick you," she said.

"He wouldn't dare kick his father."

"You wanna bet."

Chapter Twenty-Six
Deja Vu

Three days later I had to return to Quantico. I was concerned as to what the Marine Corps would do with me now that all charges had been dropped. With all the adverse publicity the Marine Corps had received from my trial, it didn't seem likely they would put me back in OCS. I had become too *conspicuous* to be a good OCS candidate. Unfortunately the alternative to OCS was Marine Corps basic training at Paris Island, S.C. Whenever I thought of Paris Island I remembered Charlie Russell. *The drill sergeants there love to get washouts from OCS,* he told me more than once. They live for the opportunity to humiliate and torment them. Obviously Paris Island was not an option. I couldn't let them send me there. It was time to get out of the United States Marine Corps.

Thinking back to my summer internship with Congressman Harmon, I remembered that he often helped servicemen get military discharges for one reason or another. It seemed to me I certainly had good cause to want out of the Marine Corps. I called the congressman and discussed the situation with him. He indicated he would see what he could do, but that it might take some time. Luckily Congressman Harmon was on the armed services committee so the Marine Corps was very responsive when he initiated a congressional inquiry into my situation. Within hours I was summoned to Colonel Swift's office.

"Candidate Turner reporting as ordered, Sir," I

said.

"Yes, come in. Have a seat."

"Thank you, Sir."

"Well, Mr. Turner, you've had a rocky military career so far I see."

"That's true, Sir."

"We just received a communiqué from Congressman Harmon advising us that he was concerned about your future in the Marine Corps given the court martial and everything. He suggests it might be appropriate to grant you a discharge. Do you want a discharge from the Marine Corps, Mr. Turner?"

"Well, to be honest Sir, I've lost my enthusiasm for serving in the Marines."

"You've lost your enthusiasm have you. Well Mr. Turner that's too bad, but I suppose that's understandable. The problem is we can't just discharge every Marine who loses his enthusiasm for military service. If we did that we wouldn't get anybody out of boot camp. It's not easy to be a Marine, but for those who are able to stick with the program, it can be quite rewarding."

"I know, Sir. It was my intention and deepest desire to get through OCS and serve my country, but it just wasn't in the cards."

"So what are you going to do if you're discharged?"

"Go back to law school. I've got one year under my belt and I want to finish up as soon as possible. I already have a wife and two kids and the longer I'm away from school the more difficult it is going to be to get back in."

"Well I can't promise you anything, but we are considering giving you a discharge. It can't be a medical discharge because you seem to be in perfect health at this time. So it would have to be a general discharge."

"That would be fine, Sir."

"You won't be eligible for veteran's benefits."

"No problem, Sir."

"You'll have to sit tight for a few weeks while we process the paperwork. You can remain in Casual Platoon."

"Yes, Sir."

"That will be all then. Good luck to you."

"Thank you, Sir."

It took almost thirty days, but finally I got notice of the approval of my general discharge from the Marine Corps. I was ecstatic that my nightmarish military career was about to end, especially since Rebekah's baby was due on August 15, 1970, just one week away.

Understandably, I hadn't seen much of Rita since I had returned to Quantico after the court martial. So I was shocked when one morning Corporal Lemaster brought me a note from her.

Dear Stan,

I need to see you immediately. You've got me in a terrible jam. You've got to help me. Meet me at the hospital today after my shift.

Love,

Rita

Rita's letter upset me. How could I have got her into a terrible jam? I hadn't made love to her so she couldn't be pregnant. What could it possible be? All morning I was sick with worry. The tone of the letter was desperate. I finally figured it must be just a ploy to see me. I considered ignoring it but my curiosity had been so aroused I had to know what was on Rita's mind.

At 3:30 I arrived in front of the hospital and waited. A steady stream of nurses, orderlies and other hospital personnel began to stream out of the revolving door as the day shift ended. After a minute Rita emerged from the crowd and walked hurriedly over to me.

"Stan, thank you for coming."

"What's wrong Rita, your letter sounded serious?"

"You won't believe what's happened. Let's go somewhere private. We've got to be really careful nobody overhears us."

"Okay, but I wish you would tell me what in the hell is going on."

"I will, after we get somewhere safe. My car is across the street in the parking lot."

I followed Rita across the street to her car. Her solemn demeanor scared me. Deep down I could sense that I wasn't going to like what she had to tell me. She opened the front door, looked at me and tried to force a smile. Then she sat behind the wheel and stuck her key in the ignition. I got in and closed the door. After we had left the base and were on the road to Woodbridge she began to explain what had happened.

"Last week I got a visit from Lt. Hooper. He said he was investigating Sergeant Matson's suicide. I asked him why he would be investigating a suicide. You know. . . . What was there to investigate? He told me General Harrison, the base commander, ordered him to find out how Sergeant Matson was able to get twenty seconal tablets."

"Oh my God!"

"Did you give them to him Stan?"

"Oh shit! I can't believe this."

"You gave him the tablets I gave you, didn't you?"

"I didn't plan it obviously, the pills were for me. If I had been convicted, I was going to save the Marine Corps the cost of a firing squad. Then when Sgt. Matson confessed, I could see his pain and wanted to help him. I figured he may want to take the easy way out too, so I slipped him the pills."

"Have you ever heard of felony murder?"

"Yes, I studied it in law school. If someone dies during the commission of a felony no matter how it happens, the person committing the felony can be charged with murder."

"That's right and Lt. Hooper says whoever gave Sgt. Matson those pills is going to be charged with murder."

"Oh God! . . . Oh God. . . . This can't be happening."

"I can't believe you gave him those pills. They were for you."

Rita began to weep.

"Does Lt. Hooper suspect that I gave Sgt. Matson the pills?"

"No, he thinks I did."

"What?!"

"Lt. Chamberlain must have seen me take the pills that night I brought them to you. He was going to overlook it, he said, but when Sgt. Matson overdosed on the same type pills he felt compelled to report it."

"Oh, Rita. I'm so sorry! Have they charged you?"

"Lt. Hooper is going to conduct a court of inquiry in a couple weeks to determine if I should be charged."

"I won't let them do this to you. I'll tell them I did it."

"No! You can't do that."

"Why not?"

"What about Rebekah and the kids?"

"What about your life?"

"It won't do any good. Even if you confessed, nothing can change the fact that I stole the pills. We'd both end up on trial for murder."

We drove into the city limits of Woodbridge, Virginia to a bar called the Rusty Nail. Rita said she needed a drink. Being in shock, I was oblivious to my surroundings. Soon I would be facing another Court

Martial, only this time I was guilty! To make matters worse now I had managed to jeopardize Rita's life as well. Rita led me to a booth near the jukebox and we sat down to talk.

"Who will you get to defend you?" I asked.

"Lt. Burden said he would do it."

"Do you think that's a good idea?"

"Why not? He did a good job for you."

"I don't know. It just seems weird.

"I want somebody I know and can trust."

You know, they're going to have a hard time proving you gave Sgt. Matson the pills. How could you have done it anyway?"

"They think since he had been my patient that he must have asked me to steal the pills for him. They figured he planned to confess all along and then commit suicide."

"But they have nothing but circumstantial evidence."

"Lt. Hooper thinks that will be enough."

"He said that?"

"Uh huh."

"Damn."

"So are they going to discharge you?"

"I think so but I don't know for sure. Congressman Harmon is trying to put pressure on them to let me go."

"It's nice to have a little clout in Washington."

"I wish I could use it to stop this stupid inquiry. I can't believe they are doing this."

After the bar maid came over and took our orders, Rita got up and selected a song on the jukebox. As she was standing there dropping quarters in the slot, I couldn't help but notice again how beautiful she was. After a few drinks she began to relax and then she let me have it.

"So what are we going to do now Mr. Big Shot Lawyer?"

"Huh . . . I wish I knew. I so sorry Rita. It just didn't occur to me that giving Sgt. Matson the pills would jeopardize you in any way. I didn't realize you had stolen the pills. In retrospect I should have figured it out, but I was just so preoccupied with my problem I didn't fully appreciate how you were sticking your neck out for me."

"You know I loved you, Stanley Turner. I trusted you. I would have done anything for you."

"I never promised you anything Rita. You know that."

"Right, but you never turned down my help . . . and you knew I wanted more."

"You're right, I ignored your motives. I should have kept you out of my life. It was wrong to involve you when I knew you wanted more than I could give you. But you're not an easy woman to resist. Unfortunately I can't change the past, I can't undo my mistakes. All I can do now is to figure out a way to save you. There has to be a way out of this predicament."

"I am so scared Stan. I don't want to go to jail. I've had to go to the brig to treat inmates before, the place gives me the creeps. I'd go crazy in there."

Rita began to cry again so I got up and went over to her side of the booth and put my arm around her. She laid her head on my shoulder and clutched my hand. I took a deep breath and prayed for a miracle.

It was almost midnight when Rita dropped me off in front of the Casual Platoon barracks. The lights were out so I quietly opened the door, walked to my bunk and laid down. Not wanting to wake anyone up I didn't bother undressing. When I awoke the next morning, I noticed an envelope laying on the floor. I picked it up and examined the return address. It was from General

Harrison, I ripped it open, I knew it was my discharge.

TO CANDIDATE STANLEY TURNER.

YOU ARE HEREBY COMMANDED TO REPORT TO BASE HEADQUARTERS AT 0700 HOURS ON MONDAY, AUGUST 12, 1970 TO COMMENCE PROCESSING OF YOUR DISCHARGE FROM THE UNITED STATES MARINES CORPS. YOU MUST REPORT TO THE QUARTERMASTER PRIOR TO THIS TIME TO ARRANGE FOR THE RETURN OF ALL MILITARY PROPERTY IN YOU POSSESSION. YOU SHOULD CHECK OUT OF CASUAL PLATOON PRIOR TO REPORTING TO BASE HEADQUARTERS AND BRING ALL YOUR PERSONAL BELONGINGS WITH YOU. YOU WILL BE PROVIDED TRANSPORTATION TO DULLES AIRPORT AS WELL AS AIR FARE TO PORTLAND, OREGON.

COL. SWIFT

It was a great relief to know my discharge had gone through, but obviously I wasn't celebrating considering Rita's situation. How could I desert Rita when she was in so much trouble on account of me. On the other hand how was Rebekah going to take all of this. Would she understand if I stayed for a while to help Rita out? I knew she wouldn't. And what about my children? If I wasn't very careful I could incriminate myself and they may well grow up without a father. I started to call Rebekah but then I thought better of it. Something of this magnitude would be better handled in person.

On Monday I reported to headquarters as ordered and received my discharge papers. Then I took a bus to Dulles Airport to return home to Portland. Before I left I called Rita to tell her that I wasn't deserting her.

"Hello," Rita said.

"Rita, this is Stan. How are you holding up?"

"Okay, I guess."

"My discharge came through and I'm going back to Portland for a few days . . . but I'll be back. I didn't want you to think I was going to desert you."

"Don't come back."

"What?"

"You heard me. Don't come back. You've got a wife and two kids. I've got nothing. It's better that I should go to prison than you."

"No. I can't let you go to prison. If anyone should go, it should be me. I'll figure out a way to save you."

"It's too late. Just get on that plane and don't look back."

"It's not that easy . . . I have to come back. I'll call you when I return, okay?"

"I won't take your call. You'll just be wasting your time."

"Well I can't argue with you about it over the phone. We'll discuss it when I return. Goodbye Rita."

"Goodbye, Stan."

Later that night when I arrived at the airport Rebekah was there to meet me with her parents and Reggi. She had made a sign for Reggi to hold that read, "WELCOME HOME DAD." When I saw them, it was all that I could do to hold back the tears. I dropped my carry on luggage and embraced Rebekah.

"Hi Babe, you look like you're ready to explode," I said.

"That's about how I feel. I can't believe you're home."

"Daddy! Daddy!" Reggi said as he held out his hands for me to hold him. I smiled, bent over and picked him up.

"Hi, Reggi! I missed you hot shot. Have you been good for your mama?" Reggi shook his head up and down. "Did you make this sign for me?" He shook his head affirmatively again and when I looked into his innocent little face the tears that I had been holding back could no longer be contained. Rebekah, who had been watching me closely also began to cry. She came over and hugged me and Reggi. As we all embraced there at the airport, together at last, I wondered how I was going to tell Rebekah I had to leave again?

Three days later Rebekah had an eleven pound three ounce boy. The nursery staff at St. Monica's Hospital immediately predicted he would someday be a lineman for Notre Dame. Rebekah and I were very proud parents. The next few days were very happy ones, playing with the new baby, getting reacquainted with Reggi and cherishing every moment with Rebekah. But lingering in the back of my mind was the harsh reality that somehow I was going to have to figure out a way to support this growing family. Before I could even start to tackle that formidable task, however, I had to deal with Rita's predicament back at Quantico.

It was too late to apply for the Fall semester at Northwest University Law School in Portland so I had to find a job until the next school year began. Rebekah and I were searching the classified ads for jobs when I suddenly felt the time was right to tell her about Rita.

"How about a real estate salesman?" Rebekah suggested.

"It would take too long to get licensed plus it takes a while to get paid since real estate salesmen work on commission," I replied.

"Hey here's a job in a lumber mill," Rebekah said and then smiled broadly.

"Thanks, I'd just love to chop down trees all day."

"It could have its advantages. Just think how big and strong and muscular you'd get."

"Are you telling me I'm a wimp."

"Uh huh." Rebekah laughed.

With that remark, I attacked Rebekah and quickly

had her pinned on the carpet.

"I can out wrestle you any day."

"You just caught me off guard. You cheated."

I looked into Rebekah's beautiful brown eyes as she smiled up at me. Then I kissed her passionately and began biting her neck.

"Hey you're giving me goose bumps, cut that out!"

"Let's go in the bedroom and I'll give you more than goose bumps."

"We can't, Mom and Dad are lurking about and the baby might wake up."

"You know how long it's been since I've ravished your body?"

"I know, but I'm not totally healed down there yet. Maybe in a couple of weeks we can leave the kids with Mom and Dad and go away for a few days."

"Do you promise?"

"Well, I can't be away from the baby too long, . . . but we could go for a day or two."

"Good. That will be great. . . . Honey, I've got a problem I need to discuss with you."

Rebekah looked up at me and replied, "What kind of problem?"

"Well, you remember how Sgt. Matson committed suicide after he confessed of killing Sgt. Foster."

"How could I forget?"

"Well, General Harrison was really upset about it and he launched an investigation into how Sgt. Matson got the twenty seconal capsules."

"Oh really, what did they find out?"

"They think Rita gave it to him?"

"Nurse Rita?"

"Yes, you remember Sgt. Matson and I both were Rita's patients while I was in the hospital."

"Boy, she's a regular Florence Nightingale, isn't she? Whatever her patients want, sex, drugs, whatever, she provides it."

"Come on, it's not like that. Rita is just a caring individual and, besides, she didn't give Sgt. Matson the pills."

"Is that what she told you?"

"No, that's what I know."

"How do you know that?"

"I know it because I gave Sgt. Matson the pills."

Rebekah starred silently at me for what seemed like an eternity.

"When could you have done that? You never had contact with Sgt. Matson and where would you have got the pills?"

"Rita gave me the pills so I could sleep. She stole them from the medicine cabinet at the hospital. Apparently Lt. Chamberlain saw her take them. I . . . I was considering taking them myself had I been convicted. When Sgt. Matson confessed he looked so desperate I thought maybe he would like them so I slipped them to him during all the commotion."

"So what? He didn't have to use them."

"It's not that simple. There's a law that says if anyone is killed during the commission of a felony, all of the participants can be charged with murder."

"What? That's ridiculous!"

"Ridiculous or not, that's the law."

Rebekah began to cry.

"Why did you give him the pills? What made you do it?"

"I don't know, it was just something I did spontaneously without giving it any thought."

"I can't believe you were going to commit suicide."

"Well, I couldn't bear to be without you and the kids. It would have been better to be dead than to rot in a jail cell or be executed by a firing squad."

"Do they suspect you?"

"No, they think Rita did it."

"That bitch better not squeal on you."

"Don't worry, that *bitch* told me to go home to you and the kids and forget about it. She said she would keep her mouth shut and take the rap."

"She did?"

"Yes, but I can't let her do that."

"What do you mean? Why not? She's single, she doesn't have a family."

"I know, but I could never live with myself knowing that someone was in prison on account of something I did."

"So you're going to run off like a shining knight to save your damsel in distress and desert me and the kids?"

"No. . . . no, I'd never desert you and the kids, but I can't desert Rita either."

"Stanley Turner, you better not leave me again. I can't take much more of this."

"Rebekah, what kind of a man would I be if I turned my back on Rita now? Come on. . . . I don't have any choice but to try to help her."

"Call Steve, he likes her. Let him go help her."

"I probably will call Steve, he'd want to help, but I can't just pawn my problem off on him. I've got to go and figure out a way to save Rita."

"Damn you Stanley Turner! Just when I think everything is okay and we can start to lead a normal life, you get into some kind of bullshit trouble! I'm sick and tired of it! I just want to be with you and raise our family."

"I know, Honey, it will all work out, I promise."

Chapter Twenty-Seven
Court of Inquiry

Steve was shocked when I advised him of Rita and my predicament. He immediately agreed to accompany me to Quantico to see what could be done. Several days later we both took a flight to Dallas and then flew together to Washington, D.C. On the airplane Steve and I discussed Rita's situation.

"When you called and told me what had happened, it immediately brought back memories," Steve said.

"What memories?"

"Ah, remember Hobo Jungle and your bright idea to ditch our bikes into the Ventura River."

"Oh, that."

"Yeah, you didn't think that plan out too carefully and we almost ended up in juvenile hall."

"Huh. That is weird. I'm in the same dilemma as I was with Sam and Red except this time the judge isn't likely to be lenient."

"What in the hell are we going to do, Stan? I've been racking my brain for days for a strategy but have come up blank."

"I know, it's a delicate situation. Our only hope is that Lt. Hooper can't prove his case. It's not going to be easy for him since neither Rita nor I will be talking."

"What if he calls you as a witness?"

"I'll have to take the fifth."

"But then he'll know he's on to something."

"Well, I'm not going to testify, that would be too dangerous. I'm not a good liar."

"I've got bad vibrations about all of this," Steve said.

"It will all work out somehow, I am sure it will," I replied.

"I hope so. . . . I sure hope so."

After we arrived in DC, we drove to Woodbridge and checked into a hotel. After we were settled, we called Rita to tell her we had arrived.

"Hello," Rita said.

"Rita, I'm back and I brought reinforcements."

"Stan?"

"Yes, ma'am."

"I thought I told you to stay away?"

"I don't take orders very well. Anyway, when I told Steve what had happened, he insisted we come for the Court of Inquiry."

"Really? That was so nice of him. Have you guys had dinner?"

"No."

"Meet me at the Wildbriar at eight and I'll fill you in on what's been going on."

"Okay, see you at eight."

"Good bye. . . . Oh, and by the way, I'm glad you didn't listen to me. It's been pretty lonely around her since you left."

"I couldn't desert you. I had to come back. I'll see you soon. Bye."

We arrived at the Wildbriar Restaurant ten minutes early so we sat in the bar to wait for Rita. Just as our drinks came, Rita popped in the front door. She smiled when she saw Steve and I and hurried over to our table. She gave both of us a big hug and then sat down.

"Hey, I'm so glad you guys came."

"No problem. When Stan told me what had happened I couldn't believe it. What rotten luck," Steve said.

"I know, I still don't believe it's happening," Rita replied. "So, how did Rebekah take it, Stan? I mean, how did she take you leaving her to come rescue me?"

"Not well, but hopefully she'll get over it in time."

"You should have stayed in Portland. I don't know why you came back."

"One thing about Stan, if he screws up he'll do whatever it takes to make things right," Steve said.

"Right. I sure hope I can make this screw up right," I said. "I can't ever bear to think of the consequences to Rita if I can't."

"Well, we've got to be positive," Steve said, "We can't get swallowed up in gloom and doom. We've got to stay up beat to be effective."

"You're right Steve. Just keep reminding me whenever I start feeling sorry for myself," I said. "So Rita, what's happened since I left?"

"Lt. Burden and I have met a couple of times. He doesn't think they can prove I gave Sgt. Matson the pills, but he's worried I'll be charged with theft of a narcotic."

"Why, because of Lt. Chamberlain?"

"Uh huh."

"Did you know he saw you take the pills?"

"No, he didn't say a thing to me."

"What's the punishment for theft of a narcotic?" Steve asked.

"A ten thousand dollar fine and two years hard labor," Rita replied.

"Shit!" Steve said."That's pretty stout."

"I'm going to see Lt. Burden tomorrow and see if there is anything Steve and I can do to help."

"I don't know what it would be," Rita replied.

"Well, he might have some ideas. You never know."

After dinner Steve and I went back to our motel

and crashed. It was only ten o'clock but it had been a long day and we needed to be fresh in the morning. During the night I had a dream.

Rita and I were in the midst of making love. She was on top of me and I was massaging her supple breasts as we rocked back and forth in utter bliss. I flipped her over and began to kiss her feverishly, our tongues engaging in licentious combat. Her moans became more intense as she neared sexual orgasm. We rolled over once again and Rita began to thrust her body back and forth frantically until she climaxed and collapsed on top of me. As she lay there I gently stroked her silky buttocks and inhaled the sweet scent of her body. A wonderful and peaceful feeling overcame me. Then I began to notice our surroundings. We were on a small bunk bed, a bare toilet decorated our abode. In the distance were the steel bars of a prison cell. I jumped up, ran to them and began screaming. No. . . . No. . . . Let me out of here! No . . . No. . . .

"Stan, wake up! You must be dreaming," Steve said.

"What?"

"You were moaning and then you started screaming. What were you dreaming about?"

"Oh. . . . I don't know. . . . I can't remember."

I was lying, but it didn't seem prudent to share my dream with Steve. He liked Rita and wouldn't have appreciated me dreaming about her, not to mention the fact that I shouldn't have been dreaming about her in the first place. I looked at the clock and saw it was six-thirty.

"I guess we better get up so we can catch Lt. Burden before he gets busy. He usually gets to work at 700 hours."

"Shouldn't we call him first and see if he has time to see us?" Steve said.

"That would be the polite thing to do. We can call

him right after breakfast," I replied.

After eating breakfast across the street at Denny's, we went back to our room and placed a call to Lt. Burden. His secretary put us right through.

"Burden here," he said.

"Lt. Burden, this is Stanley Turner."

"Stan, where are you calling from?"

"Woodbridge."

"I didn't expect to hear from you again."

"We came back for Rita's Court of Inquiry."

"We?"

"Steve Reynolds is with me."

"Oh, I see. Well, it's probably a good thing you called."

"Why?"

"Well, there's been a new development in the case."

"Oh really? Good news I hope."

"Not exactly."

"What is it?"

"You know there was a lot of press coverage at your trial."

"Un huh."

"Well, General Harrison is obsessed with finding out how Sgt. Matson got those Seconal pills so he instructed Lt. Hooper to view every piece of footage and every photograph taken of your trial. Yesterday he found something that has sent him into a frenzy."

"What is it?"

"He found a photograph of you giving Sgt. Matson a Kleenex."

My hands began to shake and I could feel my heart pounding as Adrenalin began to flood into my blood stream. I took a deep breath in a diligent effort to retain my composure.

"So what?"

"He thinks the twenty-one Seconal pills were in the Kleenex."

"That's ridiculous."

"It may be, but Lt. Hooper thinks it enough to expand the Court of Inquiry to include you as a suspect."

"Jesus Christ! I can't believe this."

"You've actually made it a lot easier for him by showing up for the Court of Inquiry. If you do show up that is."

"Doesn't he have one small problem?"

"What's that?"

"I'm not a Marine anymore, no jurisdiction."

"You didn't read your discharge papers very carefully, did you?"

"What do you mean?"

"Well, you may be discharged, but you're still in the Marine Reserves. You can be called to duty in a national emergency. The Marine Corps may still have jurisdiction over you, particularly since the alleged crime took place while you were on active duty."

"What if I don't show up?"

"Then they will have the Court of Inquiry without you and, if they elect to charge you, then they'll seek your extradition to Quantico or the closest Marine Corps base."

Utter despair engulfed me. No matter what I did I was screwed. How could this be happening? Hadn't I been through enough? All I wanted to do was go back to law school and raise my family. I didn't need all this bullshit! My despair turned to anger.

"Doesn't General Harrison have anything better to do than harass innocent citizens? This is ridiculous! With all the drug dealers, gun runners, rapist and murderers that fill up the newspapers every day you would think he would concentrate on them rather than wasting the taxpayers tracking down one stolen bottle of

Seconal tablets. What's with this asshole anyway?"

"Jail security is very important. He doesn't like the idea that someone slipped a lethal weapon into the Quantico brig nor does he like the idea of narcotics being stolen from the base hospital. These may seem like petty concerns to you but General Harrison takes them quite seriously."

"So what now?"

"Will you testify?"

"Are you still my attorney?"

"If you wish, but I may not be able to defend both you and Rita if a Court Martial is convened."

"Well, as my attorney, I am confident once you knew all the facts that you would advise me not to testify."

"Oh, I see, well then I'm sorry you wasted your time coming all the way out here. Maybe you'll get lucky and the Court will elect not to prosecute."

"The way my luck has been running, that's unlikely."

"Well, I'll contact you immediately should they elect to prosecute."

"Fine. Hey, Steve Reynolds is here with me. He'll probably hang around and attend the proceedings. If he can do anything for you he's at the Holiday Inn in Woodbridge."

"Okay, I'll keep that in mind. Have a nice trip back to Portland."

"Thanks. Don't let them do anything to Rita, okay?"

"I'll do my best to defend her but there's a lot of evidence to overcome."

"I know, but you can talk some sense into them, you've got to."

"Maybe so. Goodbye, Stan."

"Goodbye, Lieutenant."

My mind raced as it tried to fathom the complexity of the situation. Now I couldn't even do anything to help Rita. If I hung around and was discovered, I'd be subpoenaed to the inquiry and compelled to take the Fifth Amendment. That would tip off Lt. Hooper that I was the culprit. Then he would really start digging to find the evidence to put me away. I gave Steve a confused look and then tried to explain to him what Lt. Burden had said.

"I'll stay here with Rita and you go back to Portland. It's too dangerous for you to stay here."

"No, I can't go back until this mess is resolved. Rebekah would drive me nuts. I'll just hide out here until the Court of Inquiry is over."

"If they get wind that you were in town the first place they'll come looking is here."

"Maybe I'll get a motel in DC and stay there. I could hang out with Nicole for a day or two."

"You like to live dangerously, don't you?"

"She's just a friend. I just don't feel like being alone and she's the only person I know in DC. Besides, if you recall she was dating Lt. Hooper. She might know something about Rita's Court of Inquiry."

"Oh, that's right. Maybe you can get some inside information."

"Maybe so, either way she's fun to be with."

That night I hopped the bus to DC and checked into the same Howard Johnson that I had stayed in several months before while on leave from OCS. It was early afternoon so I went down to the gift shop and bought a book. I tried to read but I couldn't concentrate. I watched TV for a while but nothing could wrestle my thoughts away from Rita at Quantico and Rebekah back home in Portland. What was going to happen to all of us? Was there anyway out of this predicament? Would I ever graduate from law school and settle into a nice law practice? As I slid into a deeper and deeper depression I remembered what Steve had said."We've got to be positive, we can't get swallowed up in gloom and doom. We've got to stay up beat to be effective."

As I flipped from channel to channel on the TV I began to think of Nicole and how we had spent the night in a room just like this. What an idiot she must have thought I was for not fucking her brains out. I should call her. Maybe she can take my mind off all of this mess. I began searching the room for a phone book but when I found it her number wasn't listed. I called information and they advised me it was unlisted. Then I remembered the note. I wondered if I still it. I pulled out my wallet and began diligently searching through it. Sure enough it was there, folded up and placed carefully behind my social security card. I dialed her number and waited.

"Hello."

"Nicole?"

"Yeah, who is this?"

"Stan, Stan Turner."

"Stan, where are you calling from?"

"I'm in DC"

"What are you doing here?"

"It's a long story. I wondered if you had dinner plans?"

"Well, I was going to have left over pasta actually."

"Well, if you have your heart set on that I'll understand, but I was thinking of a couple of juicy steaks myself."

"Hell, the pasta will keep until tomorrow."

"Where can we get a good steak in DC anyway?"

"Actually there's a place about a block from the Senate Gallery Club called the *Omaha Corral Bar & Grill*. They've got the best steaks in town."

"Good, I'll meet you there at seven."

"Okay, see you then."

I didn't know exactly why I was seeing Nicole but something inside told me it was the thing to do. If I were wrong it didn't matter, at least I would have a pleasant evening and Nicole was a good listener. I took a cab to the *Omaha Corral Bar & Grill.* Nicole was standing by the front door waiting for me. She was wearing a short Navy blue dress with a slim gold chain around her neck. Several men at the bar already had their eyes on her.

"Hi, Nicole, you look great."

"Thank you. It's really nice to see you."

"Likewise. Can I buy you a drink before dinner?"

"Sure."

We left our name with the hostess and then took a seat at the bar. After a minute the bartender took our orders and before long we both were sipping Pina Coladas.

"So what are you doing in DC?"

"Rita is under investigation for allegedly stealing narcotics from Quantico Naval Hospital."

"Oh yeah, I heard about that."

"From Lt. Hooper?"

"Yes."

"Have you two been dating?"

"A little, he's pretty busy, but we've been out a few times."

"Listen, don't tell him you saw me, okay. They may try to subpoena me if they know I'm in DC"

"I won't. Did you hear about the photograph?"

"You mean the one that shows me giving Sgt. Matson a Kleenex?"

"Yeah."

"I just heard about it this morning."

"What do you think?"

"It doesn't prove anything. It was just a damn Kleenex."

"That's what I thought but Lt. Hooper was pretty excited about it."

"He was?"

"It's the first piece of evidence they've found to link you to Sgt. Matson's death."

"What? They're trying to pin his death on me!"

"Apparently. General Harrison is really upset about all the bad publicity the Marine Corps got from Mrs. Stone's articles and the national media attention she stirred up. To make matters worse some congressman put a lot of heat on him to give you a discharge. That really ticked him off."

"Oh, that would have been Congressman Harmon. I used to work for him. I just asked him to check into my situation and see if he could help me out."

"Lt. Hooper said the General was really upset about it. So when he showed the photograph to him, he got all excited about the possibility that you might have given the pills to Sgt. Matson."

"I can't believe this. And I thought this nightmare was over. I don't know what I'm going to do now."

"Well if it's any consolation, Lt. Hooper said he didn't have enough yet to prove you or Rita gave Sgt. Matson the pills."

"Thank God."

"But that was a couple weeks ago. I don't know what they might have dug up since then."

The hostess advised us our table was ready so we moved into the dining room, put in our orders and continued our conversation.

"So how is Rebekah?" Nicole asked.

"Oh I didn't tell you, I'm a father again."

"Congratulations! Was it a boy or a girl?"

"An eleven pound three ounce boy."

"Oh my God! Poor Rebekah."

"Yeah, he's already got college football coaches

visiting him in the nursery."

"I bet. What did you name him?"

"Mark."

Nicole shook her head. "Reggi and Mark, wow, I can't believe you have two kids."

"Nor can I."

After dinner Nicole and I took a cab back to her apartment. We had a few drinks and talked until well past midnight. Nicole offered to let me sleep on the sofa but I declined not wanting to create any additional problems. She promised to let me know if she heard anything new about Rita's Court of Inquiry. I took a cab back to my motel and called Rebekah to see how she and the kids were doing. They were all fine. The next morning I called Steve early to let him know what I had found out. He promised to call me just as soon as the Court of Inquiry was over.

Since I had nothing to do all day I went to Capital Hill to see Congressman Harmon. I thought I would thank him for his help and say hello to some of the staff members I had met while interning for him. As it turned out the Congressman was tied up in committee meetings all day, but I had a good visit with Mrs. Thompson, his administrative secretary.

It was about three in the afternoon when I returned to my room. There weren't any messages so I lay on the bed and watched TV. At 3:22 p.m. Steve finally called.

"How did it go?"

"Not so good."

"Shit! What happened?"

"The Judge determined their was good cause to convene a court martial for Rita. They're not sure they can prove she gave Sgt. Matson the pills but they think they have her nailed on the theft charge."

"Damn it! Did they mention me?"

"Yes, Lt. Hooper suggested that Rita may have initially given you the pills and then you in turn gave them to Sgt. Matson."

"Oh God, this is unreal. What are we going to do now?"

"That's not the worst of it."

"What? What could be worse?"

"When they saw me in the courtroom, they slapped a subpoena on me. I've got to testify tomorrow morning."

"Why?"

"Lt. Burden says they are hoping that you told me something incriminating or that I might have seen Rita give you or Sgt. Matson the pills. I was there on the day of the trial when it happened."

"Oh Jesus, what are you going to do?"

"Don't worry I have a bad memory."

"I know you would never say anything, but I don't want you to perjure yourself. I couldn't live with myself if you got into trouble too.

"There's not much I can do about it now."

"I know, we better get together tonight and plan your testimony. You're going to have to be really careful."

"Rita wants to see you tonight. Can I bring her along?"

"Of course. Get up here as quick as you can. We've got lots of work to do before tomorrow."

"All right, we're on our way."

It hadn't occurred to me that Steve might be called as a witness if he attended the Court of Inquiry. It all made sense now though in retrospect. He was there, he saw what happened and he had a close relationship with both Rita and me. Why didn't I see that sooner? We would have been better off had we stayed at home. It seemed no matter what I did I was only digging myself a deeper hole.

About ninety minutes after our phone call Steve and Rita showed up at my door. Since it was about six thirty we decided to go get something to eat before we started work. Since we were in a hurry we ate at the restaurant adjacent to the motel. Rita was pretty upset about what had happened at the Court of Inquiry.

"When do you think they will convene the Court Martial?" Rita asked.

"Gee, I don't know, probably sixty to ninety days from now, maybe longer," I replied.

"What will happen to me if I'm convicted?"

"I don't know Rita, I guess they'll take you to some military prison somewhere. But don't start packing yet, we're going to do everything in our power to get you out of this mess," I said.

"Yeah, you've got to be strong Rita, don't give up," Steve added.

"Why are they picking on me? All the nurses steal medicine."

"Nicole said General Harrison was upset over my trial and all the adverse publicity the Marine Corps received from Virginia Stone's articles. He's dying to get revenge. I'm sure he thinks going after you will eventually lead him to me."

It suddenly occurred to me what Lt. Hooper was up to. He was trying to scare Rita by this Court of Inquiry so that he could offer her immunity if she testified against me. What a brilliant plan. Obviously I had underestimated Lt. Hooper.

"You know Rita Lt. Hooper might offer you a deal one of these days."

"A deal?"

"Yeah, he might tell you that if you'll testify about my role in getting the pills to Sgt. Matson that you can go free."

"I would never do that."

"I know, but he will probably ask and you would only be human to give it some serious consideration."

"Well, I couldn't live with myself if I did something like that. I'd rather be dead than be involved in such treachery."

"I know exactly how you feel. I couldn't let you go to jail for something I did. I would go right now and confess if it would do you any good, but they would most likely try us both for felony murder."

Rita began to cry. Steve put his arm around her, looked at me and shook his head. Why was this happening I thought. What had I done so evil to deserve this? After dinner we went back up to my room to start work on Steve's testimony. As we walked out of the elevator I looked down the hallway and was shocked to see a Marine standing by my door. My first inclination was to run, but I knew that would only be a short term solution and only solidify the Marine Corps' belief that I was guilty of something.

As we approached the door the Marine looked down at a photograph he had in his hand. Then he said, "Are you Stan Turner?"

I hesitated momentarily and then replied, "Yes."

The Marine handed me some papers and explained, "This is a subpoena for you to appear tomorrow afternoon at thirteen hundred hours at the Court of Inquiry being held in the JAG auditorium at Quantico Marine Base, Quantico, Virginia."

I took the papers and the Marine quickly departed. Now we were totally screwed. If I had to testify I would have to take the fifth and then everybody would know I was guilty. If I were guilty then obviously Rita was guilty as she was the only one who had access to the pills. The situation was getting more desperate with each passing hour. For several minutes we all sat silently in the small motel room contemplating our plight. A hard rain began to fall outside and the sounds of thunder could be heard in the distance. Finally I realized there was but one course of action left to take.

"Rita, I want you to go to Lt. Hooper and tell him you'll testify against me if he'll give you immunity."

"What? I can't do that. I won't do it."

"You have to. At least you can save yourself. There is no reason for both of us to go to prison. It's the only way one of us can go free."

"What about Rebekah and the kids?"

"I'm screwed anyway. They've lost me already. There is nothing I can do to save myself, but at least your life can be salvaged."

"I won't do it! No way. I'll take my chances in court."

"Stan's right Rita," Steve said, "this is your only chance to cut a deal with Lt. Hooper. Right now they need you to testify, but down the road they might find enough evidence to convict Stan without your help. Then it will be too late."

"I don't care, I won't do it! There must be another way out."

"I hope we figure it out soon, I don't know what in the hell I'm going to do tomorrow."

"Why don't you two just flee the country?" Steve suggested.

"That's a thought but probably not too realistic. Neither of us have much money, I don't know about Rita but I don't have a passport and there may be someone watching us right now."

"It's getting late, I'm exhausted," Rita said. "I'd like to go home and get some rest before tomorrow."

"Sure, there is not much else we can do tonight," I replied. "We'll just have to let the chips fall where they may tomorrow. I'll see you guys tomorrow in Court."

"Okay, we'll see you tomorrow," Steve said.

I gave Rita a hug and she and Steve left. What a disastrous day it had been. Lt. Hooper had been one step ahead of us all day long and it was about to pay him a huge dividend. If I took the Fifth it would mean another court martial would be inevitable. I wasn't sure I could bear such an ordeal and I knew it would devastate Rebekah. Needless to say that night I couldn't sleep. My mind raced over every option available but none of them were the least bit palatable.

The next day I caught a bus into Woodbridge and met Steve at his motel. We went together to JAG headquarters. Steve was called to testify immediately and took the stand. Rita was conspicuously absent. I asked Lt. Burden if he had heard from her but he said he had not but asked if I would go call her since her presence was mandatory. He said I could use the phone in his office so I immediately went there. His secretary gave me Rita's number and I called her. There was no answer so I began to get worried. I asked Lt. Burden's secretary if there was any way I could get a ride into Woodbridge to check on Rita. She offered to take me, so we left.

Rita lived in an apartment. I had been there a couple of times before so I had no trouble finding it. Several times I knocked on the door but no one answered. I walked around the perimeter of the building and peered in all the windows but could see nothing. Finally I went to the manager's office and asked if she would let us in to have a look. She was reluctant but finally said she would go in and make sure Rita was okay, but that I would have to stay outside unless Rita invited me in.

Lt. Burden's secretary and I waited as the manager entered the apartment. After a minute we heard a scream so we rushed in to see what had happened. The living room was empty so we ran to the back of the apartment to the bathroom. The manager was standing motionless over Rita's rigid body.

"What's wrong? Is Rita all right?" I yelled.

"No, I think she's dead," the Manager replied.

"No. No. . . . She can't be dead!"

I grabbed Rita's wrist to check for a pulse but felt nothing."

"Somebody, call an ambulance!" I screamed.

While Lt. Burden's secretary called for an ambulance, I frantically tried to resuscitate her but she did not respond. With the Manager's help we pulled her out of the tub and laid her on the carpet where we could work on her more effectively."

"I'll give her mouth to mouth," I said as I checked to see if anything was blocking her air passages.

"She's ice cold. I think it's too late Mr. Turner," the manager said.

"No, let's keep trying, she may still be alive."

For ten more minutes I tried to force Rita to breathe but to no avail. Finally I just held her in my arms and cried. When the paramedics came they had to pry me away from her. I couldn't accept the fact that she was dead. As I was being escorted out of the bathroom I noticed a bottle of Seconal on the floor. It was empty! I wondered if Rita had committed suicide or just got careless. Then I saw the note. It was on a single sheet of notebook paper carefully situated on the kitchen table.

Dear General Harrison,

There is no need to waste your time or the taxpayer's money conducting a court martial on my account. I am guilty, I admit it. Like every other nurse and doctor at Quantico I have taken what medication I needed from time to time. Yes, I helped Sgt. Matson retain what little dignity he had left. Is it not a person's right to live or die? I believe it is, and I therefore will fade away into oblivion rather than be your pawn.

Peace,

Rita Andrews,

R.N.

It was a lie! The suicide note was total fabrication. I started to tear it up and throw it away so no one would ever see it. But then I realized if I did that Rita would have died in vain. Obviously she had sacrificed herself for me and I was powerless to alter what had already transpired. All I could do now was honor her memory and try to make myself worthy of her sacrifice.

"What's that you're reading Mr. Turner?" the paramedic asked.

"It's a note, a suicide note," I replied.

"You better let me have that, the police are going to want to take a look at that."

"Sure, here, take it."

The court of inquiry was canceled shortly after Rita's suicide. The Marine Corps released me from my subpoena and I returned home to Rebekah and my family. Rita's suicide was a complete shock to me. I hadn't appreciated how much she loved me. She must have been convinced that this was the only way that I could be saved. She knew I would never let her confess and take all the blame. The only way she could save me would be to make it impossible for me to stop her. She had succeeded and I felt very guilty and very sad. I missed Rita and for years I mourned her loss.

In the Fall of 1971 I finally started back to law school. If you think getting through law school was all downhill from there, forget it. Rebekah got pregnant two more times before I finally graduated. After her first pregnancy the doctor advised her not to use the pill for some medical reason. That made birth control more difficult and we ultimately failed at it. The book and movie deals that Virginia Stone was working on crashed as the public became more interested in the Sunday Night Slasher's story than mine. Then the local bar committee for the Oregon Bar Association summoned me to a hearing on my application to become a member.

It was April 8, 1973 when I appeared before the Northern District Bar Admissions committee in Salem, Oregon. I wasn't sure why I was summoned but I knew it was unusual and not a good sign. I had registered with the Oregon Bar Association for an expected graduation from law school in June of 1974. It was about an hour and a half drive to Salem from Portland and I arrived ten minutes late. When I entered the room five well-dressed men with cold solemn faces greeted me.

"Mr. Turner?"

"Yes, Sir."

"I'm Howard Hampton, the chairman of this committee. The other committee members from my left are Jake McMahon, Ron Smith, Paul Bingham and Henry Johnson."

"Pleasure to meet you."

"Please have a seat. Did you receive a notice of this meeting?"

"Yes, Sir."

"What time did it say the meeting was to begin?"

"Nine. I believe."

"That is correct. The question is why did you arrive at 9:10?"

"I guess I underestimated the time it took to get here from Portland."

"Do you realize Mr. Turner that arriving ten minutes late to a court hearing could result in your client losing a case?"

"Well, I guess I didn't realize the urgency of getting here precisely on time. You know how it is, hurry up and wait, right? I laughed."

"It's our job to see to it that every applicant who

applies for admission to the bar is not only fully qualified to practice law but is of good moral character. If you become a lawyer, what you do not only effects you and your clients but it impacts the profession as a whole."

"Yes, Sir. I realize that now and I will always be punctual in the future."

"Now we called you here today for a more serious reason. Do you recall the application form that you submitted?"

"Yes, sir."

"Do you recall the question regarding your military service?"

"Yes."

"The question was: Did you receive an Honorable Discharge? Do you recall that?"

"Yes."

"And how did you answer that question, Mr. Turner?"

"I believe I said, yes."

"Now you didn't receive an Honorable Discharge, did you Mr. Turner?"

"Well it was actually a General Discharge Under Honorable Conditions."

"Well that's not the same as an Honorable Discharge is it?"

"Well I don't know exactly. . . . I've never seen the precise definition of Honorable Discharge. I thought the key word was honorable. My discharge was honorable."

"We're not here to argue semantics with you Mr. Turner. The fact is we are very much concerned about your military record and your lack of candor on your application for bar admission."

"I certainly didn't mean to mislead the Bar Association about my military history. Although I don't know exactly what relevance my military history has to practicing law."

"It's a question of honor and integrity Mr. Turner and that is quite relevant."

"Yes, Sir."

"Now, according to your military record which we have procured from the Marine Corps you were dismissed from your OCS class on two separate occasions and then arrested and tried for murder."

"Well, that's a gross over simplification of the facts, Sir. Does that report say that I was acquitted and that someone else confessed to the crime?"

"It says all charges were dropped but it doesn't give any explanation. Frankly we are very much concerned about what actually happened to upset your military career."

"Well, it's a long story."

"Then Mr. Turner I suggest you give us a complete and detailed account of what happened if you ever expect to be a member of the State Bar of Oregon."

"Yes, Sir, I don't know how much press my story got here in Oregon but you might have heard about the Sunday Night Slasher."

"Yes, everyone has heard of the Sunday Night Slasher, but what does that have to do with you?"

"His real name was Brett Billings and he was the first person I met at OCS. Within twenty-four hours of my entry into the United States Marine Corps he had ended whatever chance I ever had of becoming a Marine officer."

"You're the Marine who was charged with killing his drill sergeant up at Quantico?"

"Yes."

"I didn't realize that was you. That was quite a court martial. Your defense counsel must have been very good."

"He was, and we had a lot of help from many other people too. But, the point is I didn't do anything wrong. Obviously after all that happened the Marine Corps didn't want me around and I didn't particularly have any desire at that point to be a Marine Corps Officer."

"Well, that certainly explains this military report. I guess you've been through quite an ordeal, Mr. Turner."

"I don't know what I could have done to make things turn out different. I wanted to have a successful military career. Some day I want to go into politics and a poor military record sure isn't going to do me any good."

"Well, I don't think this committee has any reason to cause you any more grief. We'll take your application under advisement and report back to the State Bar. If there is any problem you will be advised."

"All right."

"Thank you for coming and good luck on the bar exams."

"Thank you."

Apparently the committee acted favorably on my application as I never heard any more from them. When final exams finally came, I was ready to get my legal education behind me. Unfortunately on the last day of finals my wisdom teeth decided to come in causing me excruciating pain but that was a minor problem compared to what I had already been through. I loaded up on aspirin and finished my exams. I didn't get the best grades at Northwest University Law School but I did pass and actually received my Juris Doctor degree.

Rebekah threw a big graduation party for me and invited all our friends and families. Nicole came all the way from DC and Virginia Stone managed to stop by on her way to Bolivia. Midway during the party I asked for everyone's attention so I could say a few words.

"When I was a little boy Steve and I lived in California and every year we went to the Ventura County

Fair. One year they introduced the first computer ever made, the Univac Computer. They had the computer programmed to analyze your handwriting and from that analysis predict your future. So Steve and I decided to try it out. Steve got a real nice prediction saying he was going to be everybody's best friend and I got a damn curse! Then in high school my guidance counselor said I wasn't smart enough to become a lawyer and my Dad said I ought to be a plumber. I got drafted, joined the Marines, beat up by my drill sergeant and thrown in the brig for murder. Worst of all I almost lost Rebekah and I did lose my close friend, Rita Andrews. I know it probably sounds like I'm feeling sorry for myself, and maybe I am, but the point of all this is to thank all of you for helping me survive all these seemingly insurmountable obstacles to the fulfillment of my dream, to become a lawyer. The only thing I can say is that after what I've been through, practicing law ought to be a slice of cheesecake.

Everyone laughed and then Steve stood up beside me and began to address the group. "We have a little gift for you Stan. We know that the worst is surely over but just in case getting a law practice going is more difficult than you anticipate we want you to have this plaque for inspiration. Let me read it to you.

'Struggling in a hostile world,
Pursuing your destiny;
You will stand resolute against adversity,
Undaunted'

"Thanks a lot. This is great. All of you have been wonderful and I hope someday I can do half for you what you have done for me. So, if you ever need a lawyer, you better call me. Everyone clapped and then someone put some money in the jukebox and suddenly the room was alive with music.

"Rebekah, kids, come on up here," I said. "Rebekah, Reggi, Mark, Peter and Marcia want to thank all of you too, but enough chit chat, let's pour the champagne and get this party rolling!"

Undaunted is author, William Manchee's, second novel and the first of the Stan Turner Mystery Series. He also penned a legal thriller, *Twice Tempted*. In addition to writing, Manchee practices law in Texas where he lives with his wife of 31 years.

Coming Soon from William Manchee
Brash Endeavor

Coming in 1999
Death Pact
In Search of A Virgin

Also coming soon from Top Publications,
L.C. Hayden's,
Who's Susan?

Visit William Manchee at his website.
http://www.billmanchee.com